Reign of Melek
Book 2 of the Issur Trilogy

Reign of Melek

Copyright © Brian A. Griffen
All rights reserved.

Cover design : Danny Baker
Interior design: Devyn Maher
www.doodles.blue

ISBN print: 978-1-956305-81-1

Library of Congress Control Number: pending
Categories: Young Adult Fiction / Action - Adventure / Fantasy
Printed in the United States of America

Dedication

For Claire, Ben, and others who seek
backyard adventures

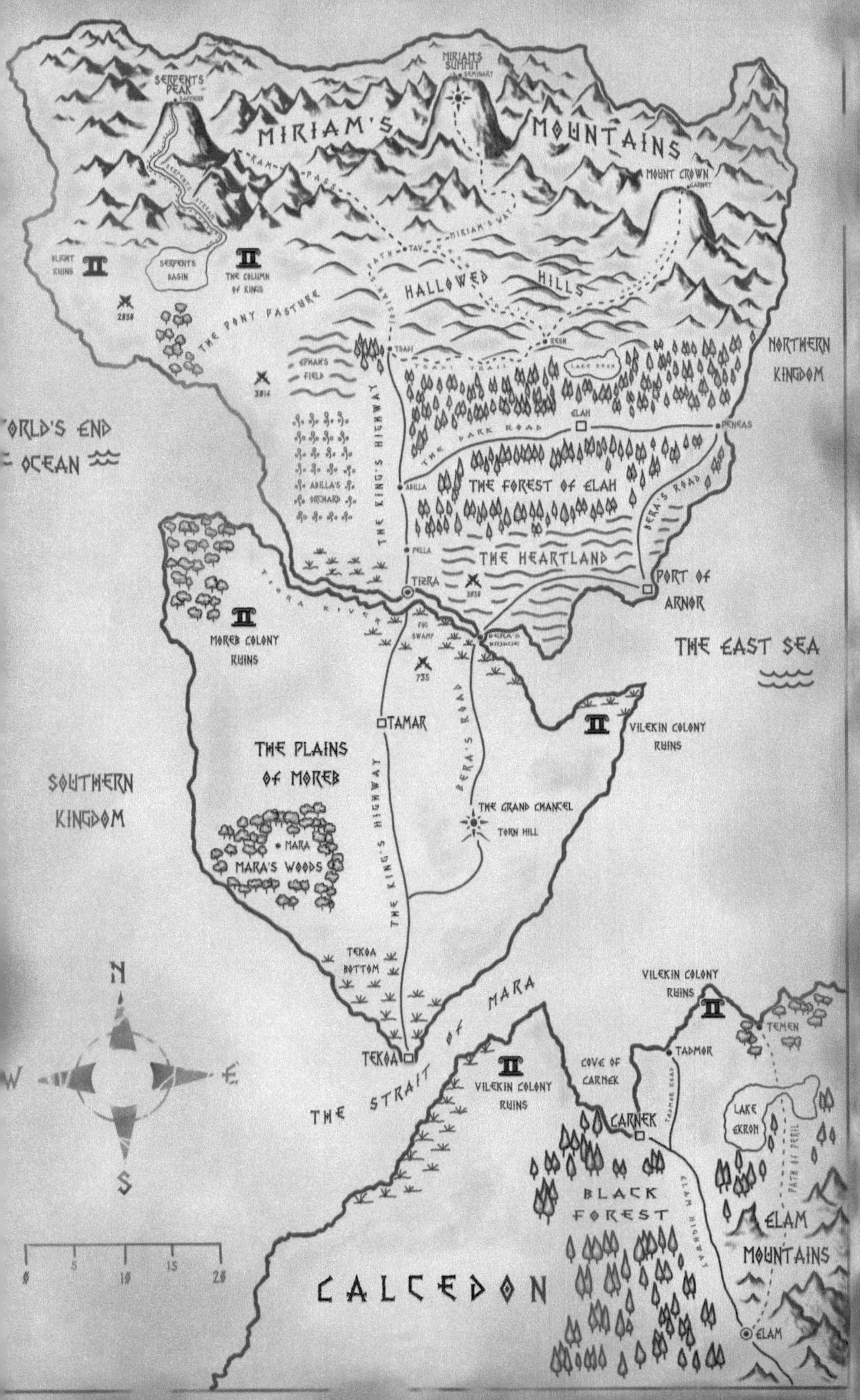

SERPENT'S PEAK
SAPPHIRE
MIRIAM'S SUMMIT
SEMINARY
MIRIAM'S
MOUNTAINS
MOUNT CROWN
GARNET
RAM PASS
SERPENT'S STEPS
BLIGHT RUINS
SERPENT'S BASIN
THE COLUMN OF KINGS
MIRIAM'S WAY
PATH
TAV
HALLOWED
HILLS
RESH
NORTHERN KINGDOM
THE PONY PASTURE
2850
EPHAH'S FIELD
TSADI
TSADI TRAIL
LAKE RESH
3814
THE PARK ROAD
ELAH
PENEAS
WORLD'S END OCEAN
THE KING'S HIGHWAY
ABILLA'S ORCHARD
ABILLA
THE FOREST OF ELAH
BERA'S ROAD
PELLA
THE HEARTLAND
TIRRA RIVER
TIRRA
3838
PORT OF ARNOR
MOREB COLONY RUINS
FIG SWAMP
BERA'S BRIDGE
THE EAST SEA
735
BERA'S ROAD
SOUTHERN KINGDOM
TAMAR
VILEKIN COLONY RUINS
THE PLAINS OF MOREB
THE KING'S HIGHWAY
THE GRAND CHANCEL
TORN HILL
MARA
MARA'S WOODS
TEKOA BOTTOM
STRAIT OF MARA
VILEKIN COLONY RUINS
TEMEN
TADMOR
N
TEKOA
THE STRAIT
VILEKIN COLONY RUINS
COVE OF CARNEK
TADMOR ROAD
LAKE EKRON
PATH OF PERIL
W
E
CARNEK
BLACK FOREST
ELAM HIGHWAY
ELAM MOUNTAINS
S
CALCEDON
ELAM
0   5   10   15   20

Table of Contents

Chapter 1 ✦ No Higher Honor

Fall 3016 of the 4th Age

Benjamin's bones ache on the stone floor. His arms and legs numb, his vision blackens with silver comets flashing underneath heavy eyelids. A cumbrous boot sinks into his sternum leaving a size sixteen impression in his black leather armor. Quit spreads throughout every ounce of his being as his body goes limp.

Captain Tobi Tamar presses his boot into the initiate, sweat-beads plummeting from the freckles on his bald head to his reddish beard. "Heroes aren't born. They're made. Crafted in the depths of a barracks. I'm going to make you a sentinel, *Ben Tav*. One worthy of protecting my king. Fate may have ordained your title but fate is no match for skill."

"I did fight a nephesh," reminds Ben, yet again.

The crass remark lengthens the disgusted captain, removing his boot from the cocky cadet. "How many times are you going to bring that up!? Worst thing to ever happen to you! Ruined you, it did!

Ben pushes himself from the floor and reaches for a bucket of water. While attempting a drink, Tobi smacks the wooden bucket from Ben's mouth.

"You live in the past, you obsess about the future. A shepherd has the luxury of daydreams; a warrior lives in the moment. Get your head right or get it removed… Now, stand opposed!"

Captain Tamar's training was different. Evan was tough but not this tough. Maybe Evan trained with love, but due to the sibling rivalry, Ben never recognized that love. His brother's swings stung his hand; the captain's attacks jolted his entire body.

Captain Tamar was curt, a man of action - not words. In fact, the name Benjamin took too long to say, therefore Benjamin became a part of the past, like his days as a shepherd.

Ben hurt like he never hurt before, worse than the days his shoulders would pop from shoveling manure-soaked hay from the stalls or from bearing an injured ewe lengths across Hallowed Hills. It was almost as if Tobi knew that Ben took a dagger in the shoulder for he targeted it mercilessly. Ben didn't know what sentinel life would be like, but he imagined it more glamorous than this.

Ben gathers his thoughts and heeds his teacher's advice. He breathes in the must of the training cellar and tastes the dab of blood on his bottom lip. He feels the weight of his armor as it fits his stance. The hilt of his sword sinks into his grip.

Tobi charges him, the captain's sword cutting the stale air like a whirlwind. Ben blocks the fury of attacks with nimble glances. The waves of his long black hair dislodge their binding to flow atop his head. He moves with purpose- strikes with accuracy. The captain finds himself in a defenseless position and concedes the duel with a nod and a sly smile.

Ben attempts to interpret the rare smile on Tobi's mug when four cadets enter the training room and fan out to cover every side of the sentinel.

They charge in sync.

Ben ducks the slices coming from his flanks. The blades of two cadets collide, causing the men to recoil.

Ben sweeps the legs out from underneath the other two cadets. They rack their fists on the cement, and their lost swords clank across the floor.

Ben presses his attack on the two rattled cadets. He disarms their weapons from their unsure hands and knocks them to the floor alongside their comrades.

Quite proud of himself, he sheathes his sword and turns to face Tobi when a giant tetherball swings down from the ceiling. WHACK! The tetherball connects with Ben's shoulder, hurling him into a wall.

The gruff captain stands atop his initiate once again.

"Now. It's always now… What time is it?"

"Now," wheezes Ben.

Tobi replaces his boot with a bucket of water. The exhausted sentinel sits up, plunges his head into the bucket, and sucks the water dry before inhaling a gasp of air.

"How long have I been down here?" asks Ben.

"You've trained twenty-three days straight."

"When is this going to end? Why can't I train with Kurion? Where are my friends? What happened to Melek?" asks Ben, slamming the bucket in frustration.

"You ask a lot of questions. You sure you're a fighter, not a philosopher?"

"Haven't I earned some answers?"

Tobi itches his thick beard and senses that the leashed shepherd prepares to snap, so he generously offers more words than he cares to.

"Your barrack's training ends in seven days, then I'll return Kurion. As for your friends, Ashira helps Aden sort out the food shortage. Ezekiel travels with the corpse of Othniel 'Wayfarer' to the crypt at Summit Seminary. Seth travels with him. King Emmerick researches this nephesh that you claimed executed Zimri. Caleb tracks Zidon. Emmerick hopes for an arrest so that he can question the magi."

The news sends wave after wave of sentiment over Ben. A burdensome wave with the knowledge of another week of pain ahead - a calming wave with pleasant thoughts of Ashira's raven-colored hair and dark eyes. A swell of distrust because King Emmerick didn't take him at his word - a tide of doubt because Melek looms in the future. A final flood of loss drowns in him sorrow for his fallen mentor.

Ben's emotions toss about like the acids in his stomach turning his face an unhealthy shade of grey. He searches the sentimental sickness and identifies the source. It's not the death of Othniel or the mystery of Melek. He longs for home in Hallowed Hills.

A white lamb with chocolate freckles on her face wades out into Lake Resh. The choppy waves disturb her confidence. Daniel hears her cry for rescue and plays the role of hero. He plods through the water and tosses the lamb behind his neck. His wolf-skin boots sink into the brown pebbles as he makes his way to the concerned mother. She lets out a bah of thanks for the return of her wayward daughter.

Daniel bows to acknowledge her gratitude, and the flock adores his charm. He turns north and enjoys a long look at the higher hills in the horizon.

Evan takes note as he scoops water from the lake and scrubs his short hair all the way to the scruff of his neck. "Based on the shadows of the mountain, the rains should come soon. Then, we will take this flock home. I'm sure Judith misses you."

The newlywed hides his lovesickness behind a forced smile to his brother-in-law.

The thought of Daniel and Judith's romance makes Evan think of Ashira. Regret resurfaces, for their rift in the ashes of Pella was bitter. Anxiety nags his hopes of reconciliation, for apologies do not come easy to Evan Tav.

A blast of thunder echoes across Miriam's Mountains and disconnects the shepherds from their longings. The flock gets antsy when the clouds rumble to blot out the sun.

"Come on now, no need to fuss over some thunder," offers the fetching shepherd.

Evan smiles at Daniel's banter with the flock when oddly he hears the whimpers of a little girl from a distance.

Evan turns to see a pale child with flowing locks of red atop a white dress. She stands barefoot on the edge of the lake, her tears sprinkling a bouquet of water lilies in her tiny hands.

His shepherd instincts kick his gut and force him to look beyond the child.

There, he spots brown fur in the tall grass.

Evan dashes around the lake as pebbles spray beneath his strides. The commotion takes Daniel's attention away from the flock while he watches Evan draw his longsword.

The wolf darts from the tall grass - saliva flings from his fangs with jaws wide ready to consume the child.

As the wolf closes on his prey, Evan's longsword swings down upon the stalker severing its head from its body.

The lost girl buries her red hair into her rescuer's shirt to weep out the terror.

The flock spooks and the sheep scatter.

Daniel turns to find the chocolate-freckled lamb in the mouth of a mangy wolf, the slobber from his fangs drenching the back of the lamb's neck and she cries out to Daniel once more.

"You will not take her!" yells Daniel, charging the beast.

He slashes the wolf across the face and the scoundrel drops the lamb. Her little legs rapidly flap before they touch the ground and bolt to her mother.

The two enemies size one another while they circle about the pebble-laced shore. The stench of the wolf heightens Daniel's senses, his survival skills liven as he waits for the wolf to make a move.

The wolf catches a scent floating atop the breeze, and the mongrel retreats with haste disappearing into the hills.

Daniel regains his nerve and the flock offers up a chorus of thankful bahs. He takes one final bow when a mountain lion leaps from the high grass and attaches herself to the shepherd's back.

"Daniel!" cries Evan. He prepares to race to his aid, but the terrified child drops the lilies and latches her fingernails into his neck. She wraps her legs around his waist and digs her heels into this back. When he realizes that the child won't detach herself, the muscular shepherd sheathes his sword behind his back to allow for mobility.

Whatever their fate would be, they'd meet it together.

Daniel clenches the mountain lion's hide. Ripping her from his back, they fall to ground. The wounded shepherd weakens from the blood loss that pours out of the puncture wounds in his neck.

Daniel gets to his feet and draws his sword. He waves the flock around him and they cluster behind their champion.

The mountain lion's brown paws swipe with the same fervor as the grunts that roar from her jaws. Daniel fends off the attacks, blood streaming down his arm and dripping from the pommel of his sword.

Daniel fights for his wits, the majestic beast blurring in his vision. The cat glares at the shepherd standing between her and the feast of sheep now cornered by the lake.

The cowardly wolf returns for revenge. He darts toward Daniel.

The shepherd lowers his sword and pierces the wolf.

The mountain lion pounces on the distracted shepherd sinking her teeth into Daniel's throat.

Death comes for Daniel as swift as the savage attack.

The redheaded child clutches Evan's back in a way that he can't unsheathe his blade, so he puts all of his rage into his boot that shatters a rib of the mountain lion.

The thick beast barely budges. Her rough tongue favors the broken rib a bit while Evan backs away. The stalker roars painful retribution at her enemy while she straitens her muscular legs toward the shepherd.

"Come on, child. You don't have to let go but I need my sword." The girl lightens her grip allowing Evan to draw the blade.

Evan draws it quickly to repel the first swipe of the lion's paw. The follow up swat catches his thigh, ripping though his black pants and tearing his flesh. Evan returns the wound by running his steel across the mountain lion's face as they pass one other.

The angry beast lunges at his back. Evan turns his body around to spare the child from the jaws of the hunter. The predator bites through his leather bracer; he feels her sharp teeth prick his bones as she rips the bracer from his forearm. Evan grinds the pommel of the longsword into the lion's eye to force the attacker off of his arm. The eye swells shut, weakening her perception.

The cat leaps, but she soars too high allowing Evan a shot at her stomach. The blade breaks skin, but fails to fell the mountain cat.

The beast fires a fury of swats that Evan repels, save one. The lion powers one vicious swipe that rips downward from the shepherd's cheekbone all the way to his stomach.

Evan's blood-soaked shirt flaps in the breeze of the lake, the crisp wind stinging his wounds. The child weighs heavier on his soul than his body. He connects with her spirit, and her breath of life renews his willpower.

The one-eyed mountain lion sniffs the adrenaline in the shepherd's sweat while she ponders another pass. Though she senses danger in the prey's resolve, the pride of a lion is not easily cast aside.

Her powerful paws spray stones as she rushes Evan.

He takes a high guard as the lion leaps with her hind legs. The lion's jaw locks onto his neck as the longsword pierces the lion's heart. The impact jars the child from Evan's back and all three fall headlong beside Daniel Tsadi in his final rest atop the crimson-stained pebbles on the shore of Lake Resh.

Chapter 2 ✦✦✦ Unwelcome Home

Ben rustles about his blanket and rolls over to grab a jagged rock from underneath his shoulder. The wound from Zimri's dagger unsettles his body and taunts his mind. The soreness stirs a reoccurring question that continually vexes the sentinel in the depths of the night. Was the wound a result of Zimri's careless aim or proof of divine intervention?

Ben sits up, stretching his hand to grasp the rolled up tapestry beside him. He runs his index finger across the heavy thread of a black and yellow tapestry commemorating the shepherds triumph in Tizra. The masterful hangings will soon grace the walls of the guild halls in Hallowed Hills.

The firewood pops, drawing his attention back to the dead of night. Shadows from the Forest of Elah to the east smother the moonlit trees scattered across Abilla's Orchard to the west.

This is the part of the trip that he dreads the most, the constant reminder of his sister's death calling out from the chattering leaves in the orchard. While extending grace to Zimri takes the edge off of the memory, it does little to alleviate his soul of the profound loss of his best friend.

There's only one sight that calms his nerves - Ashira's peaceful face at ease in a dreamy sleep.

Ben fetches more firewood from the outskirts of camp, weaving around Aden and two of his rangers sound asleep. He nods to the third ranger keeping watch near the horses.

Benjamin's gratitude for Aden runs deep, for the homecoming would not be possible if not for the prince. He convinced Captain Tamar that the sentinel could gain experience on an errand involving the prince's wellbeing. Besides, with Emmerick buried in his research of nephesh, Benjamin would not be of much service to the king.

Delivering the tapestries gives Aden Tizra a chance to honor the fallen shepherds in hopes that he might repair his last name. The task provides Ashira with a chance to sort out her future with Evan. The errand offers Ben the opportunity to celebrate with Judith and reconcile with his brother. There is much to be gained or lost on this errand, yet the companions know nothing of the crimson-stained pebbles on the shore of Lake Resh.

Ben returns with a bundle of wood and notices Ashira's empty bedding. A sting of anxiety sticks him before he hears her faint sighs of frustration.

Out of curiosity, he tracks her sighs.

"What is it?" asks Ben.

"That noise… A rapid ticking… There are hundreds, maybe thousands coming from the orchard."

"Nightjars," answers Ben, suppressing his joy to hear the

familiar chirps. "They hatch their young atop the boulders of Hallowed Hills in summer. They move them to the orchard in fall, and then, they settle in Tekoa Bottom for winter."

"How do you get them to stop?" asks Ashira, rubbing her sleep-starved eyes.

"You don't. They're trying to find their mates. They'll sing as long as they must."

Ashira perceives the direction of the conversation and seeks a change of course. The moon beans offer an out, revealing Ben's thicker arms.

"Look at you, Ben Tav... Quite fit."

"If it were only that easy," says Ben, allowing the serenade of the birds to appease his shepherd's soul.

"I know it's not easy. Aden told me about his training sessions with Captain Tamar."

"No, not training with Captain Tamar. The notion that enough chirping will eventually find a mate."

Ashira directs her sigh at Ben, gladly allowing the calls of nightjars to fill the silence.

"Have I done something?"

Ben's question lingers amidst the rapid ticking from the thickets.

"We went through so much together, then, we're apart for a while, and you've hardly said a word to me since we left Tizra."

Ashira withdraws toward her bedding.

"So that's it?"

"Why do you do this to yourself?" exhales Ashira.

Ben slides his hair from his eyes to reveal a blank stare.

"Don't play innocent shepherd boy with me. I know. I feel the current of energy coming from you; it's like the energy flowing through the flock of nightjars. I felt it in the prison cell... At the coronation too... It never stops when I'm around you."

"Why don't I feel that energy from you anymore?"

"I won't let you."

"Because you still have feelings for Evan?"

"Because I made a promise to my father. You know full well of a promise to a father, so don't judge me… Be my friend."

"A friend? Isn't that what most men look for in a woman?"

The shadows swallow Ashira's dark features when she leaves Ben alone to brood with his snide remark.

For Ben Tav the view feels long overdue but it's well worth the wait, Hallowed Hills rolling about the feet of Miriam's Mountains. As he nears Tsadi, the smell of hay and the bleats of sheep welcome him back. Ashira and Aden smile at Ben's boyish disposition as he basks in the ambiance of the hills.

Ben feels as if he's died and gone to the ether world.

As the horses clear the initial steeps of Josiah's Path, Ben senses that something's wrong in Tsadi. A thick gloom fills the air, a similar gloom that descended upon Tav after Jael's death.

Other than the few boys running alongside Aden's mount eager to catch a glimpse of the prince, the town square embodies the mood of a graveyard.

Ben notices the mound of dirt in the shadow of the guild hall and he can smell the sadness in the lavender.

"Jether Resh, what's he doing here?" asks Ben.

Aden dismounts and approaches Jether with the tapestry.

The guild master graciously receives the honor cloth, the black-haired shepherd unfolding a corner to admire the craftsmanship with his one good eye.

After Jether Resh welcomes the prince, the others dismount.

"I'm glad to see that you are finally able to return home and pay your respects," says Jether to Ben.

"I've been training as sentinel, but yes, I'm grateful every day for my brethren who perished in Tizra."

Jether's eye twitches at Ben's response.

"You are talking about the tapestry?" questions Ben.

"No. I'm talkin' about your brother-in-law, Daniel Tsadi… I take it that you haven't heard," says Jether, turning to stare at the mound of dirt and the faded stems of lavender.

Ashira clams up, rests her head against her saddle, and strokes her horse's neck for comfort.

Ben stares at the grave in disbelief before a sickness for Judith irritates his stomach.

In a show of respect, Aden and his rangers stand still.

"Wolves?" asks Ben out of his most primal fear.

"Worse. A mountain lion attacked him and your brother at Lake Resh."

The news of Evan's peril draws Ashira to the forefront. "Is Evan alive?"

"Barely… My daughters heard the commotion and arrived in time to witness his triumph. Evan spared the flock and saved a girl's life."

"What girl?" asks Ben.

"No one knows where the redheaded child came from, but she refused to leave his side no matter how hard my girls coaxed her. My daughters tended his wounds before my two sons took Evan, the girl, and the flock back to Tav."

"Was he here for the funeral?" asks Ben.

"No. But you missed your sister by a day."

"If you'll excuse me, I must offer my condolences to Ardon Tsadi," says Ben, attempting to slide by Jether.

"That's not a good idea. To put it mildly, he didn't care much for your decision to leave these hills, undermine his pact with the crown, and abandon your shepherd duties."

"And you?"

"I served alongside your father at Ephah's Field," answers Jether, adjusting his eye patch. "You'll find no qualms with me."

"I'll approach Ardon in the name of my father," says Ben, attempting at a second pass.

"Though he spoke with a grieved tongue, Ardon made it clear. He believes if you had obeyed his pact, you would've been with Daniel and Evan. Maybe he doesn't have to bury a son… Leave him be."

Aden separates Ben from Jether and motions the sentinel to his steed, "Then, we will not trouble a grieving father. Please present this tapestry on behalf of King Emmerick and know that the condolences of the crown rest with this fallen shepherd."

Jether nods in respect as the companions mount their horses.

Ashira's steed dashes out in front leading the way to Tav.

The air that hovered above Tsadi follows the travelers to Tav, and the same gloom manifests itself among the villagers. Ben hopes for a fall breeze to sweep down from Miriam's Summit to liven his senses and for a friendly smile to welcome him home, but Tav feels like a ghost town with everyone settling in for an early night.

The moonlight casts a familiar shadow over the guild hall to allow Ben a brief moment of nostalgia for he knows the shadows cast inside will offer no such warmth.

Ashira notices the soft flames in the servant's quarters and jumps from her horse in hopes of finding Evan inside.

Ben follows.

Aden dismounts in sync with his rangers. "See to the horses, and then find your way to the inn. I'll meet you there soon. I won't burden the guild master or this widow." The prince provides a handful of coin and his men follow orders.

Aden walks to the doorway of the servant's quarters and stands next to Ben. Ashira kneels, crying at Evan's side. White bandages swarm his body from neck to thigh, and three scarlet claw marks streak vertically down his right cheek. His left eye sinks into a black bruise.

Ben can't stomach the view and his eyes wander about the hovel. Not much has changed since he dwelt there with his siblings, though it doesn't have the warmth of Judith's touch as it once did.

Ashira lightly pats the unharmed sections of the flesh around Evan's face. Aden nods the troubled shepherd to the guild hall.

Ben and Aden enter the guild hall to a silhouette of Judith. She knits alone in front of the fire place, her black dress and black headscarf darkening her silhouette.

"Judith, I'm home," announces Ben.

Aden sits quietly on a stool in a corner with the tapestry across his lap.

"Lower your voice, a child sleeps," whispers Judith.

It's not the greeting he expected, but it's one he understands.

Stepping lightly across the wooden floor, he gets on bended knee next to Judith and takes her hand. "I'm sorry, Daniel was a good man."

Judith shakes off her cold disposition and stands. Taking her brother's hand, he stands with her. She embraces him with force, her fingernails sinking into his leather cuirass. He wraps his arms around her; she continues to squeeze him in a way that her anguish penetrates his armor and pierces his emotions.

The siblings drain their souls through tears, and for the first time in a long time, Judith regains a sense of who she is.

She blots her eyes with her headscarf while looking over Ben, "Our parents would be so proud. You finished their call."

He accepts the compliment with a smile afraid to wreck the moment with details concerning Melek.

"Is Evan going to make it?" asks Ben.

"I think so; he's like a stubborn ram."

"And what of this little girl that I've heard so much about?"

"I finally convinced her to sleep in Jael's bed. She minds no one but Evan, though she's warming to me. I'm guessing it was the smell of your bedding that drove her in here."

Ben smiles at the quip, happy to see some pep in Judith's words.

Judith peers over his shoulder to see Aden sitting in the corner. "Did you bring a guest?"

"This is Aden Tizra," introduces Ben.

"The prince? I look like a wreck, the hall hasn't been cleaned in days, and you invite the prince?"

Flattery always makes Aden feel uncomfortable, but it feels different coming from Judith. He steps out of the shadow with the tapestry under his arm and extends his hand. She takes it and offers a curtsy.

"No need for formality, my lady," greets Aden.

"*My lady*… Sounds formal enough."

"Aden, why don't you help yourself to some mutton stew? My sister makes the best. I'll go check on Evan and Ashira."

Ben exits in a hurry, leaving the prince in an awkward spot.

"Um… The last thing that I want to do is intrude, please allow me to take my leave. I'll join my men at the inn."

"Well, you're nothing like your father. Last he was here, he took what he wanted."

"No. I'm not my father," asserts Aden.

Judith senses the chill in the icy response.

"Sorry, my lady… I'll accept Ben's offer."

"It's not stew, just broth. Evan can't keep anything down. Neither can I," says Judith, scooping a cup for each of them.

Aden stands until Judith seats herself. She once again notices his manors but minds hers.

"Since my husband's death, I can't sleep at night."

The thought of Daniel draws out more tears from Judith's already irritated eyes.

Aden stares at the floor while she sobs.

Judith removes her headscarf, blots her tears dry, and drapes the black lace across her shoulders. The prince returns his gaze to the widow. His heart flutters at her elegance. Aden calms his heart, frustrated with himself for eyeing a grieving widow. As guilty as he feels in the moment, he can't divert his eyes from her perfectly-placed silken hair about her royal face.

"Tell me about your husband," requests Aden.

The request feels too laborious to answer, but Judith recalls how talking about Daniel to her siblings used to bring comfort.

Her hesitancy to answer convicts Aden's attempt to make conversation. "I'm sorry, I shouldn't have asked that."

"No worries… He was tall. Kind. Made me feel safe. I waited twenty-eight years to marry him, and we were married for twenty-eight days."

Aden takes their empty cups and places them on the table, giving Judith time to complete her thoughts, before he sinks back into his chair.

"He died doing what he loved, protecting his flock."

"I pray that I will be worthy of such an honorable life, and death."

"Forgive me if I appear rude, but I can't take the curiosity anymore. Why are you carrying that rug around?" asks Judith.

"This is no rug. It's a tapestry from King Emmerick, sewn together by the palace seamstress. There are only two others like it, one for each guild master."

He unfolds the hanging in front of her and she reaches out to admire the craftsmanship of the thread work.

"Based on his allegiance to Ardon Tsadi, I doubt your

brother would want me to hang this tapestry. I'll put it in the corner," offers Aden.

"My brother doesn't live in this hall. I do. And I like it. Besides, I'm sick of looking at those clunky swords above the mantle."

"May I have the honor?"

"By all means, but be careful on that stool, it's wobbly."

Aden steps on the stool, quickly perceiving her words of caution. He unhinges the swords slowly and lowers them down to her.

Judith changes out the eyesores with the tapestry.

The prince stretches himself out over the mantle to reach the highest corner, maintaining his balance as he hooks the final corner.

As Aden steps down, he crosses his feet and the stool flies out from under him. He falls across the ledge of the mantle and displaces a box of trinkets on his way to the floor.

After slamming into the planks, the plethora of jewelry showers his head.

Judith shoves her hand over her mouth to quell a laugh that would wake the little girl. She goes to the floor and gathers up the scattered artifacts. Aden shakes off his embarrassment and helps her gather in the trinkets, save one - a stone medallion with an engraved lightning bolt.

"The shepherds of old used to wear these runes for protection," informs Judith.

The rune, aglow in the fire light, captivates Aden's gaze.

In the cemetery next to the guild hall, Ben runs his hand down a lightning rune on a tombstone - at the tip of the bolt, the engraved name, *Jael Tav.*

Her cat, Smoke, lays curled against the marker. Ben's eyes

swell when he embraces the tombstone. Smoke livens and glides his fluffy grey fur across Ben's face in hopes of drying his eyes.

Thankful for the company, the shepherd removes himself from the stone and gathers Smoke into his arms. The comfort of the cat puts him at ease as he offers a confession to Jael's grave.

"So much has changed, but so much is the same. I don't think Evan will ever forgive me."

Smoke purrs loudly as if the confession is meant for him.

"I've been asked to do the impossible and I'm losing faith in Neshama's call. I doubt I'll ever find freedom, if it's even possible?"

Ben looks upon the waning autumn stars dotted about the black expanse. "Jael, wherever you are, I hope you're free."

He stands and sets Smoke next to the tombstone, the cat curling once more against the rock.

Ben returns to the servant's quarter, but thinks twice before entering. He senses what he's about to witness, but enters anyway.

Inside, Ashira sleeps under the arm of Evan. She hasn't removed her affects, and she appears as if a burdensome weight had collapsed her next to him.

Ben lies down in his bed of furs, hurting with disappointment.

Maybe it's best to be Ashira's friend, thinks Ben - though the notion offers little consolation. He pulls the Miriam statuette from his pocket and caresses her with his thumb and index finger. He holds the prophetess to his chest, then rolls over to the comfort of his old blankets with a familiar feeling of home.

Chapter 3 ✦ Obligations

Seth's lungs burn as he sucks in the mountain air. The corpse of Othniel wrapped in black burial cloth weighs on the behemoth's boots trying to gain traction on a section of loose steps.

Ezekiel blows off the high altitude and digs in with Othniel's staff to drive his feet up the stairs.

Once Seth clears the top section, he doubles over to rest. "The embalming fluids make my head ache. I can't believe I agreed to this," nags Seth.

"I did save your life," reminds Ezekiel.

"How can I forget, you've not stop talkin' about it since we left Tizra."

After catching his breath, Seth agonizes over the next long set of stairs that await him. "Maybe the prophets should consider cremation."

Planting his staff into the next incline, Ezekiel finds no humor in the response.

"What do you think Othniel meant when he said that I must learn patience?"

"Do you want me to unwrap him so that you can ask him?"

Ezekiel deflects Seth's joke like the mountain he treads upon.

"I don't know much about the ways of your order, but I do know a lot about fighting. I didn't want to be in The Pit when Zimri sent me there. I was filled with rage and I unloaded that rage on my first few opponents.

Then, I faced this old vet and that rage nearly got me killed. This guy was smart - didn't rush in, let me wear myself down. I hit a lucky shot that dislodged his jaw."

"Enough bragging, get to the lesson already," says the brash prophet, much in need of the instruction.

"Patience over passion, Zek."

"What does that mean, and how does that apply to me?"

"When things don't go your way, you lose your patience and give way to anger. I think Othniel wants you to exert more control over your craft."

"I've plenty of patience and I'm in complete control!" snaps Ezekiel, huffing up the next flight of stairs.

Seth rolls his eyes, readjusts the corpse on his shoulders, and follows.

They finally reach the mouth of crypt and Seth gently lays Othniel's corpse on a bed of rocks. "You're crazy if you think I'll ever haul your backside up this mountain."

"Just bring him in here," says Ezekiel, lighting a torch that guides them into Miriam's Cave.

Seth places the master in a humble stone coffin, before sliding the lid across the top. He senses the suffering in Ezekiel's soul when he receives the torch. He backs away, allowing the disciple his farewell.

"I'll find my way, I'll find patience. I promise, Master."

Seth explores the deep cave. A long row of tombs dug out of the cave wall contains the bones of deceased prophets. An artistically-crafted mural carved into the rock decorates the opposite wall. The mural depicts Neshama creating the world.

Seth marvels at the creation story exquisitely carved by Miriam.

Once he's able to detach his artist's heart from the mural, he walks to the Miriam statue at the end of the cave. Evidently the work of a novice devotee, but the simplicity of the piece resonates with him.

He cautiously extends his torch into a black chasm, allowing the embers to reveal lengths upon lengths of cavern below.

Ezekiel rejoins his friend peering into the abyss.

"Where does it go?" asks Seth.

"No clue. Othniel never showed me. He said that he dreaded the day that a prophet would have to venture there."

"Who's she?" asks Seth, nodding toward the statue.

"Miriam, the founder of our order. She was a daughter of a shepherd, who disowned her for believing in Neshama. She lived most of her life in this cave until she made a covenant with the Goddess. After that, she returned to Hallowed Hills and did kind acts for people, even her enemies."

"She loved her enemies?"

"That's the way of grace."

"You know what, Zek? You're pretty good at telling stories."

"It's my favorite part of being a prophet. I wish I could spend the rest of my life telling the story of Miriam and Neshama."

"I hope that will be your fate."

"Did I make a believer of you?"

"No… Go say goodbye and let's move on, this place gives me the creeps."

Ezekiel has one final moment of silence with Othniel before offering a benediction. "Master, may your journey to Neshama be swift. Goddess keep you."

Seth pats Ezekiel's shoulders as they exit Miriam's Cave for Summit Seminary atop the crypt.

"Imriel," calls Ezekiel into the dark entrance. A lone candle burns next to a stylus soaking in a jar of ink on a desk with a scroll winding down the floor. The seminary smells of the musty books shelved throughout the library and study.

The ether training center resides in the north wing. In the east wing, the kitchen and dining quarters double as a chapel. The living quarters rest in the west wing. Tiny specks of light bounce off a brass bell atop the rafters in the vaulted-ceiling of the library tower. The mountain winds swirl down from the bell tower, hissing at the visitors.

Ezekiel uses the candle to light the candelabra, which brightens the words on the parchment. Seth skims the scroll over Ezekiel's shoulder, his heavy breath sending shivers down the prophet's neck.

"You breathe like an ox?"

Seth moves in for a closer look.

"The revelation from Neshama, which she gave to her prophet Imriel, about what must soon take place. Blessed are the Issurians who hear it and take it to heart.

The end draws near. The Corrupt gather in the secret places, and Zithri's children will raise Blight from the abyss. Issur will burn and her Remnant will become orphans. Josiah's line will falter, the blood of kings will fill the gutters of Tizra, and the dogs will lap the crimson flow.

Issur will denounce Neshama, and a great whore will gather the hungry to her breasts to suckle her poisonous nectar. In that day, there will be neither king, nor precept, nor prophet. Instead, a lamb will shepherd them."

BAM! The northern chamber door opens, bumping the nerves of Seth and Ezekiel. Seth draws Peacemaker and readies himself as Ezekiel shelters behind.

A large man, in flowing brown robes, wobbles into the library. His bristly auburn-colored beard frays in all directions from underneath his brown hood. "Put that mallet down, big man, and quit hiding like a squirrel, Ezekiel."

Taking an immediate liking to the outspoken Imriel, Seth lowers his weapon.

"You made a racket down in the crypt, now you come up here sticking your nose in my work. Why did you even bother to come back?"

Before Ezekiel can answer, Imriel blows by Seth and gathers in his scroll. "How much did you read?"

Ezekiel attempts another answer.

"Did you come back for more training? If you did, you can forget it. The ether well has gone dry, and besides, I've more important matters to tend to."

The brazen prophet binds his scroll and moves out of the library towards the kitchen.

Seth and Ezekiel follow.

Imriel rummages through the pantry and yanks out a pouch of cornmeal and a jar of honey.

"Looks like you finally sent 'Wayfarer' to his death," says the bushy-faced prophet, throwing his food and a bowl into a sack.

He pauses to blow the dust out of a metal skillet before tossing it into the sack. "Knowing you, I doubt you brought me a growler of honey mead like Othniel used to do."

"If memory serves me, the jug was always empty by the time it reached the seminary."

"It was the thought that counted… Ah, forget it! I've got to go!"

Imriel wobbles back through the library, though Seth doesn't pursue, happy to remain in the seminary kitchen.

Imriel opens a closet and all sorts of clutter pelt him.

He swims his arm through the pile, pulling out a torch, and then a pipe. "That should do it," ends the conversation for the portly prophet as he moves towards the ether well in the middle of the training room. A rope secured around a column disappears into the deep well.

"Wait! You rude beast!" yells Ezekiel.

"What do you mean, rude?"

"I've got questions that you must answer, now!"

"Still an ill-tempered squirrel, I see."

The prophet's task at hand presses him, but like Othniel, Imriel has a soft spot for his innocent student. "Lilith's Journal is on my night stand. I must be going."

"There will be neither king, nor precept, nor prophet?"

"Let it go, Ezekiel."

"The opening of your prophecy is twisted, not hopeful. How can you say that it comes from Neshama?"

"That's the tricky part of prophecy. Deciphering codes, fooling with riddles, what's present, what's future? Let it go, young prophet."

"Am I the last of the Order?"

"If what Neshama reveals is true, then yes."

The air in the room stagnates with the answer and Ezekiel feels all of the souls that have passed through the halls of the seminary huddling around him. Eerily, the empty seminary feels crowded as it once did in the glory years of the prophets.

Imriel approaches and lowers his hood behind his bristly beard, leaving Ezekiel's stomach in knots at the sight. A purple streak glows through Imriel's flesh down the right side of his face, as when lightning strikes a tree - his hairline and beard scorched and parted, his eye seared shut. The purple glow pulsates with his heartbeat.

"I refused to listen to her. That's when the signs came. First, the ether in the well vanished. Next, I was brought to my knees when I felt the bones of 'Wayfarer' shatter, and I ascended from the floor when his soul departed for the ether world. Hundreds, then thousands of whispers filled the seminary, so I fled to the summit to drown the voices in the whistles of the peaks.

That's when it struck me. A bolt of ether ripped my flesh and pierced my soul. The visions started shortly after I was marked by Neshama. Now, I must follow where the visions lead, down the ether well and into the depths of Miriam's Summit."

"Let me journey with you as your disciple, as I did with Othniel."

"No. Your fate lies with Zidon. You must defeat him. Don't fail the Order. I'm simply passing through this story; you're living it. When you finish with your tale; I pray that Neshama will have you tell mine."

Ezekiel masks his confusion about the final instructions and simply nods in agreement.

Imriel plucks a candlestick from the Ezekiel's candelabra. "Remember the sacred words of Miriam. Darkness can only exist in the absence of light."

He drops the candle down the dark well. The flicker glows deep into the blackness, until it vanishes into the depths. Imriel flips his hood over his head and slings the sack over his back. He grips the rope, and slowly lowers himself into the well.

The last prophet watches until the oracle disappears into the void.

Ezekiel returns to the kitchen to find Seth partially unarmored. He wears a tiny apron and in place of his warhammer, a wire whisk.

"Did you know the seminary has a hen? And look, a jug of mix for flatcakes. All I need is a little oil on this griddle and I'm in business."

Seth's tiny apron offers the stressed prophet a chance to smile before he prepares himself to retrieve Lilith's Journal from the nightstand.

Sitting on Imriel's bed, Ezekiel finds it hard to breathe with a lump lodged in his throat while he reads Lilith's Journal.

He isn't an orphan. His parents never killed by bandits.

He learns of his mother, Lilith and his father, Lomas, jewelry makers from the mountain town of Garnet. He learns of their resilient faith in the midst of disease and death. He finds out that he's the great-grandson of the master prophet, Ezekiel 'Wind Song.' He comes from a family dedicated to the prophethood including his uncles Othniel and Zidon, both names difficult to accept in their new context.

The smell of flatcakes draws his attention away from the journal, and he exits the bedroom.

Ezekiel's vision blackens when a burlap sack shutters his eyesight. A rope binds his narrow wrists.

The little prophet musters enough might to buck his feet against a vase that shatters on the floor.

Seth rushes from the kitchen at the sound of broken clay.

An assassin draped in black robes swings down from the rafters and blows Seth backwards across the kitchen counter. The assassin's hood flies back to reveal black moon runes tattooed around his bald head. His blue eyes glisten within the depths of his black eye-paint.

Xylen was the name given to him by the Queen Mother Isavel. Like any male children born of the temple prostitutes, Xylen was judged accordingly. He wasn't scrawny enough to be discarded in a trash heap. He wasn't plump enough to be offered as a festal sacrifice.

At age ten, Xylen faced the Rat Trial. Armed with a knife and wearing only a loin cloth, he was dropped into the toxic sewers of Tizra alongside his illegitimate brethren. Their mission - survive the hellish trial and earn the opportunity to train as an assassin of Melek.

The first mistake that most boys made was giving into thirst and hunger. If the sewer water didn't kill them, the rat meat did. Many initiates were claimed by the pestilence permeating from the swarms, others by the jagged fangs in the narrow mouths of the rodents. Those lucky enough to claim a prize with their knife quickly experienced the rat's revenge as the rodent's protein shredded their victim's stomach, for no fire burned hot enough to purify such a fowl meat.

Xylen's cunning equaled his willpower to live. He waited for those sparse rainy nights when the tepid water would trickle down the gutters and into the sewer grates. Alongside the water, rotten fruits and vegetables flowed into his tight stomach.

Not only did Xylen survive the Rat Trial; he became a son of the sewer. Emerging from the shadows on the blackest of nights, he offered sacrifices on the altar of Melek – the most venomous snakes, blood-soaked leeches, and hides ripped clean from gators. After coming of age in the sewers, the survivalist assumed his place as the first assassin.

"He's not to be harmed," orders Xylen to his counterpart, forcing Ezekiel toward the exit.

Xylen draws his curved sword and dagger toward Seth, who attempts to recover his senses as well as Peacemaker.

The assassin presses his attack. He slices off Seth's apron, narrowly missing contact with flesh. With the warhammer out of reach, Xylen underestimates Seth's ability to improvise.

Seth grabs the griddle and sears it into Xylen's head. Flesh from his skull detaches when Seth rears back for another shot. The follow-up shot scrambles Xylen's brains as the yellow eggs scatter.

Enraged, more by the ruined meal than the attack, Seth hurls Xylen into the pantry.

More clatter from the library reminds Seth of Ezekiel's predicament. He grabs Peacemaker and gives chase, leaving his sleeves of armor behind.

When Seth exits the seminary, he encounters five more assassins on horseback donning the black robes and bearing the runes of Melek. The assassins begin their cautious trot down Miriam's Summit, escorting the kidnapped prophet, who lays bound across a mount of one of the attackers.

Seth sizes up Xylen's horse, a lively steed with white speckles dotted about her black nose. The horse gets wide-eyed at Seth's size and zips down the mountain.

Seth tracks the assassins.

He plops down upon a rock face hoping to go unnoticed, but the mini-avalanche caused by his heavy landing gives away his position.

The assassins draw bows and zing arrows at the warrior. Seth slides under the arrows and bunkers near a boulder. He puts his shoulder into the massive stone, which slides in the loose gravel underneath. Momentum builds quickly and the boulder bounds down the rock face gathering allies as it tumbles. One boulder turns into ten and the chunks of rock separate the abductors from the assassin detaining Ezekiel.

A force collapses down upon Seth's shoulders, planting his face into a mound of gravel.

Xylen returns from the seminary kitchen pantry.

Both men lose their weapons in the fall leaving them to grapple with their bare hands, which does not bode well for Xylen.

Seth tosses Xylen off the rock face.

In a stroke of fortune, Xylen body presses his wayward steed. He spooks the beast and the stallion rips down the mountain with his master clinging for life.

The avalanche redirects the other four assassins to another pass down Miriam's Summit, so Seth grabs Peacemaker and pursues the lone assassin with Ezekiel.

Seth takes a more cautious approach when he gets in range of his enemy - to jump down upon the assassin, too far, and to charge down upon him, too risky. A clever thought surfaces to the forefront of his mind. Though the idea seems cowardly, it ranks as his best.

Seth winds back his warhammer and launches it at the assassin. The steel bludgeon helicopters its way toward the unassuming victim.

THUD! A direct hit bashes the back of the assassin's head and chucks him from his horse. The steed rears up and dumps Ezekiel onto the ground before bolting down the mountain.

Seth rushes to retrieve Peacemaker. After securing his weapon, he attempts to interrogate the assassin. He pulls aside the black hood; he then pulls it directly back to shield his eyes from the carnage.

Seth uses the assassin's dagger to remove the rope and sack from the shocked prophet.

"We're even, Zek."

Ashira pats Ben's blanket, the warmth answers her curiosity as to where he spent the night. Her palm presses down upon the statuette of Miriam and she pulls it from the covers. She looks it over until the rooster crows to wake Evan from his sleep. She places the idol back in the bedding before he opens his eyes.

Evan senses her presence and sits up. Ashira slides to him to offer support. He embraces her with all of the strength in his tender biceps. Enraptured by her caress, his burning limbs cool.

"I'm so sorry about what happened in Pella. I didn't mean to hurt you," confesses Evan, eager to divulge his regret.

"That's the past," tenderly whispers Ashira.

"We parted in anger because of my pride. I abandoned you."

"Rest. There's no need to apologize."

"I don't have faith like you, but I still believe in us. My life is empty without you."

Ashira's desire to quell the conversation lessens as Evan opens up to her in a new way.

"Remember when we would play together as children. Me, you, Judith, Seth. Benjamin was still a toddler and my mother was pregnant with Jael. Even then it seemed like we were meant to be. I dreaded the trips back from Tizra because I couldn't take you home with me."

"Those were simpler times… good times," admits Ashira.

"That dreadful feeling returned when I abandoned you in Pella. I realize that my love for you is stronger now than it's ever been."

"Please, Evan. Don't bring this up again."

"Hear me on this… Zimri's dead, you're free. If I truly love you, I must be willing to accept your freedom, even if that means seeing you in the arms of another man."

Ashira pauses to steady her emotions. Her gentle hug conveys her gratitude to Evan for revealing his softer side.

Ben eavesdrops on the conversation outside the window with a pail of water in hand. Unsure of the cordial version of Evan, he stares at his reflection in the water. He's nearly caught in his pondering when Evan and Ashira exit the hovel and head toward the guild hall for breakfast.

The sneaky shepherd recovers by lifting the pail and marching toward a trough in the stall. "Mornin'. Thought I'd get a jump on chores before breakfast."

The black and yellow tapestry over the fireplace enters Evan's line of vision when he steps into the hall. The crossed look on his face prompts a response from Judith. "It's a gift from the new king. And no, I won't take it down."

Unsure of how to respond to the boldness of his sister, he chooses not to debate her.

Now that the mourning period has passed, Judith no longer wears her funeral garb. Instead, she wears a slender gown of royal-blue trimmed in opal lace. Every strand of her hair rests perfectly placed, as always.

After silencing her older brother, Judith turns her ire to her younger brother once he clears the top step into the guild hall. "And you…"

"What I do now?" asks Ben in the tone of a boy in trouble.

"Last night I hosted Prince Aden. This morning, Ashira. You need to tell me when you plan to invite guests to the guild hall."

"No need to fuss over me," says Ashira, embracing Judith.

Aden and his rangers trot to a stop at the hall steps.

"Duty calls us to return to Tizra," summons Aden from atop his horse.

"Not without breakfast," welcomes Judith.

Drawn more toward Judith than toward Tizra; Aden delays his return. The prince and his rangers join the Tavs for a bowl of oatmeal.

"Just the way you like," says the big sister to her little brother, serving him the first bowl.

Everyone takes in the smell of apples, cinnamon, and roasted oats as Judith serves her guests.

Once she's seated, the guests dig in. She watches her little brother shovel the oatmeal into his mouth. Taking it as a compliment, she allows the brutish behavior.

Ashira sarcastically chides his poor manners, "Hungry, Ben?"

"Ben's a sentinel, he needs the energy," adds Aden.

Judith looks at her little brother with suspicion. He stops eating when he feels her eyes analyzing him. "I like the sound of Ben."

Evan finds himself annoyed with Benjamin's shortened name as well as the sentinel necklace secured around his neck.

"What's a sentinel?" asks Judith.

"A sentinel guards the king and protects the people from tyranny. He values Issurian lives more than his own," informs Aden.

"What happened to the last one?" asks Judith.

"My father had him assassinated."

"Why?"

"A sentinel's oath to king and country is rooted in the Covenant. My father's loyalty lied elsewhere."

Judith reaches over to straighten the black and yellow knot necklace dangling about Ben's neck. "So that's what this is about."

"When we return to Tizra, Ben will be in the service of the king. Emmerick plans to call a council upon our return."

Evan continues to stare at Ben unimpressed by Aden's proclamations, but his attention shifts along with everyone else when the little girl emerges from Jael's bedroom. Hoping to discover her father's profile, she intently studies the faces of Aden and the rangers.

She begins to sob when she doesn't recognize him among the strangers. Judith's long arms gather in the child to calm her down. "Now, now, love. Be still."

Aden stares at Judith mothering the child. Her compassion for the little girl warms him more than her oatmeal.

After all of the attention shifts to the child, Evan slips out of the hall. Ben senses an opportunity for reconciliation and follows behind.

"You haven't said a word to me today," notes Ben.

Evan grabs a rake and attempts to neaten some loose hay

billowing out of the stalls. He grimaces as he twists his ribs to slide the rake. "That's a pretty necklace. Sentinel, aren't you something? And Ben, that sounds so grown up."

"Be that way, I don't know why I came out here," says Ben, returning to the hall.

"We could have used your bow," stops Ben in his tracks. "If you weren't off playing hero, maybe Judith's not a widow, maybe I don't have to be cut off from my flock, don't have to hire the Baladans again.

It sickens me how you continue to choose strangers over family. You got Jael killed and you could have spared Daniel… Look at you, choosing the crown over kin."

Ben receives Evan's words with empathy. Yes, there's anger in his brother's words, but he recognizes the truth in Evan's scolding.

Ben grabs two pails near the trough and heads for the watering hole to think on the admonishment. Evan slams the rake and returns to his hovel.

Evan reclines in his bedding when Ashira enters and sits next to him.

"I take it that you're going to this council," says Evan.

"Yes. I have to follow my heart."

Ashira waits for him to voice his displeasure.

"I think getting out of that kitchen will be good for you."

Evan shuffles about the floor and pulls out a box hidden underneath a loose plank.

He hands her a bottle of jasmine perfume. "I'll miss the scent, but I've been holding onto this since my last trip to Tizra."

Ashira squeezes his hand to thank him for the thoughtful gift. He gently flips her hand so that her palm is wide open.

Evan places a ring in Ashira's palm.

Stunned silent by the ring, she can't breathe let alone speak. Her heart pounds, lungs flutter. She buries her head into his shoulder and caresses his neck while the rings transitions from a memory to reality. "My mother's wedding ring. I thought Zimri stole it or burned it in the fire."

"Your parents gave it to me the season before they died, maybe they could sense their fate. They told me to protect it until the day I would place it on your finger."

Ashira returns her gaze to the ring resting in her palm. Evan takes her fingers and slowly covers the ring.

"My hope is to fulfill their promise and one day, place this ring on your finger."

The surreal moment mystifies Ashira's sense of time and though her thoughts should be on Evan, they drift to the past instead, consuming her with images of the diamond ring on her mother's olive-colored hand – the ring wrapped around her delicate finger, her father's thick arms wrapped around her mother.

There was but one certainty in the life of Ashira Keros – the love that her parents had for one another. One of the fondest reveries of her childhood remained the conclusion of her mother's work day after she ceased peddling the pottery wheel.

Her mother ritually washed her clay-stained fingers while her father slowly turned the lock on the shop door. He'd always approached from behind and wrapped his arms around her waist. Taking the ancestral ring from the clay dish next to the sink, Laud would tenderly slide the ring onto his wife's index finger as if he were proposing to her all over again. This routine ended every day at the Keros pottery shop.

"Ashira!" summons Aden from atop his horse, jarring the potter's daughter from her pleasant childhood memory.

She feels pressed to confess her love for Evan, but she can't, for it doesn't possess the same sense of commitment that her parents held for one another. Maybe that would come with time. For now, she shows her appreciation with a tender kiss on his claw-scarred cheek.

Ashira emerges from the hovel, her mind still spinning through time. She clenches her bottle of perfume and ring with her fists - the items anchor her once again in the present reality.

Evan holds her stirrup as she secures herself atop the horse.

"Ben! Where are you!?" summons Aden, with a little more bite in his words.

Ben arrives with a gimpy sheep over his shoulders. "This little guy twisted a leg coming out of the stall. I'm going to bind him up."

The feel of the downy wool against his neck energizes him in a way that he hadn't felt since Evan began teaching him how to shepherd. The manure in the stall livens his nostrils, and the orange sun rising over the stone chancel delights his eyes.

Ben finally feels at home.

"We don't have time for that; we must leave," says Aden.

"Can't I stay for short time? Evan's in no shape to care for the flock and the Baladan Brothers aren't here yet."

"You swore an oath, Ben Tav. You've bound yourself to King Emmerick Tizra and that yoke won't be broken until death. To stay here would be an act of treason."

The harsh reminder from the prince proves Evan right yet again. Ben chose the crown over kin.

Any resentment for Evan disappears instantly and for the first time, Ben feels his father's love in his brother's admonishment. *There is no higher call than to protect the flock* runs through Ben's mind when placing the gimpy sheep next to the trough.

Ben squeezes Judith for his final goodbye. He then reluctantly mounts his horse. Evan takes his place next to Judith, and the little girl latches onto his leg.

As the horses gallop into the horizon, Ben takes one final look back at Evan.

Chapter 4 ✦✦✦ King Emmerick Tizra I "The Learned"

Zimri's once gaudy throne room transitions into a library under Emmerick's reign. Books, scrolls, loose leaf notes clutter the space, and a pile of documents bury the wooden throne. A mass of artifacts cover the oak table in the center of the room. At the head of the table sits the professor-king.

Emmerick twists his handlebar mustache while pondering the possible existence of Melek.

Tobi enters the room and sees no sign of Emmerick. Smoke rings billow up from his pipe behind a wall of books signaling the king's whereabouts. The captain's greeting of "Sire" fails to reach the professor, who ventures deeply into his dense thoughts. Tobi fires off a second "Sire" in his drill sergeant voice shocking Emmerick back to reality.

"Is it well, my Lord?"

"No. It is not well. There's no proof, no evidence."

Tobi tugs his thick red beard in awe of the perplexed agony in Emmerick's eyes for he has never witnessed such a sight in all of his days of service – the professor, stumped.

"I can't bring myself to a conclusion that this Melek exists. That these nephesh exist," says Emmerick, lifting from his wilted disposition.

Emmerick kneels on the floor where the ether vortex once swirled. He removes a stack of crumpled notes while brushing his hand across the stone floor.

"Sire, you ordered no visitors but the High Precept has arrived from the Grand Chancel."

The announcement jars the professor from his research.

"Pass him," huffs the wide-eyed Emmerick.

High Precept Amar Divine glides through the door frame with folded arms, his pure white robe sliding across the floor - the carats of gold sparkling atop the sun embroidery sewn into the robe at the chest. A golden cord cinches his robe around his full belly, and a circle of keys dangle at his side. Light shines through the windows behind the precept as if he commands the sun.

Amar Divine was born Amar Rook in the tiny settlement of Mara nestled within Mara's Woods. His mom kindly called him 'big-boned' as a boy, but the chubby child's ego was much larger than his waistline. It was his pride that the local precept attempted to humble, for young Amar could teach holy writ with the brilliance and vigor of a seasoned precept.

The youthful boaster knew that he was good because people gathered from all over The Plains of Moreb to hear the prodigy preach. The mentor-precept accepted the fact that the large crowds boosted the boy's ego to such an extent that he could never tame. In due time, the mentor found the arrogance unbearable, so he left the settlement and placed it under the guidance of young Amar.

It was his sixteenth year when he drafted his apology on veneration - a collection of sermons about the divinity of Miriam. He proclaimed that every believer in Issur could have access to her divinity if they prayerfully approached the Goddess with a fierce faith. His followers called him 'Divine' for there wasn't a man, woman, or child in The Plains of Moreb who broke the Covenant.

News of Amar Divine's greatness reached the Synod of Paladin Precepts and caught the attention of High Precept Shamgar Ram. For Amar's high conversion rate, an apology that confounded the Order of the Prophets, and a holy fervor for Mother Miriam - Ram appointed him as Associate to the High Precept.

From that time forward, Amar Divine lived in the Grand Chancel under the tutelage of Shamgar Ram until the precepts were either killed or exiled during the Scarlet Winter. Since his exile, Amar Divine has poured his life's work into raising a new Grand Chancel on Torn Hill and digging up the roots of evil attached to Melek worship.

The middle-aged precept inspects the king's research with his glowing green eyes, which sink into his milky-white face. "Holy mysteries belong to Neshama and have been entrusted to the precepts, my King. You do believe in Neshama?"

"High Precept, I believe this is the first that I've seen you outside of the Grand Chancel. I'm certain that you have more pressing matters than a theological debate with a biologist."

"Word reached me that an imperial council would soon convene."

"That's correct. The council will convene upon Prince Aden's return."

"Now that Zimri is no more, curse his dark soul… I trust that we will return to the old laws, good King. According to precedence, a paladin precept must be appointed when imperial councils are called into session."

"You will be joining us, then," invites Emmerick with a twist of intrigue on his tongue.

"No, my mouthpiece will. His name is Ur Rothmore and he should be offered the same respect as my office."

"The Southern Kingdom rebuilt the Grand Chancel; they trusted you, why do you assume disrespect from me? I've always been a lord of the people."

Tobi nods in support as a witness to Emmerick's character.

"You never answered my question, Sire. Do you believe in Neshama?" asks Amar, his bottom lip quivering with aggravation.

Offended by the high precept's aggression, the hot-headed captain defends his king, "One of your edicts is charity. You reside in the Plains of Tamar - talk about a charity case. The poor funded your chancel when they couldn't afford to put bread on their tables. Lord Emmerick refused his lawful wage when the tax fund ran low so *he* could put bread on their tables. You tell me who is like Miriam, who follows Neshama."

The whites of Amar's eyes redden and veins boil atop his milky-skinned bald head.

Emmerick motions his captain to stand down. "Forgive Captain Tamar, he's been in the company of cadets for too long and has forgotten how to address holy men."

"Seems like a problem on every street in this city, too many souls have been infected by the plague of Melek. Judgment may be the only edict that will remedy these sinners."

"I trust that the precepts know how best to save souls and I welcome Ur Rothmore to join our council. I will see to it that you're comfortably quartered in a palace suite. I'll even have some brandy sent to your room to assure a good night's rest."

"Very well, Sire. Have a man with strong hands deliver the tonic, my back aches from the carriage ride," says Amar, smiling at Tobi.

Emmerick ushers the high precept to the door and sends him off to the suites with an escort of servants.

A sense of relief livens the researcher as he returns to his work. "Oh my, that visit was most unusual."

A final question for Captain Tamar pops into Emmerick's thoughts before he shelters behind the book wall. "Have we any word from Caleb Glade?"

"Zidon's trail went south on last report," answers Tobi.

The streets of Tekoa fill with the chatter of politics concerning the fall of Zimri and the aggression of Calcedon. Local officials anxiously supervise dock repairs and the recalibration of the ballistas. The recent raider attack puts the port city on edge. Equally troublesome, no vessels of commerce arrive from their suspect ally to the south.

Caleb Glade finds it hard to focus in the midst of all the angst. Disguised as a miller, he totes a basket of baguettes across his shoulder.

Making his way through the streets of Tekoa, he approaches a beggar perched on a fence in the town square. A stone statue of Mara, dressed in an iron cuirass over her gown, towers above him.

Caleb hands a loaf of bread to the dirty rover. "Have you seen a man with a big crooked nose, knotted beard, grey robe?"

The rover shakes his dreadlocks 'no' prompting the scout to dump another loaf on his lap with a playful glare. "Come on, the weird ones aren't hard to miss."

"I saw him this morning when I was down by the docks. He was having a dispute with the harbor master."

Caleb dumps the remaining baguettes over the beggar. "We have a winner!" announces Caleb, before racing towards the docks.

Disappointment greets him when he arrives to see Zidon adrift at sea, heading east across The Strait of Mara.

Hoping to gain access to the shipping log, Caleb enters the harbor master's office.

"What do you want?" asks the harbor master, refusing to make eye contact with the uninvited outsider.

"A gorgeous woman, I'm talkin' mermaid gorgeous."

"Does this look like a brothel?" retorts the mariner, peeling his tired eyes from the shipping record.

"That depends. How much did the man in grey robes pay you?"

"You think you can come in here and work me over with your charm? You're not gonna pry this oyster. Get out!"

"Now that sounded rather dirty. How much for your pearl, my dear?"

The much larger harbor master emerges from his desk and stands over the spy. He blasts Caleb through the doorway, and the spy rolls across the dock before wrecking into a stack of crates.

"I guess I'll have to do this the fun way," says Caleb under his breath.

Caleb sits in a dark corner of the local inn next to the harbor master's office. The sounds of bullfrogs pound his eardrums through the moonlit window next to his head, while the putrid swamp air tortures his nose. He undoes his ponytail to take a whiff of his hair. "I hate The Bottom."

"I'm not picky," says a tramp, pressing her pointy hips into his shoulders.

"That's a good thing, my dear… You see that man over

there?" asks Caleb, pointing out the harbor master. "He's going through a tough time. His wife left him for another man. She took the dog, moved to Tamar. Don't bring this up with my friend. Just buy him lots of brew, and buy lots for you too… Let's be honest, that's why you're here."

The glassy-eyed tramp smiles at his candor.

"My room is up the stairs, the first door. Bring him there after last call."

His orders surprise the tramp. After he spills some coin in front of her, the shine in her eye tells him that she agrees to go along with his plan.

A few hours pass and, as Caleb planned, the inebriated harbor master stumbles into the pitch room. The tipsy mariner plops down on the bed.

The sly scout grins at the tramp before slamming the door in her face.

Caleb ties the harbor master's wrists and ankles to the bed.

"You're a wild one," says the seadog smiling ear to ear.

"You have no idea," says Caleb in a woman's voice.

The baritone voice replaces the seadog's smile with a suspicious quiver of the lips.

The delighted look returns when he feels something slide up his pant leg.

"Is that a snake in your pants? Why yes, it is. Don't make any sudden movements, one bite and that's it," warns Caleb.

The danger of the situation sobers the harbor master.

"This would have been so much easier if you would have just taken my coin and told me what I wanted to know," sighs Caleb.

"Anything, I'll tell it!"

"The man in the grey robes, why'd you argue with him?"

"I told him that the mayor banned travel to The East Sea. Roving bands of refugees recently attacked merchants in those waters. He secured a crew on a fishing boat in defiance of the ban. Ah…"

The snake shifts in his trousers, breaking his line of thought.

"Keep going," presses Caleb.

"He paid me a large sum to look the other way, so I did."

"Where's he going?"

"Temen. It's a fishing village in Calcedon."

"Why?"

"I didn't care why."

Caleb steps toward the door.

"I told you what you wanted! Remove the snake before it kills me!"

"No chance that happens. It's not poisonous," says Caleb, opening the door to the persistent tramp - unmoved and upset by the recent slamming door. She glares at him with a vicious scowl on her mug. "I can't say the same for her."

Caleb trades places with the tramp, before she slams the door in his face.

"Wenches," snickers the spy as he exits the inn off the docks.

Caleb's countenance falters while walking across the Tekoa docks. Glowing down upon the coastline of Calcedon, the moonbeams instill an eerie sense in his intuition.

Chapter 5 ✦✦✦ The Council of Nine

“And our people dubbed you 'The Wary.' You're nothing but a fool,” says a steel-clad warrior with unkempt dark hair and pasty, dry skin. The crimson tint to his eyes looks as if something unnatural lurks inside of him. The enormous steel claymore attached to his back runs the entire length of his long body, and onyx dagger handles jut forth from his gauntlets.

The warrior turns his back on a decrepit old man dressed in sackcloth. The elderly man wears bruises from head to toe, and a strip of cloth conceals his gouged eye sockets.

“Yes, my Son. King Lars 'The Wary' of Calcedon is what

my people called me. And if I had to be betrayed, I'm glad it was by you… Your mother died so young; she was too beautiful to die so young. After we lost her, you were all that I had; I was all that you had."

"You introduced me to Melek so don't lay your guilt on my altar. You researched endlessly, you knew what he required."

"I became so devoted that I lost my only son. You were a good son before this ruination happened, and I was a good father."

The entitled prince boots the king in the gut with such force that his father's mouth spits blood.

"Melek is my father! He removed all of the obstacles before me as prince and inspired me to claim the kingship of Calcedon. Soon, I will rule an empire. The world will bow at the footstool of King Tartek 'The Destroyer.'"

The vile son imprisons his father without food or water, leaving him for dead.

It might have been his mother's death that made Tartek such a fierce competitor from an early age for he buried his resentment deep within his soul, forbidding himself to display any emotional weakness to his rivals. Most nobles in Calcedon believed that Tartek's combative spirit was birthed in the legendary last stand of his two battle-hardened uncles, Rygar and Rex. Refusing to mourn their deaths, Tartek instead vowed to best them in his future exploits.

The two Calcedonian heroes perished on the same day. With their regiments routed from Temen and outnumbered five hundred to two, the hot-blooded princes refused retreat. They slew a hill of Bactra invaders that afternoon, but the hill grew a little too high and soon they found themselves in a compromised position.

A Bactra bolt-thrower skewered both brothers on the same shaft as the cowardly seafarers drifted out of the harbor never to return to the Calcedonian coast.

When King Cator 'The Sullen' found his dead sons, their knuckles were locked so tight around the hilts of their claymores that he was unable to unhinge their fingers from their weapons. Thus, he buried them as he found them.

The next season, King Cator found himself on his deathbed, his knuckles hinged around his claymore. When the day came to pass the crown to his youngest son, Lars the second 'The Wary,' Tartek saw the regret in his grandfather's eyes. For Cator 'The Sullen' resented that an academic, not an aggressor, would inherit his throne. Unlike Cator 'The Sullen' and his older brothers, Lars 'The Wary' was a man of books, not blades.

Though Lars endured the scorn of his father and brothers, he could not endure the scorn of his son. Ever since his teenage years, Tartek's apathy forbade him from admiring his father's aptitude or from appreciating his undying devotion to his only child.

King Tartek's steel boots clank as he climbs the steps into the throne room where colorful illustrations lace the circular walls honoring the great deeds of the Calcedonian Kings.

Tartek takes his place on his smaller marble throne next to a gigantic marble throne capable of hosting a man of epic proportions. His eyes spin with the hypnotic swirl of the ether vortex in the middle of the room. The whirlwind of ether darkens as the swirls gain momentum, the strands shifting from grey to black.

Korah emerges from the vortex.

"Welcome back, Korah," greets Tartek with a tilted nod of the neck.

"What has become of your father?"

"He rots to death with resentment as Melek has foreseen."

"What of your army?"

"We wait your command… You were long in returning to me, Korah. "Has there been a setback?

"A minor setback, nothing that your army can't destroy."

"Nothing that Melek can't destroy," corrects Tartek.

"Your faith in Melek makes you invincible. You have his permission to launch the first strike according to the battle plan."

Korah's declaration of war causes Tartek's possessed eyes to burst red with visions of destruction.

"Have my warriors been prepared for the purge?" asks Korah.

"Crafted by the master's hands in the palace depths," boasts Tartek cracking a vile smile.

Black and yellow streamers flow across the ceiling of the Tizra palace dining room and twirl down the walls. The tapestries of the kings of old have been restored and the smell of refinished cedar lifts from the table permeating every corner of the grand hall.

Servants scatter about with trays of feta cheese and goblets of chardonnay. They gently divvy out the fine china at each table setting.

The court recorder enters with quill and paper, taking his place behind the desk in the far corner. He places his materials as soon as the maids sweep their dusters across the furniture for a final touch up.

The flutist softly gives breath to her wooden reed when guests begin to arrive. She stands next to the portly herald draped in a maroon velvet vest. He stands at the ready to announce the entrance of the king and his gentlemen.

Seth and Ezekiel arrive first.

"Told you that we had more time," nags Seth.

"Sorry, but I couldn't take another one of your adjustments."

"Zek! Look at this armor - black steel over silver chainmail. Notice how much nicer it is than my pitfighter gear. It's not every day that I get treated to the royal armory. Besides, I would have been in this armor a lot sooner if I wasn't on top of a mountain rescuing you."

"You have to bring that up again, that's all I heard on the way back from the mountains."

"Look at all of that cheese," says Seth, peering over the dainty portions on the saucers to locate their source. A servant turns around to find Seth with a chunk of cheese melting in his mouth. "This is so good."

Ezekiel reddens with embarrassment.

Caleb Glade approaches and finds the drizzle of cheese oozing from Seth's mouth most humorous. "Enjoying the cheese, I see. Are you campin' anytime soon?"

After Caleb turns to eye a servant-girl, Seth leans into Ezekiel, "What did he mean by that?" The wittier prophet realizes that the inner-workings of human digestion are lost on Seth.

Ashira enters and her brother smashes the cheese back onto the serving tray. Seth wipes his hand on Ezekiel's robe before he dashes toward her, the china on the table quaking at his thunderous stomps.

"Glad to see that you two made it back safely," says Ashira, receiving a tender squeeze from her brother.

Seth immediately senses that something troubles Ashira and tilts his head to signal his concern.

"We'll talk later," acknowledges Ashira.

"Looks like someone else was in the armory," says the veteran, checking out her black leather cuirass and greaves.

She wears a brace of three throwing-knives across her chest and two shortswords strap to her back.

"That's my sister, glad I could finally talk you into two blades."

"I expect you to finish your training on the use of two blades," reminds Ashira.

Ezekiel looks over the warriors with a bit of confusion and jealously.

"Zek's still mad because all he got was new sandals."

"Oh, why don't you suck down another fistful of cheese?"

Ashira chuckles at her brother's expense.

"Don't you think it strange that we're invited to a council concerning the king's research and everyone shows up ready for war?" asks Ezekiel.

"Captain Tamar said to be prepared because Emmerick tends to act on a whim," says Ashira.

As soon as she mentions the king's name, the herald inhales deeply to proclaim the royal arrivals.

"Ladies and gentleman, I give you Primus Captain Tobi Tamar and Sentinel Ben Tav."

It's evident that the captain followed his own advice, arriving with his heavy halberd slung over his black-iron cuirass. A man of superstition, he never buffs his armor. Therefore, it proudly displays the battle markings from his days as an infantryman.

Tobi unrolls a map of Issur and Calcedon along the table. He then places some markers on his corner at the table.

Overjoyed at the sight of his friends gathered in one place, Ben finds it difficult to keep a formal disposition.

Standing post while Emmerick researched for hours on end made for a long first week as sentinel. The boredom sent Ben to his training sessions with such a renewed anticipation that Captain Tamar took note of the sentinel's sharper focus.

"Behold! Prince…," before the herald completes his name or accolades, Aden covers the boaster's mouth and shakes his head 'no.'

Quickly dismissing the irreverent gesture, the herald prepares to trumpet his king's entrance.

"All kneel in honor of King Emmerick Tizra the First 'The Learned'!"

Everyone kneels, even Emmerick when he trips on his oversized yellow cloak with black trim. He plows into a suit of armor causing the metal suit to crash down upon the herald, who flattens out the tiny flutist.

Emmerick jumps to his feet, rips the cloak from his back and stuffs it into an attendant's chest. "Oh, forget it! This is silliness, enough with the formality!"

As the council assembles around the table, Emmerick notices that everyone comes armed to the teeth. He glares at Tobi, who points his eyes to the floor.

Emmerick twists his mustache annoyed by Ur Rothmore's empty place, but he calls the council into session anyway despite the tardy precept.

"I offer my gratitude for accepting this invitation; your heroics in the overthrow of Zimri speak of your quality. It's not so much the overthrow of my brother, but the manner of his death that troubles me. I researched this matter for more hours than I cared to study in hopes of reaching a logical conclusion to Ben Tav's claim that Melek is more than an idol. That he's an actual nephesh."

The king's intensity captivates the council for he speaks to their hidden desperation concerning his conclusion.

"My academic bend is towards the physical not the metaphysical, towards the seen not the unseen. My area of expertise is the field of biology, in particular nature and animals. But I put aside my natural inclinations and looked into metaphysics with an open mind. I gathered every book that I could find on nephesh. I was fortunate enough to reclaim lost writings that the scribes had stashed in the sewers."

Seth, emotionally scarred by his encounter with the sewer rats, frowns at Ezekiel; the prophet nibbles his cheese like a rodent to mock Seth's fear.

Emmerick sighs his deepest breath of frustration, which heightens the council's interest as he readies his conclusion.

"I have no proof to believe that Melek or nephesh exist."

"So you're calling me a liar," blurts Ben.

"No, a liar would be unfair… More like delusional."

"I had three encounters with a nephesh named Azor. I fought another named Korah. Another named Melek came out of an ether vortex and stomped Zimri to death."

"Yes. Delusional is the precise word."

Ezekiel removes Othniel's Book from his robe and smacks it on the table in defense of Ben's claims. "This book has been protected by the Order of the Prophets for centuries and it confirms Ben's testimony that Nephesh exist."

Emmerick rolls his eyes at the assertion.

"Show him those pages that you were telling me about," says Ben.

"Do you expect me to take seriously findings from a book of fairy tales?"

The rude response pushes Ben and Ezekiel to the brink of dissention and prompts Aden to address the council.

"I've known Ben Tav only for a short time, but I won't make of him a liar. Likewise, we can't cast off our faith in Neshama, the Covenant, or the scripture preserved by the prophets. A debate on reason or faith avails nothing at the moment. A threat does exist to this nation and we must address it, so let's cover what we do know."

Emmerick slicks his mustache impressed by Aden's resolve, "Fair enough, Nephew."

Aden continues his reasoning, "Assassins tried to kidnap Ezekiel in the mountains, their runic moon tattoos clearly identify them as Melek worshippers. Caleb saw Zidon sailing for a fishing village in Calcedon."

Tobi places markers as Aden recalls the recent events.

"It seems to me that a Melek cult still exists and Zidon appears to be their leader. He's the one that convinced my father to worship Melek and tried to turn me against Neshama. He must be dealt with."

The very mention of subduing Zidon makes Ezekiel's innards fearfully quake; he takes a rare sip of alcohol to soothe his stomach.

"Have we heard any correspondence from the ambassador to Calcedon?" asks Tobi, placing a marker on Elam.

"Nothing from the ambassador, nothing from my old friend King Lars," answers Emmerick.

"Calcedonian refugees have been attacking merchants in the East Sea, so the mayor of Tekoa has stayed all vessels," informs Caleb.

"It was a regiment of refugees that sacked Tekoa for food last summer," says Aden.

Tizra's food supply sparks Ashira's concern, "We have yet to meet the needs of this city. When I was with Aden working on the food shortage, I noticed that Tizra's on edge. Many suffered under Zimri's tyranny and others lost family defending his kingship. Most citizens were loyal devotees of Melek. It will take time for them to abandon their vices and return to the Covenant."

The grind of chain links dragging across the stone floor diverts everyone's attention to the entrance. In walks Shamgar Ram with his grey robe drenched in blood and maroon spatter drizzled across his face and gauntlets. Blood drips from the mace at his side and the shield on his back. The gruesome precept drags the severed heads of the temple prostitutes on his chain.

His crystal-blue eyes brighten from his sunken eye sockets as the old precept grins, "No worries Daughter of Issur, the eradication of devotees in Tizra is now complete."

After stomaching the gruesome sight, Emmerick announces his assumption, "Precept Rothmore, I presume."

"No. This is Shamgar Ram, the High Precept," introduces Ben.

"A position he relinquished long ago," says Ur Rothmore, strutting through the entrance, careful to step over the severed heads.

Layers on his flabby face absorb his chin and his pursed lips labor to move when he speaks. He fills out a grey robe similar to Shamgar, but the sun on his robe has a wide-open mouth. His gauntlets have a freshly polished sheen like the one atop his head, and an enormous mace with a double-handed shaft dangles behind his back.

"In fact, he's no precept at all. I'm afraid so."

Ur Rothmore's acclaim didn't grow because of his number of conversions; it grew because of a single conversion. The mouthpiece loved to talk about it more than the Goddess herself. His self-proclaimed miracle became the reason that he earned his distinction for charity. No precept could pull coins from a purse like Ur Rothmore, and no testimony could pull it more quickly than the day that he converted a forester - the only forester conversion in the Synod's records.

Holy hands reach for Neshama when the faithful hear how the precept convinced Emor Boar to walk the five stages through the Grand Chancel and purify his soul. Granted, old Emor Boar only had five more steps in him, but to die at the feet of Miriam a converted forester - no precept could top that testimony of faith. High Precept Amar Divine appointed Ur Rothmore as his mouthpiece because of his silver tongue and the gold pieces that overflowed his coffers.

Ram wrestles with the decision to punch Rothmore in the mouth or lecture him. "You should've finished the purge a month ago, but you and the other cowards locked yourselves away in the Grand Chancel."

"O you dare, we were devoted to prayer. And Neshama did speak on how we are to deal with the weak. Edict one: truth is lacking. Edict two: charity is slacking. Edict three:

forgiveness, too much grace. Edict four: veneration, way too late. So here stands the final decision. Amar Divine calls for an inquisition!"

"You rhyming fox! Now is the time for the edict of truth, this has always been the way of the Synod. Once judgment is complete, then we guide the people back to the way of truth."

Emmerick waves off the debate. "This council has already decided to move forward on this secret Melek cult, not negotiate Synod procedure."

"There is no such cult!" yells Shamgar. "Souls will take time to heal, but I assure you that any remaining devotees to Zimri's kingship are on this chain. The Queen Mother has been slain and her hags have suffered the same fate."

"Then how do you explain the assassins?" asks Aden.

Ur Rothmore demonstrates that he's indeed the mouthpiece of High Precept Amar Divine when he lets out a blood-curdling roar.

"Shamgar Ram! You must pay for the sins you committed, for all the acts of murder you inflicted! I think that Melek dwells in your heart, that's he's been there from the start!"

Shamgar drops his chains, draws his mace, and grasps his shield.

"Guards, detain this man," orders Captain Tamar. The palace guards speedily disarm Shamgar and cuff him.

"Wait, you can't arrest this man. He saved my life and he led the charge that broke Zimri's troops on the drawbridge," says Ashira.

"I can vouch for Shamgar's character. He may be cold-hearted, but he's no Melek worshipper," offers Ben.

"Take him to the prison," orders Emmerick in a hesitant voice. "If these Synod charges are true then they must be proven in court. My kingdom will be one of law and order."

The light in Shamgar's eyes dissolve into his dark circles. He hangs his head while the guards escort him to prison, his chain of severed heads dragging behind him.

After taking a long pause to gather his wits, Emmerick returns his focus to the council.

"As for an inquisition, you have my permission Mouthpiece Rothmore, but there are to be no executions - only questions. Any accusations must be entered as public record. All of the cases that you wish to try must be brought before my court upon my return."

"Where are you going, my King?" asks Tobi.

"Calcedon."

The answer silences the racing minds of the council.

"Aden is correct. Zidon is our biggest threat and he must be captured. Issur is in no condition for war, so we must seek a diplomatic solution with King Lars of Calcedon. I don't want another century of war like we saw in the Third Age. I'm hoping that a small company from this council will join me.

Ben must follow as sentinel. Ezekiel, I may need your prophetic knowledge. Doubtful, but I must be thorough."

Seth siphons wine through his nose at the insult.

"Your brawn would be of service, big fellow."

After a deep swallow, Seth refuses, "Sorry, I have plans to repair my pottery shop."

"Join me, and upon your return, I'll finance the repairs."

The life changing offer locks Seth's and Ashira's eyes in disbelief.

"Deal. But my sister comes along too. She's the best cook in Issur, and she's handy with a blade if we get in a jam."

"That makes five of us, then," notes Emmerick. "Six, including Caleb. I will need you to secure the schooner."

The scout politely nods in agreement.

"Don't you mean seven, Sire?" asks Tobi.

"If these were different circumstances then I'd say yes,

good Captain. But I need you to continue training the army, what remains of it."

"Yes, Sire," says Tobi with a little less gruff in his voice.

"Aden, you will continue to see to the needs of our people, as well as supervise the repairs to the city walls."

"Yes, Uncle."

"Precept Rothmore, you are dismissed to go about your holy work."

Rothmore exits as arrogantly as he entered.

The council disbands with a mixture of excitement and anxiety concerning the various paths ahead. As the bodies intermingle around the room, Ben notices that Aden stands frozen with his eyes glazed on thoughts from the past.

"Aden… I'll look out for Emmerick every step of the way, and Tobi can keep his eyes on you."

"It's not Tobi's eyes that concern me, Sentinel."

The prince changes the subject by raising his goblet for a farewell toast.

"To the Remnant. Goddess keep us."

The council returns his well-wish, as everyone, even Ezekiel, swirls down a drink of wine.

Chapter 6 ✦ The Feast of Hamor Chug

Seth rummages about the burned-out Keros pottery shop, sifting through the debris in the workroom. He props up a charred stool next to the potter's wheel. The ashen smells settle in his throat.

Ashira enters and attempts to look beyond the ruins in hopes to reclaim warm memories of her childhood. She connects with a fond reverie - her skinny tan legs stretched across her mother's lap, her little hands underneath her mother's hands sliding across the soft clay.

Seth's harrowed brow brings her back to reality and the two feel the need to escape to the street. Ashira takes Seth's arm and guides him over the cobblestone.

"Ezekiel said that you were here... After we return from Calcedon, you'll have this place back to good."

"What about you? You leavin' the pottery business?"

"I was never really in the pottery business. I know more about cooking than pottery."

"Open an inn. I'll sell you the dishes."

She playfully nudges his ribs with her elbows.

"You can do whatever you want, Ashira. You're free."

"That's my problem; I have no idea what to do. I thought that living without the yoke of servitude would be easier than this. Choice makes it overwhelming."

Seth slings his bicep over her shoulder and pulls her to his side in a show of support.

"I don't even know if I should be part of this company. Seth, why did you vouch for me?" questions Ashira behind her abashed brown eyes.

"You need to get away from Tizra, get away from Evan. Take a break from the past, and get lost in the moment. Freedom is all about the moment. That's what mother taught me at the wheel. The energy with which I craft a piece will exist for the moment, then, it will be captured in the vessel and be mine no longer. What's done is done. Who knows what we'll find in Calcedon, but we'll finally get to spend time together."

Ashira's demeanor brightens while she ponders the Keros family philosophy.

Night settles on the palace and after days of tiresome research and a lengthy council meeting, Emmerick slumbers in his chair behind his book wall. Head back and mouth open, his snores crackle in rhythm with the pops from fireplace.

Ben sits awake at the table reading about the triumphs of Josiah, the Shepherd King. Longings for home stir him from his spot.

He walks down the open-air hallway to catch a glimpse of the vast expanse of stars that span across Hallowed Hills. The stars seem brighter than usual and they continue to brighten as if they descend upon him.

Ben's face looks directly up, then, collapses down after connecting with the purple eyes on Azor's face, a sense of relief calming his sense of wonder.

"How I've missed you," says the scorned believer, resting his forehead against the white robes of the nephesh. "Where have you been?"

"After failing to subdue Korah, I returned to Neshama."

"What's it like to be in her presence?"

"You and your questions, Benjamin… It's like watching your earth, sky, and sea conjoin with the celestial realm. I feel the majesty of her creation pulsing within her essence. To look upon the Goddess is to adore her with perfect fear mixed with pure love. Her grace envelops my ether and validates my purpose in her eternal plans."

Ben pauses as his soul feels a faint brush with eternity.

"She feels so close and so far from me… Why did she send you back, Azor?"

"For a second chance. She treasures nephesh the way she treasures all life. She won't give up on her creations because she can't. I told you before - she's connected to her creations."

"What happens if Korah refuses to return?"

"Then, he risks falling into corruption, similar to humans who refuse to remember the Covenant."

"Has this ever happened to a nephesh before?"

"You ask of mysteries that I refuse to reveal."

"This great war in which you fought and killed nephesh?"

"Focus on the here and now, Benjamin. Why do humans obsess over the past and the future?"

"I've been told that this is a problem for me," admits Ben.

"Maybe the time will come when I reveal these mysteries, but I arrive this night seeking your help. Do you have any idea where Korah might be?" The desperation in Azor's voice gives Ben even more cause for concern.

"I have no idea. All I can tell you is that he's with another nephesh named Melek."

Azor jogs his memory brimming with names of the ether-guardians, but he can't identify any nephesh named Melek.

"You've seen a third nephesh?"

"Yes, he was enormous. Taller and thicker than you or Korah. His robes were black like Korah and he had the same yellow eyes. He emerged from the ether vortex as soon as you vanished and stomped Zimri to death."

"All nephesh are the same size, so how can this be?"

"Not you too… Most already doubt what I witnessed. After Melek killed Zimri, he proclaimed that he would bring darkness down upon the Remnant."

"This is troublesome news but there's nothing that I can do to remedy the situation. My call to bring Korah back to Neshama must be completed. I'll return to the ether world in hopes of finding the last nephesh to serve with Korah."

The plan sounds unconvincing to Ben, who feels more isolated in his plight.

"You've worked to overcome your selfishness, Benjamin. Your heart is more earnest than when we first met, but you must fulfill your call or the burden of regret will crush your soul. Zimri's dead but it appears that Melek worship still persists. You must find the root of this evil."

Azor's celestial light fades down the hallway and into the dark of night leaving Ben to ponder his divine call of Neshama, and his divine appointment with Melek.

Korah awaits Melek's arrival in the throne room at the palace in Elam. He senses his master's ether before it connects with the vortex on the floor. The grand nephesh slowly emerges from the swirling black ether and glides to a halt on the stone surface.

Korah bends his knee to Melek.

"Welcome, Master."

"Why does the prince not take his throne beside me?"

"King Tartek takes his place among the ranks of his army. He makes ready his ranks for the first phase of the battle plan."

"You may rise."

Melek has grown in stature since his encounter with Ben - his robes blacker and thicker - his yellow eyes wider.

The artistry of the wall crumbles into tiny slithers, for his massive steps create fault lines down the throne room mural.

As he sits, his robes symmetrically caress the sides of his throne. He rests his ether sword across his lap.

"King Tartek?" questions Melek.

"Lars starves to death in the dungeon, tormented by regret - a just punishment for rejecting your vision."

"Have you surveyed the ranks of your army?"

"I marvel at your brilliance with ether, my Master. Issur has never faced a Calcedonian army of this magnitude."

"True, but they are mortals. If we nephesh have but one obstacle, it's the flesh and bone of mortals."

"If only they were merely flesh and bone," notes Korah.

"Sounds like you visited my laboratory as I requested."

"Master, you promised that your secrets would become my knowledge, that you would heighten my awareness of ether."

"I've already begun; you've identified the essence of the human soul. If only all mortals were weak like Zimri and Tartek, the Covenant would be lost and Neshama forgotten. Mortals of faith like the shepherd and the prince make this a challenge that I did not anticipate."

"You give them too much respect."

"So speaks the nephesh who was repelled by the shepherd."

The words stoke an internal fire that demands revenge on Ben Tav. Korah's eyes dim with secrecy as he conceals his challenge with Azor - the reason he did not slay the shepherd.

"Is there more?" asks Melek, attempting to read Korah's narrowed irises.

"No, Master," says Korah, maintaining his stoic stare.

"The mortals in the Remnant detest my ways, but there's only one mortal that we must keep an eye on."

The thought of the magi broadens Korah's shoulders. "Zidon sent word that he comes to us by way of The East Sea, forced to take the long way."

"Of course he comes. He needs us, and we need him under our supervision. Hopefully, our magi-bait will net us some fish."

The company of Emmerick, Ben, Ezekiel, Seth, and Ashira arrive at the white walls of Port of Arnor - the city of merchants. They dismount from their horses before boarding them in a stable that overlooks the sea of corn in The Heartlands.

A skinny man in blue silks greets them with a dainty bow to the king, "Greetings, Sire. My name is Carswel, Executor Chug's steward."

Carswel ushers the company through the streets of Arnor, the luxurious town flaunting its elegant architecture.

The lavish city bustles as shoppers weave around the white columns that line the perfectly strait cobblestone streets. The citizens flow to and from their rows of townhouses topped with orange tile neatly stacked next to one another. Similar to the shops that display their conformity to the merchant culture, each townhouse corresponds to the symmetry of the port city.

The company notices a competition in the style of Arnorian dress. The wealthier wear more layers of silks. Some don trappings of furs, while others flaunt their wealth with the jewelry in their ears and noses. The smell of exotic perfumes lifts from the merchants as they pass one another on the busy streets.

The high level of security comforts the elitist merchants while they stroll through the markets. Upright guards with spears against their shoulders stand post on every street corner and a tall white watchtower in the center of the city houses a unit of archers, marking potential thieves in the streets below.

Steward Carswel delivers the company to the doorsteps of the executor's mansion.

The company enters the parlor to grey marble flooring. An exotic vase collection spans the parlor, thus mesmerizing Seth. The collection of pottery spans numerous oceans and surpasses any craftsmanship that the potter has ever seen since his mother's work graced the showroom of their family business. The thought of breaking a vase makes him nauseous, and he treads ever so lightly through the gallery.

The tiny steward ushers them up a flight of stairs to a veranda overlooking The East Sea. As Ben stares down at the vessels in the port, the softest breeze caresses his face, and he can taste a hint of salt in the air.

The sight of the white brick, the smell of the sea breeze, and the sound of the crashing waves offers serenity to the entire company while they await the feast of Hamor Chug.

"Carswel! Where are you!?"

"On the veranda with our guests, Sir."

Huffs and puffs echo up the staircase before Hamor Chug emerges with a sweaty forehead.

A handsome man with a perfect nose and thick brown locks, he was nicknamed the moonstruck merchant for he captivated clients with his suave sales pitches. He swindled miners out of the finest jewels and farmers out of their best crops. There was a time when the maidens of Arnor swooned over the fetching trader, and the moniker 'moonstruck' aptly described these weak-kneed damsels. His tales of high sea adventure and chests of treasure were enough to make any young lady get lost in his grandeur.

As time past, it was his many wives who got lost at sea that troubled the women and men of Arnor. For what at first appeared to be bad luck, turned into a troublesome pattern.

The city council threatened to bring murder charges when three cheated sailors vowed to testify against the fishy merchant in court. However, it was Hamor, who fleeced Zimri into a deal that spared the Merchants Guild in Arnor from ruination. The deal was so lopsided that the tyrant swept it under a rug out of sheer embarrassment. Instead of prosecuting Hamor, the city council unanimously voted for him to become the next executor of Arnor.

Hamor's title of executor excelled his anxiety, and that was why Carswel became the wealthiest chamberlain in all of Issur.

"The tilapia hasn't been seasoned, the wine's still corked, and my diamond stud's missing," whimpers Hamor.

"Sir, I have fresh rosemary in route from your spice shop. I uncorked the 3013 in the cellar, not the 3027 that we usually serve since we are in the presence of royalty." Carswel removes the pink diamond earring from a jewelry box in his pocket and slides it into Hamor's ear. "I had the jeweler polish your prized diamond this morning."

Ezekiel whispers to Seth, "Looks like this steward has a better meal for us than the one we had with Nebo the pig."

"What do you mean? I liked Nebo's goulash."

"Of course you did," mocks Ezekiel.

"Forgive my rudeness, good King. I want everything to be perfect and Carswel always makes it so," says Hamor, taking Emmerick's hand to welcome him.

The executor wrinkles his nose at the company dressed in their military gear. "Please tell me that this isn't your dinner attire?"

"I'm afraid so, Mr. Chug. We leave in the morning for imperial business with Calcedon," informs Emmerick.

"Carswel, take the men to the parlor and open up the wardrobe for some inviting dinner attire."

"We're not all men," says Ashira, her beauty hitting him like a sea gust.

Hamor ogles her striking features for a long moment, before wiping a dab of drool from the corner of his lip. "Moonstruck yet again," says Hamor, rising up on his toes in an attempt to be at eye level with her.

"May I have the honor of your name, my adorable doll?"

A thorn from the executor's rosy talk pricks Ben's jealousy. "Ashira Keros."

Hamor heightens all the more as the last name rolls off her lips. "You're more stunning than your mother, if such a feat were possible. Hopefully, not as stubborn."

"More so," interjects Seth, growing tired of Hamor's advances at his sister.

Hamor takes note that the siblings share the same dark features, "You have the height of your father. Looks like you inherited his hairline too."

Not intimidated by the message that Seth sends through his stature, the moonstruck merchant stiffens his shoulders while he continues to address matters concerning the Keros family. "Your father was a capable merchant. But let's be honest, your mother's talent carried that business. Loryn's pottery was unrivaled in Issur. It could have been world renown, but Laud didn't have the ambition for greatness. He never ventured too far or for too long from that humble shop. I guess if I had an elegant artisan in my midst, I would have caged her up like the rare bird that she was.

I tried to warn your parents and the other guild members in Tizra about funding the conspiracy against Zimri. I shall toast to their memory this evening."

Hamor gently takes Ashira by the hand. "Come with me, I have the perfect gown that my wife won't mind you wearing."

"You don't want to ask her first?"

"I'd love to, darling. The poor lass is lost at sea."

Hamor guides Ashira away from the men. Oddly, his charming ways lessen her disdain for him, and she feels comfortable parting from her brother.

Seth blocks the exit to the parlor, his hesitancy planting his feet on the veranda. Carswel politely waits for Seth to start walking.

"Has anyone told you that you make a good door?" prompts Ezekiel.

Seth begrudgingly heeds the prompt, and follows Carswel to the parlor. Emmerick and Ezekiel fall in line, but Ben lags behind with a protective eye on Ashira.

A thunderstorm booms over The East Sea providing an orchestra of dinner music while lightning bolts dance across the skyline of Arnor.

Colorful silks replace the drab armor of the company to the delight of Hamor Chug's eyes. Ezekiel slips and slides about the seat of his chair, longing to return to his weathered robe. Seth gradually flexes his bicep muscles hoping to stretch the silken fabric cinching the circulation of blood flow. Ben focuses on straitening his vision more than his wayward dressings for his eyes drift like the storm clouds behind him, mesmerized by the flashes of Ashira's beauty. She stuns in a black gown trimmed in garnet with her onyx earrings pairing with her onyx necklace.

Emmerick and Hamor spend most of the dinner talking trade agreements and tax rates, but the more wine the executor ingests, the more his eyes trace Ashira's hourglass gown.

"If you stayed in Arnor, you'd be the most beautiful women in the city. I'd keep you docked in my mansion though, wouldn't want you to get lost at sea."

"I happen to like taller men; it's a dancing thing… Sorry."

The conversation troubles Ben, and if it were not for the intoxicating aroma of the rosemary on the tilapia, it would bother Seth too.

"Feisty girls are my favorite," says Hamor, spraying a mist of wine through his incisors.

"I'm spoken for, so save your flattery."

Ashira's defensive words inadvertently hit Ben harder than Hamor, and she quickly regrets saying them to ward off the inebriated merchant.

"I bet he can't dress you in the finest gowns and dine you with the best meals in Issur."

"Dress, no. As for your fish, I've prepared better."

"Ha! You cook!? And you cook better than my chefs!? Nonsense. Women can't cook. Travel enough and you'll find the best chefs in the world are men."

Hamor's comment rings so offensive that Seth stops eating.

Ashira stares down Hamor as the flashes of lightning illumine her intense gaze. "Tell me, then. If your chefs are so good, why brush the fish in this lard that you pass off as butter? Olive oil would offer a much richer flavor. And why not add a hint of garlic salt to the rosemary to give a bit of kick to the taste?"

Seth looks at the fish on his fork, shaking his head in agreement with his sister.

"Is this how the women of Tizra carry themselves, Sire? I can see why you stayed single all of these years."

"No need to spoil a pleasant evening, Mr. Chug."

"No, Emmerick Tizra. It's your family who spoils all that is good in Issur. Your brother was a terror to this country. I'm still furious over the little amount of coin I wasted on that worthless pact. I expect my sum to be returned in full or this agreement of ours is void."

Hamor sucks down another goblet of white and slams the cup on the table. "Never forget this one truth. Merchants are shrewder than politicians, and the merchants of Arnor always do very well for themselves."

The executor claps his hand to summon Carswel, and the apt steward rallies to his side. "Show them to their rooms. They are to be dismissed at the first ray of sunlight," orders Hamor. Carswel balances the tipsy executor while guiding him down the staircase.

"We have a deal then," smiles Emmerick. "Let's get some rest, shall we?"

"I'll be down soon," says Ashira, as the men make for the guest hall.

"Ben, wait!" requests Ashira.

He hesitantly joins her and they watch the storm flash more bolts of golden electricity. The current swirls only in the sky, for the scorned shepherd cuts off his affectionate feelings for her.

"I'm sorry. I shouldn't have said that I was spoken for, I didn't mean anything by it."

Ben's eyes begin to water.

"You don't have to get emotional over it," chides Ashira.

"It's your perfume," reminds Ben.

"Sorry. I forgot you're allergic to Jasmine."

Ashira takes a step away from Ben to allow the breeze to whisk away her scent.

"You told Hamor the truth. I don't fault you for that."

"I do appreciate you giving me space."

"Just being your friend like you asked… It's probably not a good idea for friends to be alone on a veranda, especially after a few glasses of wine."

Flashes of lightning illumine Ashira's lonely silhouette as Ben disappears from the veranda.

The sea storm pounds the Port of Arnor, the turbulent waves tossing the boats about the harbor. The night blackens the angry clouds, and the white bolts within offer brief glimpses of the cityscape.

A watchman on patrol outside of the executor's mansion catches a glimpse of a silhouette in a flicker of lightning - a shadow skittering about a rooftop. His gut instinct refuses to allow him to dismiss the image. Hoping for another flash of lightning to reveal more of the mystery figure, he moves closer.

His wish for another flash is granted, only this time, the light reveals a clear roof. The storm begins to drift north and the rain lessens, along with the guard's tension.

Another bolt flickers and two shadows appear. A pair of assassins swiftly scales the side of the watchtower.

The watchman runs for a warning bell on the street corner. He dashes through the puddles clearing the alley.

STICK! Xylen rams a dagger into the guard's heart.

Xylen clutches the watchman's cloak and lowers him to street without making a sound.

The two assassins infiltrate the tower to find a handful of archers asleep, including the bowman on post. Their daggers slice fast and exact, sending the tower-guard to a permanent rest.

The assassins ready their bows and wait for a bolt of light to mark the other watchman on post at the entrance of Hamor Chug's mansion.

The fourth assassin prepares his next move in an adjacent alleyway. Another bolt strikes in the night, and the tower-assassins fire.

Their arrows prick the heart of the watchman.

The guard sways forward when the stalker from the alley sprints out to catch the corpse bringing it to a quiet fall.

The fifth assassin slides down the roof of an inn near the docks on the hunt for Caleb Glade. The slayer stealthily jostles open a window and lowers his legs to the floor. He places his feet precisely on the planks to avoid any creaks. The assassin readies his dagger as he removes Caleb's blanket.

The assassin's lungs release his disappointment at the sight of an empty bed.

His hopes revive when he hears a lady giggling from the adjacent room.

"Stop tickling me, Caleb!" commands the maiden in a playful giggle.

The assassin slips out of the window to eaves drop on their conversation.

"Don't be shy, my dear. I promise that a goodnight kiss is much better with the lantern on."

"No lantern," insists the maiden.

"No need for me to be picky, I suppose."

Two thuds collapsing down upon the bed call the assassin to action. He jostles open the window and readies his sword and dagger - one weapon for each victim. The slayer lunges his blades into the bed and they stick with such force that he can't remove them.

The assassin quickly perceives that he did not connect with flesh but with wood.

A lantern brightens the room and the glow reveals to the assassin that his blades have been imbedded in barrels. He closes his eyes to accept his fate that he is not the hunter, but the hunted.

Caleb's war-axes collapse down upon the assassin's neck.

"This is a real shame, you're a cute one," says Caleb to the maiden shielding her vision.

He kisses her hand, before dropping a hefty coin purse in her palm. "You're a fantastic actress. You really sold your character – 'The Innocent Wench.' The next time I visit Arnor, I may watch another one of your plays. Hopefully, no assassins will be stalking me but I can't make any promises."

Outside of the mansion, the assassins in the tower fix their attention on the mansion entrance – poised to drop any guard who might stumble upon his fallen comrades.

Inside, the company sleeps soundly for their spirits have been soothed by the comforts of fine wine. Only Ezekiel finds it hard to sleep as he slides about his silk sheets.

Xylen and his partner halt when they hear footsteps in the living quarters.

Ezekiel loses his silks for the comforts of his rugged robe. He flips up his hood, lies down on top of his sheets, and returns to his rest.

The two stalkers communicate with sign language, both agreeing that their primary targets are Ben and Seth - obstacles in their way to the prophet. They crawl along the floor in silence, which gets blown with shouts from the streets.

"Sound the alarm!" yells Caleb to the night watch in route to the mansion. "Assassins in the city!"

The untested guards hesitate, but garner the nerve to ring the warning bells that begin to echo on every street corner in the city.

The hunters in the tower think twice about hailing down arrows on the frantic guards, instead, they utilize the chaos to aid their escape towards the docks.

Ben and Seth spring into action.

The assassins launch a flurry of dagger attacks at their unarmed prey defending themselves with metal pitchers and bedpans.

"Protect the king!" orders Ben to Ashira.

She grabs Emmerick and tackles him into a wardrobe. She slams the doors behind them, dislodges the dowel-rod within, and bars the wardrobe shut.

Seth rips the door from the hinges and hurls it at the assassins. They duck in unison, and the door connects with Ezekiel, knocking him head over feet.

The timers in the assassin's heads warn them of their lost initiative, so they sprint out of the guest hall. Seth rips the hood from the Xylen, who sneers in frustration.

"You again!" yells Seth, reminded of their encounter in the seminary kitchen.

The assassins zip through the halls hanging every corner as if they had been in the mansion before. Caleb flies through the halls in pursuit. Ben speeds after him leaving the much slower Seth behind.

Hamor Chug dashes from his bedroom like a headless chicken. "Carswel, help! Emmerick betrayed me!"

Ben labors to catch the faster Caleb. The scout sprints down a long hallway after the assassins - the same hallway where Hamor Chug cowers behind a door.

Hamor sucks in his gut while the door presses him against the wall - the flowing black robes of the assassins brushing by him.

After they pass, he attempts to shut the door, but fails to close it in time.

Caleb blasts the door into Hamor's handsome face.

His perfect nose gets mashed into his face. Blood pours out his nostrils while he grovels on all fours like a pug. "Carswel, my dear Carswel," cries the disfigured merchant, catching the slightest glimpse of Caleb's face.

Ben avoids the wreckage of Hamor Chug by hanging a left down an adjacent hallway.

Ben and Caleb track the assassins up the stairs leading to the veranda. Xylen reaches the top first and turns alongside his partner to face their pursuers. In a traitorous act, Xylen sticks his dagger into his companion's back and forcefully boots him down the stairwell.

The lifeless body lumbers down the steps and collides with Ben and Caleb. After the three figures rumble to the bottom step, the two pursuers bounce to their feet and tread the steps once more. They arrive at the veranda only to watch Xylen and the two archer-assassins swim out to sea in the dim light of the sunrise.

Their counterpart steers the wheel of a schooner, anticipating their arrival. Once the men scale the netting into the boat, Xylen and his three remaining assassins sail south.

Threats of an assassination plot fume from Hamor Chug. His threats prompt the company to quickly gather their belongings and make haste for Calcedon.

Chapter 7 ⋮ Inquisitions

The fall air picks up the scent of the harvest from The Heartland and swirls it through the active Tizra streets where the merchants conduct business underneath a pristine sky. The clanks of hammers rhythmically chime across the city walls.

Aden's sweat drips into the churning grey mortar as he rolls his shoulders to stir the oaken oar in his fists. Builders sling the cement paste from the cauldron against stone blocks before shoving them into the gaping holes in the ramparts.

Tobi marches six cadets up and down the back-alleys of Tizra beneath the ramparts. One heavy-footed lass labors to keep pace with the pack. After a few growls of the captain's breath fuming of eggs and liver, the cadet picks up her pace. Aden nods to Tobi, grateful for the progression of the cadets.

Suddenly, a scream echoes throughout the north plaza, quickly summoning Aden to the source of anguish.

Ur Rothmore, flanked by a handful of devoted citizens, takes an older man into his custody. As deputies of the mouthpiece, Rothmore's attendants have sun patches sewn into their clothing. They toss the brawny man down at the precept's feet.

Rothmore stands over him with a raised mace.

"You can't do this!" pleads the young woman, before Aden steps in.

"I thought King Emmerick was clear on this. There are to be no executions until all cases become public record and tried upon his return," reminds Aden.

"If you love the Goddess, kind Prince, then why do you protest? This man worships in the dark and he confesses Melek in his heart."

"Is this true?" ask Aden of the accused.

Refusing to answer, the man covers his sweaty face with his rugged hands.

Aden turns to his daughter. "Did your father confess?"

"Yes! But he's a good man, a simple stone mason. He can't part with the Melek shrine in his shop; he believes it brings him good luck. How is that a crime worthy of death?"

"It's not," assures Aden.

"Allow me to stay my mace and with you in private make my case," says Rothmore, pulling Aden to a quiet corner.

The small following grows fond of the precept because of the way he talks, and his words resonate with the anti-Melek turnout.

"Amar Divine remembers a certain confession and how he taught you an important lesson. I would hate to let these people know about their prince and leave them to question, has his heart changed since?"

The sins of Aden's past creep up from the depths of his soul and condemnation weighs heavy on his heart. The prince turns pale before he hurries into the palace, leaving the mason's daughter to woefully watch her only hope disappear.

Aden hears the applause of the zealous mob when the deputies drag the heretic to prison.

"I will not bludgeon this man in front of your face, but I guarantee you that he will taste of my mace. So shall it be for all of you heathens, whom I will execute for righteous reasons."

Aden hangs his head while Ur Rothmore makes his way to the prison to execute his first victim of his inquisition.

Aden turns and smacks into Tobi.

"You don't look well, my Prince."

Aden can't shake the burden of the precept's condemning proclamation and therefore doesn't offer a response.

The captain raises his bushy brows with worry for the prince's wellbeing. "Why don't you have a seat and open this package that arrived from Tav?" requests Tobi.

Aden accepts the box, feels his way along the wall, and sits down hard on a secluded bench.

"Return to your troops, I'll be fine."

Aden waits for Tobi to clear the corridor before he slides out the folded note attached to the top of the package, which reads, *Thanks for making me smile.*

He unwraps the package and there before him lay the stone medallion that caught his attention in the Tav guild hall.

Recalling his encounter with Judith, Aden slides his finger over the lightning rune. He puts the medallion around his neck and tucks it under his shirt, allowing the cold stone of the rune to chill the fire of sin scorching his soul.

Judith and Evan enjoy a quiet night of sipping tea by the fireside. The little girl sleeps soundly, tucked in for a secure night's rest.

Judith sips her tea, admires the tapestry, and works her sewing needles. The routine becomes so noticeable that Evan figures the pattern.

BAM! BAM! BAM! A powerful fist bangs against the oak doors like a battering ram, jolting Evan and Judith from their chairs.

Evan gingerly approaches the door, hesitant to greet a stranger with such powerful fists. He opens the door to find two timbers looming over him. Though he's wounded in body, he's not in pride, and refuses to show any signs of intimidation.

Evan takes note of their unique raiment of red leather and bear skins. Double-handed battleaxes hang from their backs. Their fair skin and orange features inform him that the visitors travel from the Forest of Elah.

The domineering presence of the woodsmen backs Judith into the shadows.

"Isn't this a sight, not sure a forester has ever set foot in a shepherd's guild hall," greets Evan.

The bigger forester promptly sets the record straight, "We come from the guild hall in Resh. Jether Resh says you have what I seek."

"If you're welcome in his hall, you're welcome in mine."

The seven foot tall forester nearly knocks his head atop of the high doorframe. His companion, nearly of the same stature, dips his knees to be certain that his dome doesn't connect. Both men have full reddish-brown beards and wear their thick hair in ponytails. The taller forester has a face of the bear with glowing green eyes.

"My name is Erez Elk, guild master from Elah. This is my guardsman, Sorek Boar. We heard of your heroics from

Jether Resh. The scars on your face testify to his tale… Tell me. Is it true that you saved one of ours?"

Evan's paternal instincts liven as concern for the child's safety raises the stubble on the back of his neck. "You heard of my deeds from an honorable man, I have no need to boast."

At hearing Evan's response, Judith's hands tremble when she grabs hold of the kettle. "Would you gentlemen care for tea?"

"This is not a social visit. We traveled to Resh in search of a child; we were promised that we'd find her here. Did you spare her life?"

"I did," acknowledges Evan. "But I'm sorry to say that she's not here."

"Where is she!?" roars Erez.

The burly voice wakes the little girl and she runs from her bedroom. She sprints across the guild hall and leaps into Erez's arms. "Papa!" Once her giddiness wears off, she beats her tiny fists against his wide chest. "You took too long!"

Erez smiles, grateful for the beating from her tiny fists. "Iana, Pumpkin… I looked everywhere after you disappeared. Every day felt like a year. I haven't been home to see your sisters since that day."

"We were scoppin' lilies at the lake when the wolf came," confesses Iana, the memory shaking her to the core.

Evan and Judith step forward to offer comfort, but pause in step now that Iana sits securely in her papa's arms.

"There's no reward that can be placed on a loved-one's life, so I won't pay you in coin. Your name is known to me, Evan Tav. It will also be known to my people. You have my respect."

Erez extends his hand, and Evan accepts it. The forester's bear-sized paw swallows Evan's hand.

"Outsiders are forbidden in the Forest of Elah, but I

extend this offer to you and only you, once and only once. You may feast in my hall, and I will honor your deeds as a show of my respect."

Erez turns toward the guild hall doors with Iana snug in his arms.

Judith's inner-strength falters and her tears flow while watching the child depart.

Iana whispers into her papa's ears and he sets her down. The child throws her arms around her temporary mother. Judith returns the gesture by wrapping the green-knitted scarf around Iana's red hair.

After being released by Judith, Iana clutches Evan's leg and squeezes it in a show of gratitude for his bravery.

Iana then happily returns to her father's arms.

Evan sees them to the door and watches until they disappear into the hills. Feeling like a piece of her soul now ventures into the forest, Judith remains in the shadows.

"I'm heading to bed. Try to get some rest," encourages Evan.

The siblings share an embrace, and Judith closes the doors. The sound of the slamming doors reverberates throughout the empty hall before the sound dies down along with the fireplace.

Nights in the guild hall would come to embody Judith's existence – alone and in the dark.

Ben surveys the water to the south, barely able to catch a glimpse of the top sail carrying the four assassins to Calcedon. He notices that their vessel drifts southwest. Caleb stands next to him, making the same observation, "Doesn't look like they're going to Temen."

"Where are they going, then?" asks Ben.

"Carnek."

"Should we follow them?"

"Emmerick wants to avoid any entanglements; we'd definitely get noticed in a port city. Zidon sailed to Temen. He's our man, so we follow his trail."

The plan sits well Ben, though the near assassination attempt continues to unsettle his nerves. A few hours adrift on the choppy waves of The East Sea toss the earthy shepherd's nerves even more so.

The midday sun scorches the deck, but that does not stop Seth from hosting a training session for his sister. Ashira drips sweat onto both of her swords as her jasmine-scented perspiration tortures the crew. Any foolish notions by the lewd seadogs to hit on the beauty are quickly cast overboard with one look at Seth's Peacemaker.

"Swing high with right, low with left. Penetrate the armor with right swing, aim for the vitals with the left. Most warriors will try to quell your power swing, that's why your follow through attack must be lethal," says Seth, getting ready for another round of attacks from Ashira.

Ben can't help but stare. It isn't Ashira's elegance that ropes him in like it usually does; it's her perfect balance when wielding the two blades. His training as a sentinel helps him appreciate the speed and accuracy of her swings.

Ezekiel peaks up from Othniel's book and Seth recruits him. "Grab your staff. Let me teach you how to use it for more than a walking stick."

Ezekiel snarls at Seth while getting to his feet.

"What's wrong with you?" asks Seth.

"What's wrong!? You hit me with a door and I've yet to receive any resemblance of an apology."

"Well, Zek. I guess you'll move out of the way next time," chides Seth.

Ashira flips back her hair and runs her fingers through the tangles before knotting the raven-colored strands into a ponytail. She reaches for the water pale while her brother spars with the disgruntled prophet.

Ben scoops a ladle and she graciously receives it. For the first time, he notices her mother's ancestral wedding ring on a chain around her neck. Though he already knows about the origins of the ring, he can't help himself but to question her about it.

"Where did you get that ring?"

"Evan gave it to me. It was my mother's wedding ring."

"I guess that settles it, then."

"Settles what?"

"You're gonna marry him."

"I don't know."

Ben tries to find peace of mind in the horizon. When that fails, he tries to find a distraction in Seth's training session with Ezekiel, but he can't escape his jealous thoughts.

He was a war-orphan raised by a drunken uncle, who neglected him. His older siblings were too busy to cater to him. There wasn't a selfish bone in his body. He shared everything he had with his siblings and never longed for personal possessions. Kurion, the black bow strapped to his back, and his sentinel armor made him slightly uncomfortable, for these were his first possessions of significant value.

Jealousy churns his guts like a virus and he doesn't know how to deal with it, so he spews it out in sordid words. "Of course you know, so drop the act. I saw you sleeping in his arms. You're wearing the perfume he likes. You have his ring. Looks obvious to me."

"Ben, I'm being honest with you. I don't know."

"Aren't we bound to the promises we make? That's what you said in the orchard. I made a promise to my father; you made a promise to yours. We can't go back on those promises."

"Do you want me to marry Evan?"

"Do what you want, but you should drop the act."

"For someone who likes to criticize Evan, you sure act a lot like him. There's no doubt that you are brothers."

Ashira collects her weapons, readjusts her armor, and rejoins Seth as Ezekiel takes a break. Seth is aloof to what fuels the bite in her swings, but he encourages the aggression.

Caleb approaches and puts his arm around the neck of the jealous shepherd. "You're pretty smooth with the ladies."

Ben's scowl offers a few choice words for the sarcastic scout.

"Listen. If you're gonna chase the wounded ones, you gotta let 'em heal. She's all heart under that smooth, creamy, dark skin…"

Ben's scowl deepens.

"I read you… She may want to be with you, but you can't force her decision until she heals."

"How do you know so much about women?" asks Ben.

"As a spy, I spend a lot of times in taverns, which means I spend a lot of time around wenches."

The wind drops out of the main sail to slowly deflate it along with their conversation. The boat slows after the air shifts.

"Looks like we'll be sleeping on the boat tonight," informs Caleb.

A quiet night on The East Sea, the boat gently rocks most of the company and crew to sleep.

The anxiety of what waits in Temen and his sore shoulder deny Ben a long rest. He walks about the top deck and notices that Emmerick and Ezekiel study in the captain's quarters while the captain steadies the vessel through the night fog.

Ben looks in the window and smiles at the sight - Ezekiel peaking onto the pages of Emmerick's book on Calcedonian wildlife and Emmerick peaking onto the pages of Ezekiel's book about holy mysteries. One catches the other in act, so they exchange books.

The calm night reminds Ben of Tav with the slosh of waves replacing the chirps of crickets. Caught up in the mystery of the sea, he thinks on Azor's words about being in the presence of the creator Goddess.

Ben enters the captain's quarters and pours a round of tea for Emmerick and Ezekiel.

"Well, what do you think?" asks the king of the prophet.

"You know much about the natural order, but I'm not sure about your theory on leviathans. Aren't they a myth?"

"My research shows that early in the First Age, The East Sea flooded Calcedon all the way to the Elam Mountains. The artifacts that I discovered on the shores of Lake Ekron prove that leviathans are actually in these waters."

"You've done research in Calcedon?" asks Ben.

"Lars and I researched Leviathans when we were in the academy together."

"What do you think of my book?" asks the prophet of the king.

"Rubbish. It proves nothing."

"How can you say that?"

The inflection in Ezekiel's voice warns of a meltdown, so Ben calmly pats his back as well as his temper.

"Prove to me that Neshama created the world, that she authored the Covenant, that she awaits us in an afterlife," says Emmerick.

"Wait," interrupts Ben. "Why is the onus on him to prove it?"

The professor's intrigue gets prodded by the shepherd, "Go on, Ben"

"It's the same story in the hills; I have to defend my faith, defend the prophets. You have no better explanation for how humans got here, how we should live, or what will happen next."

"I've done vast research to justify my reasons," says Emmerick.

"I was mentored by a prophet, who compiled the pages in this book that justify my faith," says Ezekiel.

Ben smiles as an endearing thought pops into his head.

Emmerick and Ezekiel grin at the joy on his face.

"My father believed in the power of questions. In fact, he made me promise that I'd never stop asking them."

"You're losing me, Ben," warns Emmerick.

"Emmerick, your existence is based on science. Ezekiel, your existence is based on faith."

Both nod in agreement.

"We spend all of this time debating which is right, which is wrong, when one is hypothesis and the other hope. Isn't that what existence is about? Guessing and hoping. Why can't we simply talk about the questions and enjoy the conversation?"

"Land ahoy!" crows the captain, who ends their conversation and wakes the crew.

"Let's see what questions get answered in Temen," says Ben, brightening with the sunrise.

Chapter 8 ✦✦✦ The Unexpected

Ben fathomed a myriad of possibilities concerning their arrival at the meek fishing village of Temen but complete abandonment never crossed his thoughts. No boats dock at the fishing village and no harbor master emerges to register the company's transport.

As their gaze lifts over the harbor master's podium, they detect no signs of life in the village.

The company crosses the docks under thinning fog - their steps light, their mouths quiet. The sound of woodpeckers hammering the trees around the village loosens the tension bound in their muscles.

The captain and crew remain on the docks while the company ventures into the village square. Not a soul stirs in Temen, and a deeper investigation reveals that the houses sit empty - supplies wiped clean.

The company fans out to look for clues.

A statue of Rygar and Rex sidetracks Ezekiel, who marvels at the two brothers immortalized in stone and song. The Calcedonian heroes stand back to back with claymores raised high above their heads atop a heap of dead Bactra soldiers. The prophet reads their battle anthem inscribed on a stone slab at the base of the monument. The words strike him as profound so he commits the lyrics to memory while attempting to imagine the tune.

Caleb leans down and waves his hand over a fire pit in one of the brown plank houses. Inspecting the ashes, he sifts the black dust through his fingers when he notices specks of crisp tobacco leaves on the floor near the pit bricks.

Caleb exits the residence to deliver his analysis to the company. "Whoever lived here has been gone a while, but someone slept here recently - either Zidon or those who transported him to Temen."

"The five of us will move on from here," informs Emmerick.

"Sire, if I may. You'll need a scout if you're gonna trek to Elam," says Caleb.

"I've done it before; I'll get us there."

The company tries to suppress their uneasiness about Emmerick's plan, but their hesitant eyes tell of their uneasiness.

"I need you to stay with the crew. Don't let them talk you into deserting us if we're long in our return. Promise me that you'll stay the course."

Caleb nods to the terms.

"Stay away from the port city of Carnek. In fact, stay out

of sight. Hide the boat in the Vilekin Ruins west of here for a time. We'll find you at the other fishing village of Tadmor on the rising of the seventh sun."

"Yes, Sire."

Caleb offers farewell handshakes and hugs to the company. His remorseful eyes watch his friends disappear into the woods moving south towards Lake Ekron.

Ben stops in his tracks at the sign that points towards Elam. *Path of Peril - 23 Lengths.*

"Problem, Ben?" asks Emmerick.

"No, Sire. None, whatsoever."

Horror grips the professor's instincts and stirs him to action. Emmerick grabs Ben and tosses him aside, "Look Out!"

The company readies their weapons to unload on the pending threat.

"Ben Tav! You're trouncing all over that anthill!"

The company moans at Emmerick's overdramatic antics. He motions them together and lifts his magnifying monocle to examine the ant colony.

"We don't have time for this," says Ben.

"In the wee hours of this morning I contemplated my existence with Ezekiel. Well, it made me think of ants. This anthill tells me that I should believe in the Creator Goddess."

"What holds you back?" asks Seth.

"Rats. How could a loving Goddess bring such filth into existence? Mice I get, but rats are mangy bloodsuckers."

"You are 'The Learned' indeed," says Seth.

Ezekiel avoids eye contact with his musophobic friend.

"Get back to the lesson," pleads Ben.

"The brown ants of Calcedon are peaceful workers. They exist to create. When a moron comes along and steps on their hill, they become frustrated."

The professor passes the magnifying monocle around to his students. They watch as the ants swarm the hill to identify who dented their dwelling. The ants steady their angst and return to work.

"Then, they rebuild." Emmerick marvels at the anthill with a childlike glee about his face. "Nature was formed in harmony, but there's some force within us and possibly beyond us that corrupts her. Yet, despite millennium after millennium of getting stomped, nature recreates herself. This is true of what Othniel 'Wayfarer' wrote in your book of Neshama concerning redemption. Is it not, Ezekiel?"

"Indeed, Sire," says the prophet, warming to the professor.

"If only this lesson had an aardvark," sighs Ben.

"Silly shepherd, they're no aardvarks in Calcedon."

Emmerick adjusts his pith helmet with a grin as Ben's eyes roll in the direction of the next destination.

The woods surrounding Temen end at a clearing of tall grass, except for a cluster of trees in the middle of the plain.

Ashira follows an unbeaten path into the trees.

Curiosity gets the best of the company and they follow her.

Their first glance rises to the orange leaves spread about the autumn trees. Their second glance lowers to the ground where they identify black footprints and their noses sour at the smell of ashes.

They follow the steps into the cluster of trees and find three posts imbedded in a burned-out circle. Ben points out the Melek runes etched into the bark. Rotating all of the stages of the moon, the runes orbit the posts. Emmerick kicks up some ash and Seth lends a foot. Together, they uncover skeletal remains.

"Looks like we figured out what happened to the villagers," notes Ben.

Ben's bluntness speaks to the fear that torments the company's morale.

"Wilson Wysong loves to gamble and finds his marriage all in shambles. Oli Torn makes Melek idols, which might turn him homicidal. Tara Tanner is a liar, and that is why I have to fry her!" announces Ur Rothmore, frightening the citizens in the north plaza of Tizra.

The precept's minions disperse to arrest the heretics.

An inquisitor drags the first victim from his assignment on wall repair. Aden mixes mortar with a stone mason when witnessing the detainment.

Tobi tutors a male and female cadet on their halberd technique when one of Rothmore's inquisitors serves the captain with papers. The inquisitor's mob of henchmen escorts the trainees to the north plaza.

Aden and Tobi arrive to find a large crowd praising Rothmore and cursing the condemned. Rothmore stands atop a newly constructed stage with a large tree stump in the middle. Two of his attendants serve as relic salesmen; they move about the crowd selling Miriam statuettes.

Rothmore steps onto the stump and the faithful settle their curses. "You have been charged with dirty deeds, please tell your precept - how do you plea?"

"Those soldiers are innocent!" yells Tobi with his gruff voice. "Free them!"

"The captain trains Melek worshippers in his ranks, does he even offer Neshama praise and thanks?" questions Rothmore.

The gathering jeers the captain while Tobi turns to Aden in desperation. "Gambling's not punishable by death, aren't you going to stand up for your builder?" asks Tobi.

Rothmore takes note of Tobi's desperation and shines his devious smile at Aden.

Tobi struggles to make sense of Aden's timidity.

Rothmore steps down from the stump and orders his assistants to place the head of the alleged idol worshipping cadet on the stump. The precept raises his mace with both hands high above his shiny doom.

THUD! The mace slams into the skull of the accused.

Once the shock of the execution wears off, the faithful praises Rothmore for his righteous deed.

Tobi stares down Ur to vent his anger over the death of one his cadets.

Aden hangs his head in shame.

"No more blood will be shed to today, but I assure you - these other two are going to pay. I will torture them behind closed doors, and you will see them never more," concludes Rothmore.

The Path of Peril leads to a ford across Lake Ekron. The lake runs about five lengths long and a length wide. The rocks of the ford stack high, cutting the lake in two. An evening fog settles over the water while the travelers stop to judge the distance across against the remaining daylight.

"I say we go for it," suggests Ben.

"Crossing at evening troubles me," says Emmerick.

"Morning. Evening. What's the difference? I think it's foolish to waste this sunlight."

The other companions have no strong opinion on the matter. With silent lips, they await their king's decision.

"I've studied these waters and my research leads me to believe that there may be a leviathan in the lake, and like most aquatic lake-life, they prefer to feed in the evening."

"You're joking, right? A leviathan, the mythological sea creature?" questions Ben.

"Not the mythological one, the biological one."

"At the council you accused me of being delusional for seeing nephesh. Now, you're afraid to cross the water because of a mythological sea monster."

"Technically, it's a lake monster."

Seth's stomach rumbles, drawing Emmerick's attention.

"What say you, big fellow?"

"Let's put it to a vote," decides Seth. "I vote stay. Let's make camp and eat."

The idea sounds as good as any, and because the king doesn't prefer to pull rank, he raises his hand with Seth to stay.

Ezekiel, in defiance of Seth, votes with Ben to cross the lake.

Ashira notices the forest on the other side of the water and raises her hand to join with Ben and Ezekiel. "I need firewood to cook."

Since she factors her decision with food in mind, Seth changes his vote.

The fog thickens and the rocks on the ford thin when they reach the midway point of the lake. The company wades through the knee deep water.

"This can't be good for my armor," says Seth.

"Why not?" asks Emmerick from beneath his rust-marked iron cuirass.

The water stirs around the professor's feet. "Was that a pike, I saw? Northern or southern, I wonder?"

"I didn't see a fish," says Ezekiel.

The stirs become more fluid and develop into swirls that flow across the ford. A larger ripple in the current rocks their knees. Ben notices two lanterns skim underneath the water, brightening as they draw near the ford.

Then, as if Mother Nature sanctions the encounter, a leviathan emerges from the lake with eyes glowing, tongue lashing, body twisting.

The serpentine monster flips in the fog, smacking down upon the water. The company shields their faces from the splash, except for Emmerick. His eyes lock onto the glorious creature as it soaks him.

Ben offers the professor a look of disbelief mixed with an apology. The shepherd prods the catatonic king like a sheep to get him moving across the ford with the rest of the company.

Fins embedded in the spine of the beast surface first when the leviathan catches air once more in hopes of splashing his dinner from the ford.

Seth steps into the monster and slogs Peacemaker against its dragon-like head.

"Big fellow, why would you do such a thing!?" scolds Emmerick.

"Don't worry. He won't be back for seconds."

The waves settle and the atmosphere fills with serenity once more. Frogs and bugs cheer for the company atop their lakeshore log-bleachers.

The rush of the attack tightens their muscles and it takes a few deep breathes to unlock their knees.

The survivors take a few steps before the leviathan launches itself out of the water and crashes down on the ford with a thunderous SMACK!

Rocks spray across the lake as Seth grabs hold of Emmerick and leaps to more secure footing.

Ezekiel offers the warrior his staff and he pulls the prophet to safety on the rocks.

Ben and Ashira splash about the water attempting to keep their head above water for their leather raiment sinks them a tad.

"Hurry, it's coming back!" warns Seth as the monster unhinges his jaw to reveal a mouth filled with razor-sharp triangles.

Seth stands poised for another shot. Emmerick remains enraptured with the lake monster. Ezekiel lifts his helpless eyes to the sky. He sees a flock of sparrows migrating over the lake and that's when it hits him.

Ezekiel closes his eyes and offers the mystical chant.

"A lot of good sparrows will do, Zek!" mocks Seth.

"What dialect is that?" asks Emmerick.

"He's trying to talk to that monster!"

"Oh, rubbish."

Despite the doubters, Ezekiel continues to chant. A pike swims to the surface, white-spotted scales speckle its beige body. The fish lengthens, ready to receive the prophet's orders.

"I do believe that one is of the southern variety," says Emmerick, taking out his book on Calcedonian wildlife to confirm his findings.

The leviathan dives at Ben, who takes a deep breath and slides under the monster. Its mammoth tail crashes down next to his prey and jettisons the sentinel onto the ford.

The creature takes a wide turn for another pass while Seth and Ben encourage Ashira to swim hard. As she nears the rocks, the leviathan snakes around her body and pulls her under.

The silence maddens Seth and Ben, their hearts pounding against their armor. Ezekiel leans on his staff in prayer. Her disappearance lifts Emmerick's nose from his book.

The waves smooth beneath the ominous fog, dampening the hope for Ashira's survival. Despair drops Seth to his knees.

Adrenaline purges his despair when ripples stir in the water. Vengeance sharpens the company's focus as they ready their weapons.

Suddenly, she springs forth from the lake and collapses on the ford. "It released me," gasps Ashira.

Seth gathers her in with his arms. The professor-king moves towards her, sniffing her face, neck, and hair. A revelation bursts in his eyes as he wildly flips the pages in his book.

"Jasmine! It's allergic to jasmine! Do you have more!?" requests Emmerick. Ashira hands him the bottle of perfume, and despite Ben's objection, Emmerick dumps it all over himself and his companions.

The leviathan returns for a final pass. He rears up at the stench of the jasmine and back flips away from the company. The monster buries itself deep in the lake, repulsed by the scent of his dinner.

After a long sigh of a relief, the group makes their way to the other side. Emmerick approaches Ben, who readies himself for an 'I told you so' from the professor.

"Magnificent! Never in all of my days would I thought this possible! A leviathan! A real leviathan!"

Recalling the mystery and joy of his encounters with Azor, Ben smiles at the king for the creature becomes Emmerick's nephesh.

The company makes camp under a harvest moon on the edge of The Black Forest.

Ben gathers more firewood while Ashira stirs her potato soup. Ezekiel gets her approval before dropping a handful of wild mushrooms into the soup. Seth looks over her shoulder as if his presence will make the soup cook quicker. Emmerick attempts to jot some notes in the fire light.

The men stifle Ashira's flow and she disperses them with the look that she used to motivate her kitchen staff. The men retreat to their sleeping spaces and wait for their meal.

"Hey Zek, why don't you summon us that pike for the soup?"

The prophet bites his lip in hopes of controlling his temper while the group shares a laugh at his expense.

"I thought you were studying on the boat?" asks Seth.

"I was, before I became interested in Emmerick's book… It's quite good by the way."

The professor offers a nod of gratitude to the prophet.

Hellish yelps whistle through the forest and Ben leaps to his feet.

"Afraid of wolves?" asks Seth.

"What's it to you?"

"Oh, the irony is grand. A shepherd that's afraid of wolves," says Emmerick, drawing laughter from the company.

"Let's hope for your sakes that there are no rats in the forest."

Ben's retort silences Emmerick and Seth.

Ashira serves her soup, quieting the mouths and stomachs of the agitators.

Soon after, the exhausted company falls fast asleep - except Ben. The howls of the wolves cause him to nervously toss about his blanket and the lingering scent of jasmine stings his eyes. And though Ashira sleeps an arm's length away, she feels so distant from him.

Chapter 9 ✦✦✦ Ungodly Wolf Packs

On the lookout for Ur Rothmore and his henchmen, Tobi Tamar sneaks down a palace hallway in the dead of night. His size sixteen boots tread lightly down the stairs into the dungeon.

The prison area divides into palace crimes and precept crimes. Palace criminals remain under the supervision of the royal guard, where as precept heretics fall under the supervision of Ur Rothmore in the holding room, which now doubles as a torture chamber and inquisition headquarters.

Relieved to avoid the chubby boaster, Tobi arrives at the prison to find one guard on duty, and luckily, a guard that he recently trained. Free of worry about word getting around concerning his secretive visit, the veteran draws a look of bewilderment from the rookie.

"Odd time to visit the dungeon, Sir. Is this one of your surprise inspections?"

"I'm here to interrogate Shamgar Ram."

The rookie lets him pass, too frightened to ask the aggressive captain about the nature of such an unusual visit.

Tobi finds Shamgar wide awake as if he anticipates a guest. "The vigilant Tobi Tamar, on time as expected."

Tobi's face darkens with thoughts of betrayal.

"No need to fret, this is no ruse. I know why you've come. Unlike your king, you're suspicious of Amar Divine and Ur Rothmore."

"My suspicions have only been strengthened by Rothmore's actions… Wait! How do you know as much!?"

"The sewers were not the only place that I lurked. I paid Amar Divine a visit while he slept in this palace. I read his orders to Rothmore. Amar knows Emmerick doesn't wholeheartedly believe in Neshama. You already knew that, so you came to your king's defense when Amar pressed Emmerick about it."

"Who is it that can know the soul's of men? Only the Goddess," says Tobi defiantly.

"If only the inquisition believed that. Take note of who Rothmore killed."

"A stone mason and soldier," answers the grizzly captain, raking his beard, trying to make sense of the inquisition.

"The stone mason was an easy target. He provided the spectacle to draw a mob - a mob that grows daily and will continue to grow. Here's what should trouble you… Think about the value of a man with such a skill. And your count is off on the casualties… Two soldiers are dead."

"No. Only one died by Rothmore's mace."

"Last night I heard the faint screams of a woman when flames consumed her."

Tobi bows his bald head to pay bitter respects for another lost cadet.

"Rothmore doesn't want the walls repaired or reinforced with new recruits. This is only the beginning of your problems."

"There's no bigger problem than losing two cadets," bites Tobi.

Shamgar waits for the red splotches atop Tobi's forehead to fade before revealing his dire prediction.

"You're next, Captain Tamar."

Shamgar's prediction stuns the veteran for the truth behind the words demand his consideration.

"Once you're dead. There will be no one left to protect Aden Tizra. Rothmore will take control of the royal guard and I will no longer be protected by the law. Amar Divine will finally be rid of Shamgar Ram."

The prediction now the plot - Tobi feels more stupid than stunned.

"Free me. Give me my mace and I'll rectify all of this."

The evidence supports Shamgar's release but the captain swore an oath to the rule of law. "I can't do that. You've been charged with murder, you must stand trial. I'd be no different than Rothmore if I set you free."

Shamgar retreats to the corner of his cell until all Tobi sees of the precept are his crystal blue eyes piercing the darkness. "Like your king, you value intellect over suspicion. You trust your head when you should trust your gut. Your devotion to duty will cost Aden his life."

Shamgar's blue eyes dim in the shadows.

Aden stares at the gathering mob from his bedchamber window. The sun rises, shining a bolt of light behind the stump where Ur Rothmore will condemn another heretic. Judith's sentimental medallion offers little comfort as condemnation rips open the scar on his soul. He squeezes the stone rune until his knuckles whiten.

Aden looks over his canopy bed, the origin of his regret. His fingers slide across the smooth tan linens flowing down the bedposts. The cloth glides across his prints, as her flawless skin did that fateful night.

Aden's grandfather warned him about Melek; his father welcomed Melek into his son's bedroom. The false god was far from the appearance of the statue that once dominated the throne room. Melek wasn't revealed in a bedtime story from "The Book of Blight." These were far too crude for a pure-blooded sixteen-year-old boy. Melek came to Aden that night as a gift from his father in the form of an adolescent girl.

The prince was born a month before her. He attended writing sessions with her as a child under the tutelage of scribes. Much to the dismay of the scribes, he liked to chase her through the palace hallways in their middle years.

Abigail Locke was from the prominent house of Locke, which attained the status of Tizra nobility for Captain Norris Locke's accolades in the Glorious Battle of 2344. She was inches taller than him with long blonde hair and emerald eyes. She was not only more confident in her skin than him, but also in her ability.

Aden knew nothing of the charm by which Zimri wooed Rizpah and therefore lacked tact on how to approach girls, a problem that continued from his sixteenth to his thirty-first year. The upbringing of princes doesn't condition them for rejection, so when Abigail scorned his hand to a moon festival, and even worse, boasted about the rejection to all of the noble families in Tizra - Aden retreated for a week behind the curtains flowing down from his canopy.

Had his grandfather been living, had his uncle not been part of a diplomatic council in Tamar, and had he not been too embarrassed to talk with his mother, then maybe he would have been spared of his nightmare. For the first and only time, he confided in his father.

It wasn't that particular night when Zimri introduced him to Melek; that night arrived on the following eve.

Aden came to his room the following evening to find the silhouette of his father under the white cloth hanging from the canopy. As he drew near the bed, two silhouettes became known to him. He studied the curves of Abigail Locke enough to know that she was lying in his bed. When he pulled the cloth back, he realized that she wasn't there by choice.

Her eyes glazed like water over glass and her body trembled, for Zimri rested his sword on the linen that covered her nakedness.

"My Son, here lies the brat that scorned you. You have a decision to make - a weak choice, or the choice that a real man would make. I was sixteen once, you're my offspring, so I know of the energy in your loins. You're my proof after all," spoke Zimri with haughty breath.

"Neshama would want you to make the weak choice. She would require of you to forgive this damsel, exercise self-control over your passions, and allow her to walk unscathed from your chamber. Melek demands that you condemn this brat, exert your dominance over her, and force her from your chamber on your terms."

Aden's newfound acceptance from his father weakened his morals allowing Melek's temptation to slip by the watchful eye of the prince's conscience.

Aden stole more than her innocence that night and when

they awoke in the morning, Zimri was there to applaud the sin. It was the first time in his life that Aden felt truly loved by his father. In fact, the sensation of his father's acceptance was more fulfilling than his veniality with Abigail.

Zimri removed a brand that smoldered in the fireplace throughout the night; it was in the shape of the quarter moon that witnessed his son's conquest. With his new found acceptance, the prince followed his father's orders and his victim left the chamber on his terms, with a seared rune on her hip.

If the night of horror wasn't enough for Abigail Locke, she found more misery the following day. Zimri confronted her father about her willful disobedience that stole his son's purity. It was the case of the confident young lady versus the shy prince. Embarrassed by his daughter's promiscuity, Norris Locke cast her out of his house and entrusted her keeping to Aden.

The timing couldn't have been worse as the events of 3016 proved to be disastrous for Zimri's kingship - his brother, Emmerick, sided with the southern separatists and Zimri failed to defeat Oren Tav's shepherd army at Ephah's Field.

Aden feared losing his bond with his father, so he immersed himself in Melek homage, leaving Abigail to feel the brunt of his worship. After the truce with the shepherds, Zimri returned home weakened in faith. The tyrant blamed his failings on his lack of devotion to Melek. He also turned his ire on his son, who he blamed for not doing enough to invoke the favor of Melek.

Aden made a decision that would forever haunt his soul. To appease his father's wrath, he offered his most prized possession to Queen Mother Isavel and her harem, who were at that time housed in a lounge near the throne room.

The vixens fought over Abigail like wolves. They shredded her blond hair and ripped her flesh with their claws. The sight of her demise swelled the acids within his stomach forcing Aden to vomit on his boots.

Guilt drove Aden to the Grand Chancel, where he flung open the doors of the high precept's quarters, but Shamgar Ram had disappeared. Instead, Aden found comfort in the Associate to the High Precept.

Amar Divine.

After Aden confessed his iniquity, but before he was offered forgiveness from the precept, Zimri's assassins stormed the Grand Chancel. The prince aided Divine's escape. It was because of Aden's quick wits that Amar Divine survived The Scarlet Winter.

Aden returns to his window to watch Rothmore's ruffians pluck another young woman from the captain's ranks. They pull her blond hair and tug her limbs like a pack of wild dogs. The inquisitors slam her head onto the stump. Her body trembles as her judge looms over her with mace in hand.

The mob demands to know why the hub of Melek worship occurs among the cadets in Captain Tamar's academy. Ur Rothmore raises his hand to silence the ever-growing crowd.

"You are good to question the source of this infection. I think the captain must answer, why he is the source of all this cancer. This inquisition has come so far, we must now question Captain Tobi Tamar."

The company hastily travels across a dirt path through The Black Forest, weaving around full ferns underneath the thick fur trees that block the sun. A pack of wolves stalks every step - their yellow eyes glowing within the depths of the murky timbers.

"Incredible, was it not? I know it tried to eat us, but

we can't fault nature's urges. Poor thing was hungry. How splendid would it be to see another one in The East Sea on the way home?" suggests Emmerick.

Oblivious to the constant eye rolls of his companions, Emmerick continues his morning long ramble about the leviathan.

The professor pauses to pluck an unusual ruby leaf from a unique fern. The discovery plants a new thought his head; he quiets down and the company enjoys the silence.

Ben notices the absence of yellow eyes and the faint howls from the depths of timbers, "It's quiet. The wolves must have returned to the lake."

"Timberwolves are vicious predators. They don't announce their attacks like their weaker cousins that live in your backyard - the brown variety that preys on helpless sheep. These wolves never had their pack mentality beaten out of them by shepherds," informs the professor, still examining the ruby leaf.

"I'll beat it out them," boasts Ben with a shaky conviction in his voice.

"You still sound like a shepherd, thought you were a sentinel now," says Seth picking at Ben.

Before Ben can respond, two timberwolves charge down the path. He draws his bow and zips a yellow-feathered arrow. It sticks the hind leg of the wolf, but it keeps coming. Another arrow rips into dog's thick hide. The third arrow penetrates its heart and the wolf crashes into a bed of ferns.

The companion of the fallen wolf leaps into the air toward Ben.

Seth smacks the wolf away from the sentinel.

"Told you they were vicious predators," says Emmerick of the obvious. "Wonder where the rest are?"

"The rest!?" asks Ben.

"They don't use the term pack for nothing."

A dozen wolves blitz from the depths of the forest. They assault the company's flanks from both sides of the path. Ben identifies the opening of the mountain pass and barks orders, "Get to the high ground!"

As they make for the pass, two wolves emerge to block their path. Ben, Seth, and Ashira clash with the wolves. The hunters nip and twist as they engage the warriors, but quickly find that their hides are no match for steel. Despite the sound of shattering bones and tearing furs, the wolf pack continues to pursue their meal.

The heroes reach the high ground and find it easier to repel the wolf attacks. Seth crowns two wolves, bashing in their skulls. Another wolf tastes of Kurion. Ashira dices up a wolf with her double blades. The pack leader calls off the assault and his tribe retreats into the forest.

The path turns purplish-grey as the company works their way up the rocky terrain of the Elam Mountains. Using the assorted sizes of the evergreens poking out from the rock face, they pull themselves up the steeper inclines.

Their labor pays off when they reach the first bluff that offers a view of the forest, the lake, and the woods. The view spans all the way to The East Sea. They bask in the glory of such a view, but only briefly.

Oddly, a shadow descends on Seth.

The warrior notices his space darken and looks up to find a wolf lunging down upon him. Seth catches the beast and speeds its journey the rest of the way down the mountainside.

Seth hurls the wolf into the forest far below.

The group gets caught off guard while watching the beast plummet from the heights. Two more wolves drop onto their bluff. The tenacity of the timberwolves pushes the company off of the path and backs them to a gorge. The stalkers struggle to land a fatal bite, but it doesn't keep them from trying.

The warriors can't find balance to power their counter attack until Ben and Emmerick secure their footing and repel the assault. Kurion glows purple when it tags another wolf and the king's saber claims its first kill of the trek.

The wolf attack removes the company from the mountain pass. If they could somehow scale the three bluffs above, they will reconnect with the Path of Peril.

Emmerick offers the scouting report, "This first bluff is but a trivial task. If my memory's correct, there's a bear cave on the second bluff. We'd be well served to keep quiet. The third bluff is going to be an issue for some of us."

The king eyes the smallish prophet to count him among the some of us.

The company stares up at the steepest bluff. Ben and Seth feel confident in their ability to scale the rock face.

"Let me and Seth scale the bluffs. We'll drop the rope down and haul the gear first. Ashira can anchor the rope for Emmerick and Ezekiel. Then, we'll pull her up," instructs Ben.

Ashira's eyebrows heighten in agreement with Ben's plan.

Ben's plan worked perfectly, but it took a lot of daylight to execute. The first crag was an easy crawl. The second bluff was a steeper climb and took more effort to conquer. Seth's heavy breath stressed Ben on account of the bear cave. The third bluff was brutal because the sun scorched the rock, making the crag tough to grip.

The midday heat tried to drain the energy from Ben and Seth, but they powered through and secured the rope around a thick evergreen. The weapons, armor, and supplies went up easy enough as Emmerick, Ashira, and Ezekiel made it to the second bluff without fail.

"Guess you're it, Sire," says Ashira as the swaying rope chooses Emmerick to go first up the third bluff. She steadies the rope as he plants his boots into the rock. Ben and Seth start pulling, Emmerick starts walking. He's half way up the third bluff when the three remaining timberwolves follow their alpha down a hidden trail onto the second bluff.

Ezekiel races to a ledge atop the mouth of the bear cave, cursing the two wolves that leap for him.

The alpha wolf and his accomplice corner Ashira onto a ledge near the gorge. Securing her hands to the mountain, she makes herself as narrow as possible. Defenseless, she regrets the decision to relinquish her gear. The wolves chomp at her heels hoping to catch a tooth on her leather boots.

"I'm going down there," says Ben, after Emmerick releases the rope.

"You can't! They'd rip you to shreds before your feet touch the ground!" warns Seth, frustrated by the hopelessness of the situation.

Ben casts off Seth's advice.

Seth grabs Ben's attention by clutching his arm. "You can't help if you're dead!" Though the advice is accurate, it doesn't make Seth feel any better about the threat facing his sister.

"Zek, do something!" shouts Seth.

The call to action prompts the prophet to chant, but his recent failure at the lake cancels the notion. He looks into the starving eyes of his predators and a revelation hits him. His inspiration comes not from Othniel, but from Emmerick.

"This is a reckless idea," voices Ezekiel, swinging down from the ledge and disappearing into the cave.

The two wolves consider chasing him but their instincts forbid them to enter the cave. They join their comrades and take a shot at dislodging Ashira. One connects with her heel, but she's able to slip from its grip. She latches onto a tree root to pull herself away from her attackers.

Ashira reaches the final notch on the ledge. One more retreat will solidify her grave in a shallow stream below.

Ben, Seth, and Emmerick hurl rocks and insults at the wolves, but neither connects to make an impact.

Ezekiel returns from the cave with faint claw marks across his face and a bear cub in his arms. He places the cub in front of the cave and dashes for the rope.

Ezekiel dodges a wolf and leaps for the line.

Ben and Seth swiftly yank the prophet to safety.

The wolves shift their attention from Ashira to the easier prey, a cawing cub. His mother surfaces with a spiteful snarl upon hearing the cry for help. The first timberwolf acts carelessly, quickly lunging at the mother. One swat from her monstrous paw removes the impulsive wolf from the mountainside.

Fearless, a second wolf tangles with the grizzly bear. He uses his quickness to snap a few shots at the hind legs of the bear. The hunter underestimates the speed of the grizzly and she snaps its neck with a twist of her powerful jaws.

The alpha sinks his fangs into the bear's muzzle. The pain straitens the mother before she enfolds the wolf with her thick arms. The alpha struggles to break the hold, and the grizzly snaps his spine.

The crunch of broken vertebrae terrifies the lone survivor, who flees the fate of his pack.

In the midst of the mayhem, the company pulls Ashira to safety.

They watch with grateful eyes while the mother returns her offspring to their cave.

Undone by Ezekiel's heroics, his friends scramble for words.

"I have to give credit to Emmerick… His research on grizzly bears is exact," admits Ezekiel.

The company follows the Path of Peril until the last ray of sun settles behind the Elam Mountains. They stumble across a large wooden lean-to crafted from the surrounding pines. A fire ring sits near the shelter, and a spring gushes water from an overlook above.

Ashira carries her pot to draw water for another meal of potato soup.

Ben drops a bundle of wood into the ring and notices specks of tobacco leaves on one of the rocks in the circle. He motions to Emmerick. Seth and Ezekiel follow anyway.

"I guess this solves who the tobacco belongs to," says Emmerick. "Zidon could've gone unnoticed by the leviathan, but how'd he survive the wolves?"

"He controlled their untamed ether," says Ezekiel.

"Not that rubbish you tried at the lake."

Ashira shakes her head and counts the seconds before the next argument. After she fills her pot, she explores the overlook. Curiosity to catch the first glimpse of Elam gets the better of her.

After a glance of Elam, Ashira drops her pot. It clanks down the mountainside and rolls to a stop at the fire ring.

Ben bolts towards the spring to find her at the overlook.

"Wolves!?" yells the shepherd, rushing to her side.

Ashira stands unresponsive, paralyzed by the view.

Like Ashira, Ben becomes stricken with the paralysis. His heart freezes, causing his blood to clot and his face to turn purple. Before the overlook he was hungry, thirsty, tired, and sore. All those ailments vanish with one glimpse of Elam.

Emmerick, Seth, and Ezekiel join Ben and Ashira – only to suffer the same shock of terror.

Elam appears before them, a ruined city.

Thousands of vultures circle above waiting to devour the next citizen to perish. The stench of death lifts off of the city and overpowers the smells of autumn. Fires, scattered about the landscape, scorch any vegetation.

The walls and gates lack a guard presence, leaving the four round towers that bookend the walls unprotected. A few citizens skitter about the barren streets like mice. The only light in the city emanates from a tall thin tower grounded in the depths of the palace that houses the throne room and overlooks the city.

The sight of Elam rattles the company's confidence - the spectacle of Korah's army wrecks it.

A hundred soldiers wide - a hundred ranks deep, ten thousand ironclad warriors in all. Many a variety of spear tips - a plethora of scarlet banners. All united in one mission, all marching toward one nation.

Chapter 10 ❖ Cursed

Judith felt the scrutiny of the dozen gawking buzzards with every piece of fruit that she inspected, every vegetable. They followed her to the yarn stand and over to the bakery. Their brows raised, voices low, but she knew what the women of Tav were saying about her.

Cursed.

There was no other explanation for why her husband was killed on his first rotation after their marriage.

Judith makes her final purchase on what was supposed be an enjoyable morning of shopping. "Good morning, Mrs. Finch. Two bricks of tea, please."

Judith slides her coin across the counter. The saleslady looks over the silver coins from underneath her grey hair yanked tightly into a bun. She frowns at the 'cursed widow.' Judith remains silent while her confidence diminishes under the judgment.

"I guess your hex can't be passed through coin."

Judith gathers the bricks of tea into her arms and minds her manners on the way out.

On her dash from the market, she makes a vow to herself never to return. She scurries down a path toward the guild hall. Before she makes it home, her stomach can no longer hold her breakfast and she loses it on the path.

The isolated widow sobs on the path when Evan finds her. He pulls her into his arms. "It's going to take a long time to heal from Daniel's death."

"It's not just Daniel. The women in the village think I'm cursed, even Mrs. Finch. She used to invite me for tea in her garden."

Judith's tears soak Evan's white shirt around the shoulder for she fails to regain her composure.

Evan and Judith return to the guild hall. An elder shepherd with grey eyes and a bushy grey beard greets them, "Morning, Master Evan. I see scars, the welcome signs of healing."

"What brings you to my hall, sir?"

"I'll be blunt. I know you'd prefer it that way. The elders met last night and we're concerned. Your father and I had many talks about the Baladans; he trusted those wild boys, the elders never did. They're about as shiftless as Tinkers."

"There's no love lost between me and the Baladans, but we respect one another. Baladans are nothing like Tinkers," corrects Evan.

"I was afraid that the conversation would go in this direction."

Judith senses the same condemnation on Evan that followed her through the market.

"Why do you choose them over the shepherds in Tav?" asks the elder.

"It's a large flock. Shepherds in this town have their own worries, I refuse to burden them."

"Burden us? We wonder if you don't trust us to get the job done."

Evan refuses to answer; the fact that he hires the Baladans speaks of his lack of trust.

"I guess you're too much like your old man."

"Thank you, sir."

The elder rolls his lips at Evan's cocky response. "Maybe not in every way. Your father may have believed the Baladans were reliable shepherds, but I don't ever recall him welcoming foresters into his guild… What kind of deal are you striking with those treefolk?"

"No deal. I rescued one of their children at Lake Resh. They came for her, nothing more."

"The elders can overlook your poor judgment about the Baladans, but we won't hesitate to hold a gathering to execute the Law of Eviction if we hear of anymore interactions with those forest clods."

"You have my word."

The elder angrily pulls Evan into his chest. "I lost a son in Tizra while they hid in their forest instead of fighting Zimri… Hiding instead of fighting… Sound familiar? I've no time for cowards. We're watching you Evan Tav; you better start acting like a guild master of shepherds if you and your cursed sister want to remain in that hall."

The elder shepherd releases Evan and stomps away.

Seeking shelter from the condemnation, the steps of the guild hall soothe Evan's and Judith's berated souls.

Aden walks about the palace unable to sleep, his sin torturing his soul. He enters the palace suite where High Precept Amar Divine last slept and plops down the bed. Longing for confession, he lights a candle on the night stand and meditates on the simple white flame.

Was his sin the root of the Tizra judgment? From his sixteenth year, not a day went by that he didn't feel remorse for offering Abigail Locke to the harem of witches. Was it Ur Rothmore's condemnation or Neshama's grace urging him to relinquish the shame? Of all the questions burning within his soul, none were more terrifying than a query concerning Zimri. Was he doomed to suffer his father's fate? Was he… cursed?

All of these thoughts lead to one man at one place. Aden must seek forgiveness at the Grand Chancel in a confessional with Amar Divine.

The closet door creaks, drawing the prince's attention.

"Who's in there?"

"It's me," whispers the gruff voice.

Aden opens the door, sighing in relief to find Tobi.

"Have you been hiding here all day? The inquisition is tearing the city apart looking for the 'apostate' captain. You disappeared as if you knew they were coming."

"I was warned."

"By who?"

"That's of no concern. Before I retreated to this closet, I was talking with a sergeant. I'm certain that he tracks you as we speak… Tekoa has been ransacked again."

The news deflates Aden's shoulders. "How many raiders?"

"They were not raiders this time. The assault took place under Calcedonian colors."

"How many troops occupy Tekoa?"

"None. A tactical force slaughtered the city guard, cleared the wall defenses, and then returned to their fleet."

The news arrives at the worst of times for the conflicted prince, but the news itself doesn't come as a total surprise, for Aden had grown suspicious of their unreceptive ally to the south.

"I'll find this sergeant; see if he can't march a couple hundred troops to aid Tekoa," offers Aden.

Tobi reads Aden's worrisome face, perceiving it has more do with his soul than his citizens in the swamp.

"I will join the reinforcements and see what I can do to help the Tekoans. But first, I must visit the Grand Chancel."

The plan strikes Tobi as profound. If Shamgar's prediction stays true to form then Aden's next on Ur Rothmore's list. It may be best for the prince to leave Tizra.

"Goddess go with you, Aden. I'll survive Rothmore, get back to training cadets, and have the walls ready if an invasion were to reach Tizra."

"How are you going to do all that from a closet?"

"As much as it pains me to say it, I'll have to break some laws in order to break some bones."

Tobi unlocks the shackles of Shamgar Ram while the rookie guard babbles on, "Sir, I have orders from the king. This man has yet to stand trial. Captain, this man is convicted of murder and for being a Melek worshipper. The inquisition is after you, and I don't want to be next."

As soon as Shamgar's hands drop the shackles, the precept presses the rookie guard into the cell wall. "Hush. I'm going to show Ur Rothmore a real inquisition."

"Shamgar?" asks Tobi, having second thoughts.

"You broke your oath to the rule of law. I sense how

that troubles you. Hand me my mace and you won't have to worry about breaking any more laws."

The captain hands the precept his mace and shield, then steps aside.

Shamgar walks toward the torture chamber with his shield and mace in hand. A handful of Ur Rothmore's henchmen flog a builder with scourges. Another builder suffers, sprawled out on a rack. Both denounce any association with Melek worship, but that doesn't stop the brutality.

WHAM! The oak door quakes the room when it collides with the stone wall.

The henchmen fire their lashes at Shamgar Ram; the whips dangle about the precept as they try to ensnare him, the chords cracking against his shield as he advances. One line wraps his forearm and yanks away his mace. Another line wraps likewise around his shield arm.

One henchman breaks rank and charges with his dagger aimed for Shamgar's neck. The precept lowers his crown to ram his attacker in the nose and the henchman drops like a rock.

Shamgar secures the dagger and frees himself from the cords. He reclaims his shield and repels an array of attacks from a henchman armed with a wood-ax. The precept grabs the man by the scruff of his neck and shoves him into the fireplace.

Two henchmen rush Shamgar while he rearms himself with his bludgeon. He ducks their charge and tosses them overhead as they roll over his shield. Claiming their souls, his mace charges a charcoal-color due to their corrupted ether.

The last henchman chucks a spear that sails off target and sticks into the door. Shamgar plants his shield into the brute's throat bringing him to his knees for his final judgment.

The two deformed henchman continue to grovel on the floor. One cups a handful of blood that drains from his nostrils and the other douses his melted flesh with water.

Shamgar frees the builders.

"Take your time," instructs Shamgar.

The battletested precept exits the room to the cracks of a scourge and the snaps of ligaments.

The morning fog swirls about Ur Rothmore observing his inquisition from the judgment stump. The eager crowd purchases fistfuls of Miriam statuettes. Awaiting the arrival of Rothmore's henchmen, the fanatics buzz with intrigue over the next victim. A collective gasp sucks the fog from the north plaza when Tobi Tamar arrives to bring charges against Ur Rothmore.

"I have two witnesses, the two builders that you tried to kill last night. Both claim that there's no evidence of Melek worship against them. I'm shutting this inquisition down until King Emmerick returns from Calcedon."

The devotees lift their anxious faces, clamoring for an eloquent retort from the Mouthpeice.

"This is exactly what I'd expect from a captain who bends his troops to the will of Melek. My children, if you want your sins removed then this is what you're going to do. Take a dagger and end your life, for this is the only remedy for Tizra's strife."

The sinister order blindsides Tobi. He underestimates the Mouthpiece's affect on his followers and realizes the danger they pose to themselves. Tobi would have to take to the stump or the mob would take to the streets in a mass suicide.

Rothmore gloats over Tamar while he comes forward.

The Mouthpiece readies his double-handed mace for his high profile heretic.

"Stay your hands, for my words were but a test. Tobi Tamar suffers, and now he longs to rest."

"Not gonna happen, fat man!" yells Shamgar, smacking a

box of Miriam statuettes from a relic salesman. "Tobi, Aden, me… Isn't that your plan?"

The blubber on Rothmore's double-chin spasms in anger.

"There can be only one High Precept and it won't be your papa, Amar Divine. You twisted our synod edicts to slaughter the innocent. I've come back to reclaim my seat as High Precept, and I'll expose your soul to this crowd."

"Precept to precept we shall fight. Let the Goddess shine her favor on who is right," offers Rothmore.

The proposal reeks of Melek worship, heightening Shamgar's suspicions. He accepts the challenge with a nod and braces for the duel.

Rothmore comes down from the stage and the crowd expands to form a circle around the combatants.

Tobi steps in to receive the terms.

"No armor. We fight with the instruments in our hands. We fight to the death," says Shamgar with Rothmore nodding in agreement with every word.

"No forgiveness. Only judgment," announces Tobi.

The crowd stands silent, bewildered yet engrossed by the unfolding events.

Tobi's joints lock with worry for his fate lies sealed in the mace of Shamgar Ram.

The precept gains the initiative with his smaller mace, but the mouthpiece blocks the attacks with his bludgeon in a move that surprises the precept. Shamgar lowers his defenses for a more aggressive approach. It pays off when he slugs Rothmore in the gut, but his robes and layers of flab absorb the blow.

Rothmore counter attacks with a giant swing that Shamgar blocks with his shield. The powerful mace crushes the shield and numbs Shamgar's nerves so badly that the precept can't feel his left arm. Nerve pain throbs up and down his entire left side.

Rothmore presses his attack and his next blow fractures

Ram's left arm. Shamgar's roar from the affliction deafens the crowd as the misery from the strike drops the precept to the cobblestone beneath.

Rothmore lifts the weighty mace high above his head and sends it crashing down.

BOOM! Shamgar rolls out of the way - shards of cobblestone explode around him.

BOOM! More shards spray the plaza - the mace narrowly missing Shamgar's skull.

BOOM! Chunks of debris sink into the precept's head but he rolls away from the killing blow.

Shamgar notices the head of the mammoth mace trapped in the stone; Rothmore pulls with all his strength, but the mace won't dislodge from the ground.

Shamgar springs to his feet for retaliation. He explodes his mace into Rothmore's mouth knocking him backwards away from his weapon. A bloody chasm opens, replacing his thin lips.

"You glib fox, what do you have to confess before this mace turns black with your corrupted ether?"

The mouthpiece swallows some teeth to free his airway - not for a confession but a curse. "Get ready for a historic disaster. King Tartek 'The Destroyer' will be your new master."

The warning sends shockwaves through the crowd, but no wave swarms larger than the jolt of energy that powers Shamgar's arm as he collapses the skull of Ur Rothmore.

Thus ends the inquisition.

"I must see Aden," says Shamgar, favoring his broken limb while maroon streams flow from the shards of stone stuck in his bald head.

"He left Tizra to assist Tekoa, though he mentioned a visit to the Grand Chancel first," informs Tobi.

"Why would he visit the Grand Chancel?"

"Something's been eating at him. A matter of the soul, I presume."

Shamgar rips shreds of cloth from Rothmore's robe. He wraps them around his head like bandages, and then uses a larger shred of cloth to set his broken arm in a sling. He grips his mace with a heightened sense of duty.

"Make ready the city, war is coming… Aden's in danger. I'll try to reach him before he enters the Grand Chancel… As for your king and his companions in Calcedon, Goddess help them."

Chapter 11 ✦✦✦ The Anarchy of Elam

Sitting atop a scorched boulder, Ben stares intently at a tiny violet iris. His mission directs him to scout Elam, but the purple petals capture his gaze – a sign of life in the midst of so much death.

A closer look at the city only confirms the view from the mountain top - a city of anarchy where everyone takes what they want with complete disregard for their neighbors. Few guards patrol the city and their actions make it difficult to tell them apart from the pillaging ruffians.

Ben notices a shadow of what appears to be a person fastened to the ramparts of Elam. Edging closer to the walls, his curiosity nudges him to investigate. The black wool tights, the yellow velvet jacket, the black and yellow feathers flowing from his cavalier hat – the distinct style of clothing identifies the corpse as the Issurian ambassador. Vultures dig their claws into his flesh, shredding his fabrics and snipping his tendons. The vile sight forces the sentinel away from Elam.

On his return to the company, Ben recalls the words of Othniel when they entered Pella looking for Nebo Korse 'The Pig.' If the ashes of Pella were only the beginning of Melek worship, Elam had to be the end.

"I found the corpse of the Issurian ambassador fastened to the walls of Elam," reports Ben. "The chaos inside the city poses more of a threat than the guards, if you even want to call them that."

"Did you see Zidon?" asks Ezekiel.

"No. My guess is that went to the Sanctuary of Melek."

"Did you see Kings Lars?" asks Emmerick.

Ben shakes his head no and let's the king have a moment to plot their next move.

"Did you see any butcher shops or bakeries?" asks Seth.

Focused on the king's decision, Ben disregards Seth's appetite.

"There's a secret passage into the palace through a nearby cave; Lars and I used it all of the time to escape the mockery of his brothers back in our adolescent years. But we're going to have to split up.

"Why!?" blurts Ben in protest.

"Because, big fellow won't fit through the entrance… This may work to our advantage. Ben will come with me to find Lars. The three of you will go to the Sanctuary to detain Zidon. One of them must know why this city went mad."

The idea of a split frustrates Ben for it's not what he expected. Sadness frustrates him as well because he's not ready to leave Ashira's side. As much as he wants to let go and let her be. He can't.

"Hope there aren't rats down there," says Seth, clasping Ben's hand for a farewell. Ezekiel offers Ben his best attempt at a manly clasp.

Ashira hugs Ben. There's little affection in her embrace, but for a brief moment, her energy transfers into his soul.

The current cuts when Ashira withdraws.

Ashira watches Ben and Emmerick disappear into the cave while Seth and Ezekiel hide the hiking gear.

Ben and Emmerick crawl on hands in knees through the pitch- black cave.

"I'll get the torch burning once this space opens up," says Emmerick.

Ben finds it terribly embarrassing that every time Emmerick stops to speak, his face butts into the king's backside.

A sliver of light meanders down into the passage and offers them a target to crawl towards. Ben squashes another plump spider with his palm as the claustrophobic space begins to stifle the shepherd. Before he busts, they drop out of the cave and onto stone tiles.

The new opening allows them to partially stand, giving Emmerick the opportunity to spark his flint against the torch. "When Lars and I were adolescents, we would use this tunnel to sneak out of the palace so that we could go explore the wild. His brothers thought our adventures a waste of time."

The sentinel bends his head towards the palace to get his king moving.

The passage opens up a little more and after a stint of walking like a duck, Emmerick rears up to pop his back into place. Ben sighs at the slow pace of their progression.

"Yes, Lars and I were palace outcasts."

Though the sentinel can't stomach more details, the king feeds them to him anyway.

"Most princes learn military tactics or diplomacy, but we preferred libraries over war rooms. Strange thing though, my brother is dead and so are Lars' two brothers. Huh, I guess academia was the better path."

"Back to your story," pleads Ben.

Emmerick retraces his thoughts to find it.

"On one particular visit I found Lars badly bruised. Rygar, his oldest brother, said that he needed to toughen him up. So Rygar beat Lars with a rod… Lars and I decided to get some revenge. We went into the forest and sacked a wolverine. While his brother slept we tucked some rotten meat under his covers."

With a big grin, Emmerick twists his mustache quite proud of his dastardly behavior. "Shall we move on, Ben?"

"What did you do with the wolverine?"

"Oh, I left him out."

"Right, kind of important to the story."

"No. I literally mean that I released him under the covers to fetch the rotten meat. Let's just say his brother looked a lot worse than Lars… He never made sport of us after that."

Ben's smiles, masking his trepidation of Emmerick's darker side.

Sneaking through the alleyways that lead to the Sanctuary, Seth, Ashira, and Ezekiel come face to face with the dysfunction of the Elam. Ashen smells emanate from the soot of the burned out shops. Boards stamp the windows of nearly every residence and debris barricades the doors.

A solitaire shadow walks down an adjacent street. Lamp light reveals the curves of a woman. A man accosts her from behind with his burly arms. He gropes her hips while he kisses her neck.

Ashira has a flashback of Rezon Scar's mutant face hovering over her lifeless body. The helplessness of the memory prompts her to act. She draws swords and readies herself to rescue the woman.

Upon taking her first step, Seth yanks Ashira back to his side.

The couple falls to the ground and the woman bites the man's ear and claws his back. Faint giggles crescendo into mischievous chuckles underneath the scrum. The woman locks onto the man's lip for a sensual kiss. He lifts her from the ground, her legs wrapping around his waist.

Ashira's eyes are quick to thank Seth.

The three trespassers finally connect with the street that leads to the Sanctuary, but find the terrain difficult to navigate with hundreds of drunkards passed out in heaps. There's constant quarreling as men and women throw fists over liquor and lovers.

In the midst of the tumult, Ezekiel spots Zidon. Seeing the distant silhouette of his uncle agitates the prophet's stomach.

Zidon brings Seth's and Ashira's attention back to the mission when they watch the magi move towards a rickety wooden tavern that looks strangely out of place among the brick apartments. At some point in time the inn existed to attract thirsty Melek worshippers exiting their house of worship. Now, the wasted patrons sleep on the street.

Zidon enters the rickety inn.

"After some brew. He's Othniel's brother, indeed," notes Ezekiel.

"Let's go in there and get him," says Seth.

Ashira readies herself for action.

Ezekiel's feet stand firm. "A tavern like that might be a welcome sight for a brute like you, but it's definitely no place for a woman."

"Brute!? I take offense to that. I'm an artist."

"Woman!? As if I need a man to protect me."

Ashira and Seth make for the tavern leaving Ezekiel behind to reconsider his poor choice of words.

Emmerick's torch dwindles, only a few flickers of embers remain to cast a faint light in the passageway.

"Almost there, about a half length," informs Emmerick.

The king's boot squishes what feels like a wet sponge. The fur balls squirm beneath him and high pitch squeals confirm his deepest fear.

Rats.

The vermin flee from the dancing king, as Emmerick toe-taps in a circle over the pack.

"You clog like an ox," chides Ben, letting out a chuckle.

Suddenly, an inmate drops from the crawl space above and collapses on Ben's back. The man plants Ben's face into the stone panels.

A criminal swings two rocks in a maniacal frenzy, his chains dangling and rattling about his arms. A swift shot knocks against Emmerick's jaw and spins him to the ground.

Ben gets to all fours, but flattens one again when the criminal gets on the sentinel's back to rain down a barrage of kidney punches.

Emmerick's keen sense of smell activates at the scent of oil. He reaches towards the smell and pulls a miner's lamp from a crevasse in the wall. The king smashes the oil lantern across the psychopath's shoulders.

A tiny ember from his torch engulfs the criminal in flames.

The fire only fuels the madman's rage and he rears up to rain blows at Emmerick. The madman's knuckles shatter as they connect with the king's iron cuirass, causing the criminal to recoil into the sentinel.

Ben rips him away from the king and whirls him down

the passageway. The gust of air invigorates the flames. The new surge of flames brings the deranged inmate to his knees and eventually to his death.

Emmerick revives his torch on the maniac's corpse. Ben takes note of the chains, "This is bad."

"Indeed, a horrific odor."

"He's a prisoner. It makes me wonder if we took the correct path when the tunnel split about a length back. Makes me think we're near a dungeon."

"And your point is, Sentinel."

"You are aware of these places called dungeons. Dungeons hold criminals. Criminals are guarded… by guards."

"Oh, you think too much, Ben Tav."

Emmerick moves down the same path leaving the shepherd to wonder why he ever agreed to become the sentinel.

Emmerick removes a stone panel from the floor and peaks his head into a well-lit chamber to find a table topped with dinner scraps on dirty dishes. A few books lean on a sparse bookshelf and a rusty sword clings to a mounted rack. He steps off Ben's thigh to drop down into the tunnel.

"All clear," proudly announces the scout-king.

Emmerick takes a rudimentary ladder and shoves it upward into the floor opening. Ben watches with arms folded.

"We're infiltrating a guest room. How could there be any danger in that?" speaks the king, blowing off his sentinel's silent protest.

Emmerick shimmies up the ladder.

Ben waits for another 'all clear' but it's never spoken. "Emmerick? What are you doing up there?" whispers Ben.

The soft light invites Ben into the room, convincing him to drop the paranoia. He steadies himself on the ladder and rears his head through the floor.

Six spear tips greet his face.

"I think too much," reminds Ben to Emmerick, as he paces about the cell, careful not to brush against the scum that spans the walls.

"Now what!?"

The king reengages his inner professor and blocks out his sentinel while he studies algae growing down the wall.

"Prokaryotic Cyanobacteria. Beautiful is it not?"

"Sire! We don't have time for this!"

"Oh, I think we do."

"That's it, you're just giving up!?"

The day of claustrophobic adventure takes a toll on the free-range shepherd and he can no longer control his animosity. He directs his wrath toward the algae and claws it from the wall.

"What did that algae ever do to you!" shouts Emmerick as the king and the sentinel engage in a shoving match.

Two guards rush into the cell to break up the scuffle. As the pushing intensifies, the guards join the fray. All of the jostling in the cell loosens the jailor's key. Before it rattles on the floor, the shrewd king nabs it.

The jailor detains Emmerick and the guards reassign him to another block. Two more guards flank Ben and haul him away toward the throne room.

Wilting candles dimly light the rickety tavern as Seth, Ashira, and Ezekiel enter the inn. The decaying wood stinks of mildew and vomit. Spiders dance across their masterfully-spun cobwebs that serve as drapes over the four filthy windows in the front wall of the tavern. Ants scatter across the circular pine tables spread across the dining area. Termites chew the wooden walls, graying from rot. The same drab wood rounds the barrels that once contained the barley ale.

Ashira looks around the inn with the eyes of a cook and imagines how the inn once hosted her guests. "I bet this place had a bit of charm back in her day."

"I'm going to add to the smell if I don't get out of here," says Seth dashing for the door. He jostles the door, but it won't open. He then wrecks his shoulder into the wood, but it won't budge.

A large cart loaded with debris blocks the exit.

Seth loses his stomach on the door. After the groans of Ashira dies down, Ezekiel hears Zidon ranting atop the Sanctuary steps.

The prophet looks around the tavern for a back entrance, only to find that the collapsed wall of an adjacent shop seals off the kitchen. He walks up a shaky set of stairs to the loft above and puts his ear to the crack of a boarded window. Ezekiel's eyes widen as he listens to the tongue lashing of Zidon 'The Absolute' atop the temple steps.

"Xylen! You're an embarrassment to Melek! You failed to snatch him in the seminary. You failed again in Arnor while he slept… While he slept! I deliver his companions to your blades, now you will deliver them to my feet. I will pour Melek's wrath into your skull if you don't bring my tribute of two severed heads and the prophet. He best be alive - not a scratch!"

Ezekiel calls down from the loft, "We got to get outta here!"

"Really, Zek. Hate to tell you, but there's no way out."

"It's a trap. Zidon got in, he had to get out," says Ezekiel, looking for any secret outlet.

The prophet takes his notched-staff and taps along the floor behind the bar. "A hollowed spot!"

Ezekiel gives the spot a strong whack to dislodge a trap

door, which reveals a ladder leading into a sewer tunnel. "Found it!"

Ashira rallies to Ezekiel's side and drops a candle into the hole.

Ashira and Ezekiel exchange grave stares.

"What's that grunting sound?" asks Seth.

"What sound?" denies Ezekiel with a shrug of his shoulders.

"You don't hear that annoying squeal?" asks Seth, moving towards the source of the sound.

Seth's knees weaken at the sight of the rats.

"Nope. Not going out that way."

"Assassins stalk us outside, this is the only way out," says Ezekiel while Seth scans the layout of the tavern.

"Through the windows, that's how they'll enter," says Seth, arming himself with Peacemaker in one hand and holding a table like a shield in the other.

"What are you talking about?" asks Ezekiel.

"I ain't goin' into a sewer again, rat boy!"

Glass shatters across the room as the four assassins plunge into the tavern. They roll into shooting form and fire a volley of arrows.

Seth absorbs the arrows with the table while Ashira bunkers behind her brother.

Ezekiel leaps down through the trap door splashing into the sewer water.

The assassins adjust their angles and their arrows narrowly miss Ashira's hips.

"Cover me!" orders Seth.

He drops the table and sprints for the bar. Ashira hurls a throwing knife that removes an assassin's ear. She readies a second knife but has to duck as another round of arrows graze her raven-colored hair. Seth rolls over the bar; the arrows clear his flesh, sticking into the wall instead.

Seth returns fire with the rotted-wooden barrels.

The assassins dive for cover. One doomed cutthroat leaves his head exposed and Seth nearly removes it from his body, for the force of the behemoth's throw empowers the barrel to soar with great speed. Connecting with the assassin's head, the barrel shatters. Splinters and skull fragments spray across the tavern.

The Keros siblings take advantage of their improved odds and seize the initiative in close combat.

Ezekiel slogs his way through the rat-laced sewer under the tavern and finds a ladder that leads to a manhole in the street above. The slab slides just enough for the prophet to wiggle his thin frame through the crack. He uses his staff to roll a drunkard from the slab in order to exit the sewer.

The stench of soured hops seeps from the skin of the drunkard that slumbers atop the manhole. The annoyed sloth rises to his feet in search of a new spot to snooze. Humming a battle anthem, the drunkard trudges toward a trash heap.

Marching toward the cart of debris, Ezekiel picks up the catchy battle anthem tune.

Ashira readies a dagger like a kitchen knife and flings it at the earless assassin. He stops in his tracks when the blade sinks into his shoulder. Ashira advances with her two swords, careful to avoid the debris and the counter attacks from the wounded assassin.

Seth finds the quicker swords of the assassins to be an awkward match up for his bulky warhammer. He relies on his armor to glance many blows. He struggles yet again with Xylen. Seth is unable to land a death blow, but his patience keeps him safe and centered.

Ashira wiggles her way toward the windows but the assassin won't let her get to an exit. Her nerve diminishes as his attacks intensify, but the days in the palace kitchen prepare her to handle the heated exchange. Ashira remains mindful in the mayhem.

Outside of the tavern, Ezekiel tries in vain to move the cart from the entrance. His face turns plum red with blood vessels poking out his wrinkled brow.

The cart refuses to budge.

Ezekiel puts his hands on his knees and pants for air. He looks upon the drunkards with disdain when a revelation straitens his spine and tingles his imagination. The tune of the battle anthem matches the lyrics from the Rygar and Rex monument that he memorized in Temen.

"Ale! Barrels of Ale!" shouts Ezekiel.

The proclamation stirs the drunkards like bears coming out of hibernation. They slowly clear the street and wobble toward the tavern. Ezekiel hums the war tune to motivate the troops while he mingles about the mob.

"Let's move this cart, so we can get some brew!"

The prophet's battle cry for beer carries throughout the street and hundreds of bums surround the tavern like zombies. They put their flabby muscles into the shove, but the cart still won't budge. Therefore, the feeble bums quickly surrender.

Ezekiel shakes off his shy persona. He taps his staff in rhythm against the cart and belts out the battle anthem to rally his army of alcoholics. After a few words into the song, the choir of patriotic Calcedonian pipers joins the prophet.

"Hack. Maim. Kill. Slay.
Hack. Maim. Kill. Slay.
Rygar and Rex… Princes of death… Boots atop skulls,
they made a mess.
Rygar and Rex… Brothers in death… Blades bathed in blood,
from the Bactra that bled.
Rygar and Rex… Stood to the test… Five hundred men,
covered in red.
For brave Calcedon. We sing this song. We vow our best. Like
Rygar and Rex…"

The anthem pumps their adrenaline and they plow the cart onto its side, smashing a dozen drunkards underneath when it crashes down. Ezekiel leaps onto the rubble as the army of alcoholics plugs the tavern entrance.

Ashira tangles with her assassin while Seth absorbs more blows from Xylen and his counterpart.

Ashira and her adversary connect with an equal force that knocks them both to the ground. They jump to their feet and draw daggers. Ashira and the assassin hurl their blades at the exact time - the cutthroat's toss soars fast but high, zipping over her shoulder - Ashira's throw soars brisk and on target, nailing her enemy in the eye.

The bottleneck in the doorway becomes a brawl when the sots begin to knock heads and fists. The bums distract Seth allowing his adversaries to close on the veteran.

Suddenly, Xylen's counterpart drops his blades and flails his arms in an attempt to detach something from the back of his neck. Seth instantly recognizes the choral-blue sea snake attached to his enemy's neck.

Adding to Seth's surprise, a javelin sticks in the assassin's spine, thus ending his existence.

Xylen hits the floor when another javelin flies. The javelin sails through the tavern and nips Seth's neck before it pins the wall.

Xylen crawls along the floor to avoid another incoming missile.

A third javelin removes strands of hair from Ashira's ponytail as she dives from its path.

Seth assesses his wound by how much blood he sees on his palm when a shark tooth whip rips through the shoulder pad of his armor, tearing his flesh. His reflexes block the follow up shot by raising his gauntlets; the strand of shark teeth wrap around his forearm. The sea snake, the jagged whip - it's clear to the pitfighter that a Vilekin corsair hunts him.

Ashira charges the corsair's flank, but the agile sea hag dodges her attack and smacks Ashira face down onto the floor.

The corsair puts a javelin tip to Ashira's throat. "You killed my sister, now I kill yours," says the Vilekin to Seth. She lifts Ashira's head by her ponytail to slice her throat when the brawling sots spill into the tavern and the sea of drunkards drowns the corsair.

Seth belts a few sots out of his path and pulls his sister from the sea of drunkards.

Retreating towards the palace, Xylen jumps from the window through which he came.

Ezekiel calls to Seth and Ashira. The three friends rush down a secluded alleyway toward the palace.

The mob settles for a moment allowing the corsair to come up for air. The Vilekin reclaims her javelins before she exits.

The mob realizes they've been deceived by Ezekiel, and the drunkards express their frustration through another riot.

"Sounds like angry customers. Not sure it's good business for a holy man to lie," jokes Seth.

"Othniel enjoyed a good barroom scrum. My uncle must be rubbing off on me," smiles Ezekiel.

Ashira takes a moment to assess her brother's neck wound. "Nothing that four or five stitches won't close."

She lifts his torn shoulder pad and removes a shark tooth from his flesh. She marvels at the jagged triangle glazed with an unusual alloy.

The despair on Ashira's face informs Seth that his shoulder will require more stitches than four or five… Many more.

"Who was she?" asks Ezekiel.

"A Vilekin Corsair. Guess I killed her sister in The Pit. Not that I had a choice."

"How'd she find you here?"

"I'm certain Zidon has something to do with it."

Ezekiel senses the inevitable. He'd avoided three abduction attempts, but the time drew near to face his uncle.

"Well, we found Zidon," says Ashira with a hint of sarcasm. "I wonder if Ben and Emmerick found Lars."

Chapter 12 ✦✦✦ The Melek Mystery

Emmerick mopes about his newly assigned cell with disappointment that no algae grow on the walls. The smell of a pungent perfume distracts the guard on duty. A tramp whispers her invitation to him and the guard can no longer contain his urge to be with her, so he follows the scent.

Once the scent distances itself from the professor's nose, he unlocks his cell, careful not to alarm the guard and his mistress.

Emmerick glides about the dungeon for the exit when a faint call for water stops him cold. He knows the voice well - his old friend, King Lars of Calcedon 'The Wary.'

Emmerick scoops a ladle of water from the guard's bucket before unlocking his friend's cell. The thought of rescuing his mate disappears with one look at the emaciated king. Emmerick understood all too well the cycle of life, and Lars nears the end of his.

Emmerick puts the ladle to his friend's mouth and the water slightly rejuvenates the fading prisoner, though his neck still lacks the strength to hold up his head.

"Lars, it's Emmerick."

The blinded king returns to the floor, drained from sitting to drink the water. Emmerick slides underneath him and props him up against his shoulder.

"Remember the wolverine in your brother's bed," prompts Emmerick.

The mischievous memory activates a brain cell and a slow smile forms on Lar's face. He comments on the memory with slurred words.

"Old friend, what has happened to Elam?"

It takes a few swallows before Lars can project his regret to Emmerick. "I ruined my country, my people, my son…"

The fragile father weeps, his ribs poking through the sackcloth as he labors to breathe the air to tell his final tale. "It all started when I ventured into metaphysics, studied it day and night. I came across this god from Issur named Melek, introduced by a renegade prophet named Zithri. The illusion became the reality when a nephesh called me to follow Melek."

The testimony hits Emmerick as profound, until guilt creeps into his conscience. Maybe Ben isn't delusional as he once thought.

"Korah promised that if I allowed Melek to be worshipped in Elam then I'd be rewarded with the knowledge to explore the universe."

"He offered you omniscience?"

"How could I refuse? We're scholars at heart, Emmerick. This was bigger than searching for the leviathan in Lake Ekron. This was a chance to know more than natural science, for it offers us but a glimpse into our understanding of this world."

The risk of the endeavor reminds Lars of what it cost him, so he pauses his story to weep.

"I allowed Melek to be worshipped and watched as it took a toll on my people. I tried to end it but I was too late, and Elam fell into anarchy. Tartek, my only son, betrayed me for my crown - all for the glory of Melek."

Emmerick attempts to stay his emotions but his tears mix with Lar's, wetting the sackcloth tunic.

Ben bowed the first time that he saw one - the majesty, the mystery, the wonder of such a being. Azor was unlike anything he'd ever seen. It was almost as if he looked upon the Goddess herself. All of the mystique, even the majesty was present when Melek emerged from the ether vortex while Othniel lay dying in his arms. Instead of wonder, though, his soul was stuck with terror.

Ben smells the ether in the room, a peculiar scent like that of a warm spring rain. It looms over him like a gathering storm and swirls behind him like a tornado. He has no choice but to lift his head and look upon the source of chaos.

"You're a monster," becomes the best the chained sentinel can muster when he peers up to find Melek lording over him from the majestic throne.

"It's most unfortunate that you paint me with a brush of false assumptions."

"How can I see you as anything different?"

Melek rises from his throne and towers over Ben, who

recollects the death of Zimri. Ben tenses up ready to be crushed in one swift stomp.

"If I wanted to destroy your flesh, you'd be dead already. Your soul would be in the ether world," says Melek, hanging his head, troubled by the sentinel's assumptions. "Your soul intrigues me, mortal. Therefore, it remains in this world, but only because of my mercy."

Melek slowly circles the ether vortex spinning on the floor.

"I was once a loyal nephesh, a steward of Neshama's creation, assigned to your world to assist mortals at the dawn of creation. I shared my knowledge of ore, and how to fashion metals at a forge that I constructed in the depths of Mount Crown.

After the mortals corrupted the earth, I ascended to the ether world along with the other nephesh. We returned to Neshama and the sight of her pain was unbearable to look upon. Mortals will never fathom her remorse when they reject her. I never realized how interdependent she was with her creations, especially mortals."

The tone in which Melek speaks draws Ben from his shell, his body language opens and he finds himself oddly comfortable in the presence of the foreboding nephesh.

"As time passed I began to resent her. It became difficult to serve a being so fragile in heart, and all for a race of mortals that despised her. Then I got word of the Covenant; I couldn't understand why she refused to abandon mortals after all of the pain that they caused her."

Intently observing Melek's dim eyes, Ben perceives that he shares in Neshema's suffering.

"Worse yet, she forged a partnership with your pathetic race. I was consumed with rage when I learned of Miriam and how Neshama shared with her the knowledge of how to manipulate ether, a skill she that never shared with the nephesh. All of this led me to a truth that I did not want to accept."

The candor of the conversation allows Ben to connect with his inquisitive nature. "Neshama doesn't completely trust the nephesh, but why?"

Melek pauses before his response, for few mortals have ever spoken to him in a direct way, yet he respects Ben's boldness to question.

"There was a rebellion of nephesh, who Neshama condemned as the Corrupt. They waged The War of Rayah over a valley in the ether world."

The mention of the war sends chills over Ben, but he minds his tongue not to reveal his encounter with Azor or his minimal knowledge of the conflict.

"I was on assignment in your world when the war raged, and at the time I was furious with the Corrupt. I see things differently now that Neshama has wounded me."

The swirling breeze within the vortex becomes turbulent as the ether connects with Melek's emotional scars.

"As time passed I became intrigued with the secret knowledge of ether that the prophets possessed. I might even go as far to say that I became obsessed. Opportunity availed itself when Neshama sent me to assist a prophet, who made a discovery underneath Miriam's Mountains."

The childhood story was all too familiar to shepherd boys and Ben could easily connect the dots. "Zithri, the rogue magi. The one Josiah was called to kill."

Melek takes to Ben, enjoying his curious nature. He stoops down and raises the sentinel by the shackles around his wrists.

"Walk with me."

Ben follows Melek down a flight of stairs while he continues his saga.

"The first matter that I had to attend to was how to disconnect my ether from Neshama. I couldn't have her sense that I was missing and risk a nephesh being sent to search for me."

The first step of Melek's plan collides with Ben's knowledge of Azor's call to reclaim Korah. The thoughts of his nephesh ally vanish when Melek walks Ben into what appears to be a laboratory.

Two chambers break the space in half - the smaller chamber, sealed off by a bronze door and the bigger room, rowed with cement slabs that look like beds. Deceased Elamites rest atop some of them - odd instruments poke out of their corpses.

A few deranged citizens huddle in the corner of a cell that lines the near wall and piles of bones stretch across the far wall. A black marble altar of Melek sets dead center in the room and Ben notices Kurion atop the altar. Maybe it's a sanctuary and not a lab, maybe it's both. Ben can't figure. But whatever happened to the victims looks cruel and unusual.

"For the next two centuries I studied ether, using myself as the source when necessary. Over that time I mastered it, to the point that I could create an ether vortex. I traveled to the ether world to share my findings with Korah and he agreed to become my adherent.

After I mastered ether, I focused my attention on matter. I wondered what mortals were made of and if their souls were woven together from ether. This palace became my laboratory and the plan worked to perfection."

Ben looks across the pile of bones and feels remorse for all the Calcedonians who perished in the diabolical experimentation. His remorse also extends to those in the cage, who will soon become the next victims.

"I disguised myself as a false god and with Korah's help, deceived Lars. I offered the people of Calcedon what their bodies wanted but to a deeper level of degradation that they never knew existed. I learned that flesh is easy to corrupt for there is an element in the biological makeup of mortals that drives them to consume – gluttony, lust, greed. Such urges are foreign to the nephesh."

Ben's soul begins to feel exposed by Melek's diagnosis of humankind.

"I was surprised, however, when I learned how difficult it is to corrupt the soul of a mortal. Your soul is indeed made up of ether but it's formidable, and unlike a nephesh's ether, it's extremely difficult to manipulate. Extracting souls from mortals takes a lot of focus, but I do find that human souls yield a powerful benefit.

Likewise, when a soul becomes corrupt, a mortal has no chance of returning to their original condition by their own volition."

"Why do all of this experimentation in Calcedon and not Issur?"

"Issur is the prize, children of the Covenant, the favored ones. I didn't want to leave anything to chance. My first step with Issur was to find an ally in a prophet. I found a willing follower in Zidon, who then gained the confidence of an easily corrupted prince in Zimri. Once again I disguised myself as a false god and exactly like Lars, I deceived Zimri. Korah acted as my intercessor."

The name of Zimri curdles Ben's stomach as he digests Melek's scheme that destroyed his family.

"As a prince, Zimri wove Melek worship into the fabric of Issur. As a king, he blanketed the country in Melek worship. My first goal was to destroy Issur's religion. Living according to the Covenant, according to the codes of grace and justice only strengthen the soul and a nation. The shepherds knew this and once more Neshama had to stick her nose into the affairs of Issur. That's when she called your parents to lead a resistance."

Ben's knees weaken. The dead bones, the corpses on stone slabs, and the reminder of his parents' death make the laboratory spin. Each frame of Melek's plot sears into Ben's mind as if Melek hammers a piece of metal atop a steaming forge.

"When your father's revolt failed, Zimri was able to assert a modicum of dominance. Emmerick's defiance was a nuisance, but it was only a matter of time before the Southern Kingdom would fall. Once the worship of Neshama was banned and replaced with Melek worship, all of the pieces fell into place."

Ben's emotions plead for mercy from the painful history lesson, but his curiosity empowers him to endure it.

"The next step was to destroy knowledge, so that's when Korah instructed Zimri to dismantle the Hall of Knowledge and replace it with The Pit. Zimri exchanged education for entertainment.

The next step was for Zimri to control the wealth, so Korah ordered him to seize control of the Merchants Guild in Tizra. After that, Zimri was able to control the food supply when he crushed the Farmers Guild. I had a nation of people desiring wealth and food. There was only one man who they could turn.

Zimri's ego raged out of control and the people worshipped their false god Melek with a fierce faith."

Ben's joints struggle to bear the weight of Melek's scheme, so he sits on the edge of a stone slab.

"The final step was to turn Zimri against his son and his wife - the remaining voices of reason capable of saving his soul."

Ben wants to disregard the plan as sadistic, like he wants to pin Melek as a monster, but he can't, for he finds the plot brilliant. Ben ceases his questions, fearful of the answers.

"Come. Let me show you my favorite few of Elam."

Melek and Ben scale the spiraled stairs that lead to the pinnacle of the tower overlooking Elam.

Melek presses his hands on Ben's shoulder.

The night air sweeps a welcoming sensation across Ben's face, but the stench of death makes him nauseous as the vultures continue to circle underneath the yellow moon.

"While Zimri destroyed Issur from within, under the watch of Korah, I assembled an army of corrupted souls - mortals with no conscience, no drive to consume resources. My army from Calcedon would rage across Issur while Zimri would sit idly as his country was destroyed."

Ben realizes the plan didn't work to completion and attacks the tiniest chink in Melek's armored-clad plot. "But that's not how the plan went."

"You refer to this insignificant remnant of yours bent on remembering the Covenant… Once again, Neshama shows her pitiful nature by calling a son of Oren Tav. Your guilds are divided and the Issurian army is weakened. Neshama's children will soon become extinct."

The tension on the tower thickens along with the clouds blotting out the moon light.

"I guess you're doing all of this to get back at Neshama for the hurt that she's caused you."

"No," blurts Melek, annoyed by the assumption. "I'm freeing mortals from Neshama."

"You've created anarchy," corrects Ben.

"The purest form of freedom. Where is freedom in grace and justice? Where is freedom in bowing down to the Goddess? There is no freedom in being a slave to the Divine."

"Grace and justice are the corner stones of freedom. We must sacrifice our selfish desires to protect freedom for all."

"Mortals will only attain freedom when they worship themselves - not Neshama. I'm setting them free from a shallow and needy creator."

Melek turns Ben around by his shoulders. Taking to one knee, he looks through the shepherd's eyes. "What would it take to free your soul?"

"I am free," answers Ben with suspect conviction.

"Really? No resentment that Neshama's selfish need for relationship has robbed you of your parents, has claimed your sister's life, has burdened you with a call impossible to fulfill.

I perceive that you are like every mortal. Your brief existence is one of deficit and loss, always trying to overcompensate for the flawed being that you are."

Ben refuses to look away as Melek's golden-eyes penetrate the depths of his soul.

"Greed? No. Your work is sustained by a sense of loyalty… Gluttony? No. Your desire for food and drink can't compete with your drive for adventure… Lust?"

A twitch of Ben's brown-eyes reveals a hint of carnality within his otherwise pure soul.

"I can free you from these shackles, not only the ones around your wrists. I can free you to fulfill your desires void of guilt. You must understand Ben, ridding yourself of Neshama means ridding yourself of sin. If no Goddess exists, then no iniquity can be committed to offend her. You become your own god. You take the girl, exert your dominance over her."

Desire for Ashira enters his being through his toes and numbs his knees. Desire caresses his loins before it grips his heart. The throbbing vibe eventually settles in his throat.

His mind flashes pictures of his inner lust while he imagines the power of an encounter with Ashira, but his conscience resists the demeaning images. The lustful energy intensifies, overpowering his self-control. It pulses visions of his future with Ashira.

Ashira stands arrayed in a gown as white as her teeth, her dark eyes and raven-colored hair veiled, an aura of joy dances about her frame. As Ben moves to her side, the aura blackens. He removes the veil to see bruised eyes and blood trickling from her lips. She shudders with fear in his presence.

Ben reaches his hands to his head and digs his fingertips into his skull, attempting to alleviate the agony within his mind. He condemns the way of Melek into the moonlight above, "I don't want your freedom!"

Melek smashes his fist down on the railing of the tower and chunks of stone plummet to the streets below. "Then I will take your soul by force! I refuse to waste anymore time trying to persuade you to accept my freedom... Guards!"

The tapping boots of the two guards spiral up the staircase when a lesson on ether from Othniel reminds Ben of the laws governing the divine substance. "You can't take my soul, it's not corrupt. Only corrupt souls can be banished."

"I don't intend to banish your soul. I will consume it. Like I said, the souls of mortals are of great benefit to me."

Finally, the last piece of the puzzle fits and Ben makes sense of Melek's mystery. "That's why you're larger than other nephesh; the human ether that you consume fuels your growth."

"And soon, I will be rid of what little matter exists within me. I will become pure spirit like Neshama. I will be God."

Melek turns his back on Ben as the guards yank him away.

"Vilekin whore! You killed one of my men!" accuses Xylen at the ready with his sword and dagger.

"He shouldn't have been in my way!" defends the corsair with a javelin in each hand.

Zidon marches onward to the palace entrance with a company of guards, who dismiss the mob of onlookers hoping for a duel.

The corsair sheathes her javelins behind her back as a show on concession; the cutthroat buries his blades underneath his robes in response to her unspoken concession.

"We had them cornered until this Vilekin filth washed ashore to poison one of my men. Zidon, she claims that you brought her to Elam."

"I did. She fights with a vengeful heart and from what I hear she's the only one to draw blood."

The corsair's eyes sparkle underneath her purple-hooded cloak at Zidon's praise.

"She was a stowaway on the boat that brought me to Calcedon. Zimri paid her sister a hefty sum to eliminate Seth Keros, but it appears that failure runs in her bloodline."

Xylen's eyes twinkle under his seared scalp at Zidon's rebuke until a slap across face from Zidon removes the twinkle, making known whom the magi finds more impressive.

"I warned you about failure. You know the demands of the faith and you will now face retribution."

Seth and Ezekiel listen to the conversation from an adjacent alleyway. Ashira scouts the palace entrance through the window of an abandoned apartment.

A net falls from a balcony above the palace entrance to entangle Xylen. The guards point their spear tips on the netted assassin and disarm him.

Xylen trembles at the judgment on the high magi's face. "Prince of rats, only now in your failure will you come to understand the ways of Melek."

Zidon shoves his index finger in the corsair's face, "You're next if you fail to deliver my nephew."

The Vilekin immediately disperses into the city on the hunt for the prophet.

Zidon returns to the palace with his guards dragging Xylen behind them.

With the magi and the guards transposed, the assassin neutralized, and the corsair on the prowl in Elam - none remain to guard the entrance. Ashira gives the signal for Seth and Ezekiel to break cover, so the three friends infiltrate the palace.

Zidon marches to the dungeon with a guard on each hip. He arrives to find Emmerick caring for Lars in the prison cell.

"Two fools masquerading as kings, if only a magi could garner such a title."

The guards yank Lars from Emmerick and his frail body smacks floor. They pull Emmerick out of the cell while Zidon takes a spear from one of the guards and shoves it through the heart of the Lars.

Emmerick solemnly fathoms the tragic life of his old friend - scorned by his father and brothers, betrayed by his son.

"I suppose you're in Elam for me," says Zidon.

"You're at the root of this mystery and I have questions," asserts Emmerick.

"There's only one question to this mystery, and you'll soon learn the answer."

Chapter 13 ✦ Night Flight

As Aden makes his ascent up Torn Hill, he marvels at the moon beams brightening the golden-dome of the Grand Chancel. In the background, the Plains of Moreb drift for as far as his eye can see. The air feels calm, as does Aden, for his soul senses that forgiveness draws near.

Aden looks about the high walls to see a glowing room within the dark sanctuary and marks the light as his destination.

Aden enters the narthex and lights a torch to guide his path down a long corridor leading to the inner sanctum. The embers illuminate the mosaics that chronicle the history of the paladin precepts.

Aden takes a few steps before his boots alert him that he treads atop milky white marble floors with swirling gold etchings. His torch illuminates the cedar cathedral rafters towering overhead. He processes to the inner sanctum feeling as if enters the very presence of Neshama.

Aden approaches the doors to the holy sanctuary when High Precept Amar Divine appears to greet him. "Welcome, my valiant rescuer from days of yore… I had little doubt that Rothmore's inquisition would expose the sins of Tizra. It is a right and a good thing that you seek me.

Dear child, how heavy the burden you have bore for fifteen years. Your judgment ends tonight. Are you ready to enter the Stages of Edicts?"

"Yes, Holiness," admits Aden, narrowly able to make eye contact with the High Precept.

"Then we begin… Your confession, though spoken years ago is known to the Goddess. So we will begin this session with the edict of truth."

The precept examines the prince and takes special note of Royal Blue on his hip. "You know the ways of our order, no bladed-weapons allowed in the inner sanctum. In fact, you should relinquish your sword and your armor for the ceremony."

Caleb nods in agreement and Amar shows him to a changing room. The prince slips into a white robe and cinches it with a gold-colored chord. He removes a garnet gem secure in his armor, and palms the burgundy stone in his hand.

After Aden exits the changing room, the High Precept slips a black blindfold over his eyes. "You must not see by sight, but by spirit."

Aden hears the locks turn before the doors of the sanctuary open. Inhaling the intoxicating aroma, the incense buckles his knees.

"You now walk the path of truth. Confirm your vows," instructs Divine.

"There is one Goddess. There is one Covenant. From material to spiritual, from temporal to eternal, from death to life, we pass. I believe the truth that Neshama revealed grace to the prophets and justice to the precepts. I believe that charity flows from the hand of Neshama. I believe that forgiveness is the way of Neshama. I believe in the veneration of Holy Miriam. I believe that all will be called to reconcile with Neshama at the final judgment."

Aden completes his vows at the foot of a set of stairs, his heart thumping with anticipation.

"You may climb the steps of charity."

The prince prostrates himself and crawls up the steps on hands and knees while Amar Divine walks behind him, pleased by Aden's devotion.

Aden feels his way to the top step and touches the cedar coffer to confirm his next stop of the stations. He produces the flawless garnet and Amar Divine marvels at the quality of such an offering.

"Your generosity is noted, glory to the Goddess for all of the mouths that your gift shall feed."

Divine leads Aden to a marble altar and the prince kneels with arms stretched out and hands folded in prayer. His head bows low, ready to receive the blessing of forgiveness from the precept. Aden's soul floats within him as the burden of his iniquity lifts from his body.

"Neshama forgives you. If only I could do the same," says Amar Divine, clamping shackles on Aden's wrists.

Aden tries to rise from the altar but the cuffs are grounded into the marble floor by a chain. The precept stands behind the prince to remove the blindfold.

It takes a moment for the pupils in his blue eyes to funnel the light of the inner sanctum. Aden stares at the feet of a statue made of black marble with flowing robes. He raises his eyes to find an ominous Melek idol towering above him.

Strapped to a cold stone slab by metal bindings, Emmerick twists his neck, sending sensations down his numbed spine. He rolls his gaze to the Signet Ring of Issur. He grinds his middle finger against his ring finger to work the golden circle from his hand. The signet ring jingles across the brick floor of the ether lab.

"If by some statistical anomaly you survive what's going to happen in the next room, I want you to take this ring to Aden," instructs Emmerick.

Ben affirms the request with a regretful nod.

"You know what's coming, don't you?" asks the king.

The sentinel remains silent and stares at the cracks in the rocky ceiling. Metal bindings dig into his wrists and ankles while the muscles in his back deaden atop the stone slab. Ben rolls his head to see Kurion on the Melek altar, thoughts of heroism race through his mind if he could but grasp the blade once more.

Ben slowly rolls his head to face his king, answering Emmerick through the gloom in his eyes.

Zidon's guards usher Xylen into the main chamber. Insults flow from his tongue like the black robes that flutter about his body. His anger transforms into remorse with every step. "Zidon was wrong to doubt my faith in Melek! Please, I beg you! Allow me to reason with Melek!" The guards exchange crooked smiles, knowing what awaits the disgraced assassin on the other side of chamber door. The bronze door creaks open to receive the next victim of Melek's retribution.

The guards exit the lab but the heavy door remains cracked. Emmerick and Ben stretch their necks to get the best possible view of inside the dark chamber.

After a long pause, Xylen bawls in horrid agony. The anguish in his shrieks panics the caged citizens, who huddle in the far corner away from the dark chamber.

An onyx glow bursts, before being swallowed up in the quaint chamber.

"Ben, I must know. What happened to him?"

The sentinel hesitates until his sense of duty nudges him to inform his king. "Melek consumed his soul."

The professor takes a while to process the magnitude of the statement. If his hands weren't chained, he'd give his mustache a good twist to extend his pondering. Out of nowhere, a laugh rumbles in his stomach, so he releases it.

"Why do you laugh?" questions Ben.

"Don't you see? Melek is my leviathan."

Ben smiles as best he can, trying to find humor in their bleak condition. "I have to admit. I thought being your sentinel would be boring, thought I'd be watching you do research in a laboratory all day."

"Sorry to disappoint you, Ben. But the irony is grand, isn't it? Seems fitting that I should die in a laboratory."

"How can you joke in a time like this?"

"All life cycles end, my Sentinel… Though, something that I read in the prophet's book made me think. In fact, I haven't stop thinking about it since we reached Calcedon. The words were scientific in nature and struck me with a bolt of hope."

Darkness can only exist in the absence of light."

The words of Othniel comfort Ben as two attendants emerge from the room, their long crimson hooded-robes covering their faces and bodies. They unchain Emmerick and walk him into the chamber, again leaving a crack in the door.

Ben rolls his head to focus on Kurion and the divine mantra, but his loyalty to Emmerick inspires him to glide his eyes to the split in the adjacent room.

Emmerick moans in misery. His suffering brings tears to Ben's brown eyes. The salty drops roll down onto the cold stone. A purple glow bursts, then gets swallowed up in the dim chamber.

The space falls silent.

Ben Tav's term as Emmerick's sentinel ends.

Seth, Ashira, and Ezekiel enter the throne room in search of Zidon but his whereabouts vanish from their curiosity when they spot the ether vortex swirling on the floor.

"It's beautiful, yet terrifying. What is it?" asks Ashira.

"An ether vortex," says Ezekiel as Zidon makes his presence known to the company.

"Holding class, Nephew? I hope you're a quick study because I'm about to school you in the dark arts."

"It's me you want, Uncle."

"Only because of my affection for your mother. Don't assume that I have the same affinity towards you."

"Then let them go, this is between us."

"A plea of sacrifice. I see that my brother has infected you. It sickens me to hear you spew the beliefs of 'Wayfarer.' I didn't want to get my hands dirty, but since the assassins and the corsair failed, I'm left with no choice."

"There are more in the Remnant than us," boldly proclaims Ezekiel.

"You're a fool, young prophet. Follow the ways of Melek and you will become wise to the ways of manipulation… Your prince will be sacrificed on an altar of Melek - that dagger will fall with Amar Divine. Your king and his sentinel will die in the ether lab below us. And now, your friends will die by my hands."

Zidon pulls ether from the vortex into each hand and slings it at Ezekiel and Seth. The shots speed quickly, but lack the power to maim them. Seth and Ezekiel stumble backwards while Ashira runs for the door.

Zidon channels a thicker strand and launches it at her.

Ashira dives out of the doorway as the ether crashes into

the frame dislodging the door from the hinges. The entire frame collapses down alongside the rubble, blocking Seth's and Ezekiel's escape route.

Another blast drops Seth and Ezekiel to the floor.

As the two slowly return to their feet, Zidon calculates the precise amount of ether to incapacitate his nephew. Once the orb of ether thickens in his hand, he casts it at Ezekiel.

Ezekiel closes his eyes in preparation of the incoming affliction. His reflexes force his hand to wave over the vortex. Miraculously, the prophet weaves a white web that consumes the black orb.

Seth's mouth drop opens, shocked by the prophet's resolve.

Zidon's teeth sneer. The magi flings a massive ether orb into the ceiling above Seth, dislodging a boulder of debris aimed at crushing the warrior.

Ezekiel widens his opal net and slides it across the floor. The net hovers over his friend and repels the boulder that bounces onto Tartek's throne, shattering it on impact.

Zidon channels a cone-shaped ebony strand as Ezekiel returns the netting to his defense. His white magic lacks the power to stop the master's blast and the prophet gets blown backwards into a wall - his bones and wooden staff rattle against the stone.

A rush of rage crashes over Seth. He throws a fistful of dirt into Zidon's eyes before charging him. The blinded magi fires on instinct as Peacemaker descends over the behemoth's buzzed head. The ether strand slows the blow, sparing Zidon's life, but the force lands great enough to bruise the magi's sternum when it knocks him against Melek's throne.

Zidon's old bones collapse on the floor while Seth bashes down the tilted door stuck in the rubble. He punches a big enough hole for an exit and scoops his unconscious friend from the floor.

Zidon lifts his head from the floor. His sign of life bites

Seth with disappointment. The warrior calculates his odds of victory while factoring in the source of ether. Seth realizes that while flight goes against his instincts to fight - it's the course of action that he'd have to take on this night.

Ben settles his neck one final time to catch a glimpse of the stars twinkling through a cell window. Failure torments him more than the thought of dying.

Had he been loyal to his guild, then he wouldn't be facing the throes of death. Instead, he'd still be hiding in the shadows of an ether chancel. Jael and Daniel would still be alive. He failed Evan and Judith. All of his training as sentinel meant nothing, for he couldn't protect his king. He failed Emmerick.

Overwhelmed by failure and doubt, Ben whispers his common prayer, "Neshama. Are you there? Are you listening?"

The slashing sounds of blades spill into the chamber along with a dead jailor.

Ashira emerges with a cell key in hand.

She frees Ben. He jumps into his boots, adjusts his armor, and reclaims Kurion from the altar. He scans the room for his black bow but he does not locate it.

"Where's Emmerick?" asks Ashira.

Ben retrieves the signet ring from the floor while thoughts of defying the odds jingle in his head. He holds up the ring for Ashira as his answer.

Ben readies his exit but compassion for the prisoners halts his steps. He takes the key from Ashira and goes to cell door to free the Calcedonians. Before he turns the key, they rush him. The deranged Elamites pull his arms and claw at his armor through the bars like wild animals.

The creaky bronze door widens, so Ben wastes no more time, he grabs Ashira and bolts for the stairs.

The attendants mill about the chamber in their crimson robes looking for their next victim. Horrified by the two men, the savage citizens flee to their corner. The open chamber door reveals a neck brace attached to a chain dangling from the ceiling, along with two wrist clamps at the end of two more chains dangling from each wall. The corpses of Xylen and Emmerick lie next to one another.

Melek ducks through the doorframe to enter the lab. He bellows in fury at the sight of Ben's empty slab.

"Open the cell!"

The attendants follow orders to secure another citizen. They draw their scourges before they enter. To their dismay, Melek shoves them in the cell and slams the door behind them. The demented Calcedonians rush them and shred their red vestments before sinking their starving teeth into their dinner.

Zidon peels himself from the floor and blinks out the dirt in his eyes, his chest throbbing with soreness from the warhammer shot.

The ether vortex angrily spins like a cyclone as Melek enters the throne room. The destruction testifies to an ether duel, but with no apparent casualties, the missteps of the magi appear obvious to the nephesh.

"You are the only mortal that I hold in high regard but your failure is an embarrassment."

"Failure!?" interrupts Zidon. "Must I remind you of my deeds? It was I who played Zimri like a puppet. Look at the depths of his tyranny. It was I who held the strings. After Zimri failed to kill Othniel, it was I who eliminated 'Wayfarer.'"

"The flight of the Remnant is in motion. You have failed. You will now face my retribution," affirms Melek, unrelenting in his judgment.

"Ungrateful wretch of a nephesh! I delivered the Remnant into your black palms and they slipped through your grip!"

Wrestling with feelings of intrigue and hatred, Melek searches Zidon's soul.

The magi lengthens with confidence. "If you want to call my deeds into judgment then prepare yourself to feel the full force of my ether skills. I may not emerge victorious but I will maim you."

Melek releases a rare chuckle from beneath his black hood.

"Zidon, how I still admire your spite. It was your disdain for Neshama that launched my campaign to destroy Issur; it only seems fitting that you should be there to watch it fall. A mortal with your mastery of ether will be of use to this operation. Board Korah's fleet in the Cove of Carnek. He will know exactly why I send you."

Ben and Ashira collide with Seth inside a palace corridor. The jolt of the collision fails to energize an unconscious Ezekiel slumped across Seth's shoulders.

"Is he alive?" frets Ben.

Seth's nod of affirmation dismisses Ben's fear.

As they dash for the exit, the snorts of the assassins' horses call to them from the palace stables.

"Wait, where's Emmerick?" asks Seth, placing Ezekiel across Ben's horse.

The sentinel hesitates to answer while the behemoth saddles the biggest stallion of the lot.

"He didn't make it," says Ben.

"Great. Then this whole trip was for nothing. Now I'll never get the coin to repair my shop."

"Seth Keros!" scolds Ashira like she's his mother. "You can worry about yourself later!"

The three horses dart from stable toward the city gate.

Zidon sees them flee and mounts the remaining horse to give chase.

Two guards at the gate step forward to halt their escape.

Seth and Ashira ride to the front. A quick slice of her blade whirls a watchman in the breeze of her stallion.

Seth grabs a stumbling drunkard by the scruff of his neck and hurls him into the other guard. The watchman and the drunkard tumble together into a trash heap.

The company thunders down The Elam Highway into the fading night while pines glide by them on both sides of the road. Ben looks back to see Zidon in pursuit along with a mysterious figure on horseback. The magi's hood whisks back and his grey robes flutter in the rushing wind.

"We've got company!" warns Ben.

Seth looks back to see Zidon and identifies the mysterious horseman.

"She's back!" complains Seth to Ashira.

A javelin screams by Seth's ear and over his horses head.

Zidon closes, chanting the mystical language. Within a few tongues from his lips, he's able to connect with the untamed ether in Ashira's horse.

The steed bucks wildly, attempting to throw her off, but she jumps from the mount on her own terms.

Ben and Seth wrestle with their reins to slow the momentum of their steeds.

"I can't fight on one of these," says Seth, stepping down from his grateful horse.

Ben lowers Ezekiel to Seth, who places the injured prophet behind him and securely grips Peacemaker with both hands.

Ben races back to support Ashira.

Zidon boast the mysterious chant again to connect with a handful of vultures circling above. Ben hugs his stallion's neck as the vile birds swoop down from above. One vulture yanks a claw of hair while the others slow his rescue. Dashing with purpose, his steed blasts through the feathered-wall of fowl.

The magi disconnects from the ether within the vultures

and regains control of Ashira's horse, the steed rearing and bucking harder than before.

Ashira's agility keeps her from getting wrecked by the stallion's powerful kicks, but the distraction forbids her from drawing blades to attack Zidon.

Ashira squats down for a fistful of dirt and sprays the particles into the magi's eyes. She uses her final throwing knife to remove Zidon from his horse.

With his sense of sight diminished, his sense of hearing sharpens. As the knife nears his head, he leans back and the blade nips the tip of his crooked nose. He loses his balance and racks his backside on the ground.

Ben's eyes widen at the easy target as he unsheathes Kurion, but an exact javelin throw makes him aware of the imminent threat. The corsair takes Ben by surprise when she leaps from her horse and tackles him from his steed.

Their bodies bounce across the dirty highway causing Ben to lose Kurion in the collision.

Zidon takes advantage of the chaos by remounting his horse and riding off.

Ashira's horse finally calms, allowing her to support Ben. She draws blades and charges the corsair. The sea hag leaps into action with a javelin in each hand - her purple cloak hovering behind her.

The women clash. Javelins lunge, swords thrust.

Ashira finds herself in a position of power and strikes high with her right sword. Forced to use both javelins, the corsair attempts to stop the critical blow. As Ashira's sword connects with the javelin shafts, splinters of wood spray the shadows. Her left sword strikes lethally with pinpoint precision that would make her brother proud. Ashira's blade slides under the corsair's ribcage dropping her immediately.

Ben finds his sword and surveys the carnage. "Guess that's two I owe you."

Out of instinct, he reaches behind his back for his bow

with thoughts of sinking an arrow into Zidon, but he's quickly reminded of another lost bow.

Zidon bears down on Seth but the notion of claiming his nephew is short-lived when his bruised sternum reminds his brain about the knock he took from Peacemaker. Zidon rides to the low side of the road accelerating around Seth.

The company regroups and gives chase into the rising beams of the seventh sun, but Zidon rides too far out front. They split north onto Tadmor Road while Zidon completes his route to Carnek.

Ben's worry vanishes when he sees the sails of the Issurian schooner on the coastline of Tadmor.

Caleb waves to them from a row boat.

They abandon their horses to board the boat and the scout quickly realizes that they're down a man, a very important man.

Ben shakes his head, freeing Caleb of the uncomfortable question. "We must hurry to Issur; Aden's in danger." Ben's warning motivates Caleb, who pulls the oars of the rowboat at a fleet pace.

Aden throttles and twists the shackles, but no matter the angle he can't break free. He looks over his shoulder to see Amar Divine sharpening a silver dagger with a crescent moon on the hilt. It's as if the High Precept has suddenly gone deaf, for every question from the prince goes unanswered.

Aden runs scenarios through his head as to why Amar Divine accepted heresy, but nothing makes sense. All he can figure is that Zidon has something to do with it.

The precept scrapes the flint one final time before examining the blade in the torchlight. He pricks the tip of his index finger for a final check of the dagger's sharpness.

As Amar Divine moves towards Aden, a racket echoes down the hall. He places his dagger next to the prince and grabs his claymore before investigating the noise.

Divine moves about the hallway and stumbles across the source of the dissonance. His nose finds them before his eyes for the rancid stench nearly causes him to vomit - three rotten corpses of precepts from the undercroft defile his marble floor.

"Traitor," accuses a voice from the entrance of the sanctuary.

Divine walks towards the threat to find Shamgar Ram holding Aden's sword and armor. His mace dangles at his waist and his left arm dangles in a sling. The wounded precept moves up the stairs toward the chained prince under the Melek idol, his righteous blood rushing with indignation.

Divine enters the sanctum, closes the doors, and locks them with a key on a brass ring attached to the golden-colored cord wrapped around his bloated stomach. Shamgar scans the room for the key to free the prince while Divine moves around the perimeter of the sanctum, putting his torch to the five great bowls that burst into flame.

"You'll have to rip his freedom from my dead body," says Amar Divine, lighting pungent incense in an orb attached to a chain. He swings the orb in such a manner that the sacred fragrance thickens the air of the sanctuary.

The fumes press Aden's eyelids shut and irritate his nostrils.

Shamgar breathes deep unaffected by the ritual. "Do you hope that the incense will cover the stench of your murder?"

"Rothmore accepted Melek, they refused. Those precepts suffered in chains without food or water, yet they never ceased their prayers to the Goddess. They called on her with their last gasps."

"Rothmore is dead, the inquisition is over. Tobi Tamar

lives, Aden Tizra lives, and I live. Your plot failed."

"Says the one-armed precept," snaps Divine.

"You played on Emmerick's preference of knowledge over faith knowing full well that he'd allow the inquisition. Then, Rothmore waited for the council's decision before calculating his strength. You played on Aden's guilt and pure heart, hoping to lure him here. You wanted the wall fortification stalled and the guards protecting it dead… Your plot has Zidon's fingerprints all over it."

Aden fights the intoxicating incense in hopes of keeping his wits to learn of Amar Divine's sinister scheme.

"You're a cunning one, Shamgar Ram. You survived The Scarlet Winter, survived Rothmore's inquisition, but you haven't offered the why?"

"Your lust for coin of course."

"Avarice… Yes. But spite made the deal so much sweeter to my soul. Zidon paid handsomely, but spite is why I bowed my knee to Melek."

"Why Zidon?" asks Shamgar.

"Zidon spoke to my heart. For his faithful service as a prophet, Neshama blessed him with a dead sister."

"I fail to see how his struggle is your struggle."

"The faith of the precepts is fierce, unrivaled in Issur. Yet the Goddess calls shepherds to lead the Remnant. When she called Oren Tav, she rejected us. The Synod was massacred because he failed to overthrow Zimri. The final insult was when she called Benjamin Tav, and not me, to lead the Remnant. She chose a boy of doubts over a man of faith."

"I was frustrated with her choice, believe me, but look at what the Tav boy has accomplished. It's evident that Neshama's hand is upon him, that she is with the Remnant."

"We are the Remnant! Neshama turned her back on Issur and the precepts, now we turn to Calcedon and to Melek. The Tizra line will die with Aden. King Tartek's army will purge Issur of the Remnant and I will remake the Synod as a disciple of Melek."

"First, you'll have to remove my mace from your face."

"Glory to Melek, god of the dark, god of the moon!" professes Amar Divine with spittle flinging from his lips.

No longer able to siphon the fumes of the incense, Aden blacks out.

Shamgar readies his bludgeon. Divine lengthens his claymore with his white knuckles latched across the hilt. Shamgar throws a shot that the long blade easily turns aside. Divine allows another shot from Shamgar that he easily blocks. After two swings, Divine realizes that Shamgar's broken arm creates an imbalance.

The hefty precept whirls his claymore at Shamgar, who narrowly dodges the strikes. The wide blade slices the incense as it whistles in front of its target's nose. Divine lands a shot into the broken arm and painful bolts charge Shamgar's body.

Amar Divine presses his attack by wrecking his blade into Shamgar's right forearm. The heavy swing disarms Ram's mace.

Divine backs Shamgar away from his weapon. He grabs the mace and hurls it out of the sanctum through a stained-glass window. Jagged shards spray the Melek idol before raining down around Aden's flaccid body.

Shamgar frantically looks about the sanctum for a weapon. He identifies the dagger on the Melek altar and Royal Blue among Aden's gear, but he fails to identify any blunted weapons.

"Come on Ram, take up Aden's sword or perish with your pathetic precept oaths."

Shamgar refuses to violate the oath of the precepts not to battle with bladed weapons. He improvises his assault when he kicks over a bowl stand that sends a wave of flames at Amar. The chubby precept stumbles out of the way and barrels across the floor - his belt unknots sending the key on the brass ring toward the altar.

Shamgar shoves another bowl from its stand, but sends it with too much force, causing it to sail high and land in a vat of lamp oil.

The explosion knocks both precepts over and blasts flames up the wall vestments and into the cedar rafters. The explosion also jars a third bowl from its mount, which strikes another vat causing another eruption of flames.

The latest blast bursts all of the stained-glass windows. Shards of glass rain down, shredding the robes of the three men, while planks of cedar plummet from the ceiling around them.

The relentless Shamgar sears the flesh of his hand to a flaming mass of lumber from the rafters. Taking a stout swing, he dislodges the apostate's jaw. Divine falls to the floor under the weight of a falling plank while Shamgar rushes to the altar and frees Aden with the key on the brass ring.

Shamgar backhands the prince across the face, jarring him back to reality. The smell of smoke overpowers the incense allowing the prince to revive his senses.

Only one segment of vestments has yet to catch fire, a strand of white linens flowing down from behind the large statue. Aden straps his sword to his side and removes the cord from his waist to string his armor across his back.

He runs and leaps onto the dangling cloth.

Aden pulls himself up to a ledge that leads to an open window. The head of Melek blocks his departure, so he rocks the idol with one leg.

Below, Shamgar, armed only with the key ring, turns to the sanctuary doors for his only escape route when Divine's claymore cuts through the haze to chop off his rival's hand.

Shamgar donates his bloody hand to the steps of charity.

The heretic raises his blade to add Shamgar's head to the collection when the idol dislodges from its mount. The statue explodes the altar and the coffer before fragmenting down the steps.

The fallen idol separates the two precepts.

The back draft from the totem invigorates the flames. A large flare cuts a weakened plank of cedar which falls down upon the fourth bowl, tipping it over and spraying flames across the sanctuary doors.

The blaze encompasses the entire inner sanctum while the rafters splinter and debris rains down from the ceiling.

Aden reels in the intact vestment and shimmies across the ledge as bricks crumble underneath his footing on his way to the opening.

Amar Divine gets to his feet with claymore raised. The maimed precept's crystal-blue eyes glow through the thick smoke. Shamgar lowers his head and charges Divine like the mountain herds rack horns in his hometown atop Serpent's Peak. Shamgar rams the apostate into the fifth and final bowl.

Flames engulf the heretic in judgment.

Aden watches Amar thrash in agony, before he fastens the vestment around an opening in the window frame. He makes one final connection with Shamgar. Aden shines a glance of gratitude, then repels down the outer wall, dropping safely onto Torn Hill.

The inner sanctum implodes, washing a tide of conflagration over the remaining structure of the Grand Chancel. Within moments, the blaze consumes the temple.

Fire incinerates the flesh of Shamgar Ram, flame purifies his soul.

Chapter 14 ✦ Voices from the Past

The East Sea steadily slides the swift Issurian schooner across her waves toward the marshes of Tekoa. Full white sails, filled by a northern breeze, flap like linens stretched about a clothes line. With no sign of the Calcedonian fleet, the trouble in the souls of the company settles.

Seth refuses to sleep while keeping watch over Ezekiel.

Caleb paces nervously with worry for Aden.

Ben opens his eyes to find Ashira asleep on his chest. His mind races to remember how they feel asleep. Sheer exhaustion removes the memory, so he simply takes the moment to enjoy her closeness.

Ashira lifts her head when she feels his energy stir. They rise together and smile in unison at Seth watching over the injured Ezekiel.

"How long before Tekoa?" asks Ashira.

"Not long. Let's just hope we don't see smoke like Caleb warned. The Calcedonian army will take time to mobilize, which should allow us to reach Tekoa first."

Ashira overcomes her anxiety about the future with her gratitude for the past. "Thanks for saving me from Zidon."

"Couldn't let the cook die," smiles Ben. She nudges his ribs, her playful interaction softening his jealous edge. "I wasn't of much help. You saved me twice."

Though Ashira appreciates the lighter moment, the question that haste forbade her to ask nags her curiosity. "Did you see Melek?"

The darkness that shades his countenance appears obvious to her. She senses he did, but yearns to know more about the black nephesh. Ben realizes that he'd eventually have to give a report to the others, so he entertains her interest.

"Melek is not the monster that I imagined him to be. After I watched him kill Zimri, I thought him to be the same as the tyrant - a mindless barbarian on a conquest to ruin Issur and end the Covenant."

"He doesn't desire those things?"

"No, he does. But it's bigger than that, much bigger than us… Melek wants to replace the Goddess. He wants to be God."

The answer throttles Ashira to the core. Her dark skin whitens as her blood vessels stagnate, turning her ruby lips blue.

After watching Melek's oppression dampen her aura, Ben second guesses his decision to answer her question.

Another look at the grief-stricken Seth prompts Ben to rescue Ashira from her grave thoughts. "I'm not telling you what to do but we're going to need your brother when we get to Tekoa. Is there any way that you can make him something to eat so that he can get a little sleep?"

Ezekiel makes the task easier when he opens his eyes to the relief of all, especially his guardian. The conscious prophet draws a rare smile from Seth. Ashira lifts her brother alongside his sigh of relief. They walk arm and arm to the galley.

Ben takes Seth's place at Ezekiel's side. The prophet's hands tap about the deck to feel for his possessions. Ezekiel secures the staff in one hand and grips Othniel's book in the other.

"Do you think Emmerick would like to have another read before we make it home?" asks the dazed prophet.

"Sorry, Ezekiel. Melek killed Emmerick."

Like Zidon's ether blast, the news hits the prophet hard. Instead of his bones aching, his soul throbs with pain.

"If it makes you feel any better his last words to me were the sacred words of Miriam – Othniel's mantra."

Ezekiel smiles to acknowledge the contented sentiment.

"Where do you think Othniel is right now?" asks Ben.

"The ether world," says Ezekiel, trying not to sound snarky.

"I know that much, but where in the ether world."

"The Book of Miriam teaches that when we die our souls take a journey through a realm in the ether world called Emunah. It tells of plains, meadows, and forests filled with majestic creatures. Eventually, our souls journey to the Great Judgment Bridge."

"What happens there?" asks Ben behind wide eyes.

"This is where we meet Neshama. If we remember the Covenant, we cross the bridge. Prophets debate what happens to those who don't remember. Othniel always said that humans get one final chance to accept her limitless grace. Imriel always protested Othniel's theology. He claimed that once you die, it's too late for grace."

"What do you think?"

Humbled by the notion that Ben places his theology on the same level as his mentors, Ezekiel hesitates to answer. The prophet closes his eyes, allowing his soul to sink deeply into his most powerful conviction.

"I believe grace to be the most powerful force in the universe. No barrier can block it. No enemy can destroy it. Not even death can contain it."

Ezekiel's words convict the doubt in Ben's soul as he continues to share his beliefs. "Othniel said that there are some who will never accept grace. Those souls descend into a cavern that runs under the judgment bridge where they'll wander for eternity. He made it sound a lot like homelessness."

Upon hearing the word 'homelessness,' Ben's thoughts shift from the ether world to what he witnessed in Elam. "Melek makes an entire nation homeless. He seeks to do the same to Issur."

"I can see it on your face, you spoke to him. What troubles you, Ben?"

"His concept of freedom is the opposite of what Othniel taught."

"Can he be defeated?"

It was the question that Ben wrestled with ever since the fateful day Melek descended into the vortex. He knows the answer and the recent encounter with the nephesh only confirms it, but the resistance in his soul refuses his tongue to speak the answer.

"I can sense the hesitancy in your soul. It's not wrong to doubt."

Ezekiel's permission to doubt turns Ben's beliefs upside down. All of those years in the pews of the ether chancel, along with the scolding by Shamgar Ram, led him to believe that doubt was the enemy of faith. Nothing struck his soul with guilt more than his struggle with doubt.

"After everything that I witnessed, my faith should be so strong, but it's not. I feel powerless," confesses Ben.

"Do you think that you will fulfill your call?"

"A part of my soul says, yes. The rest doubts."

"Let Neshama help you. That's what she's there for, that's what faith is there for. We want to believe, but there's something in our nature that hinders us from doing so. That is why we must rely on the Goddess."

Ezekiel chuckles to himself as he rubs his fingertips together.

"What is it?" asks Ben with a smile.

"I can still feel the ether in my finger tips. Othniel taught me that balancing the ebb and flow of ether is like balancing the tides of faith and doubt. If a prophet allows himself to be drown in doubt, he risks losing his faith."

"You know, you're starting to sound a lot more like him," says Ben, standing and stretching. "I hope he has found his home in the ether world. I sure miss mine."

Ben leaves Ezekiel to bask in the sun, allowing him to enjoy his first success with ether magic. He moves to an isolated section of the deck when more lessons from his mentor cause him to reflect on what has come to pass.

Ben's desire for grace increases, while his longing for justice diminishes. Othniel taught that the two forces were rooted in sacrifice, but Ben scarcely understands what the master prophet encouraged him to seek. He lacks the courage to willingly lay down his life for his friends. Assuredly, he fights beside them, but to die with them or to take a blade in their place appears quite daunting.

The memory of Othniel's sacrifice haunts Ben's psyche.

As far as having a sense of wonder and imagination about

who he's becoming, that grows more problematic with every step of the journey. He's a sentinel, or at the least a soldier now. In his heart, he longs to be a shepherd once again. There isn't a whole lot of imagination needed for a son of a shepherd to follow in the footsteps of the family craft.

Thoughts of shepherding darken Ben's countenance for he doubts that Hallowed Hills will survive the impending onslaught.

Water dribbles down the sides of the wooden troughs and the scent of fresh fall hay fills the stall. Evan clutches his ribs to silence a groan at the final twist of his rake.

Many of his wounds were healing, but like his head, his ribs were stubborn and wouldn't fuse back together. He had endured many long days in the guild hall, reminiscent of the time that he was twelve and stricken with the mountain flu. It never crossed his mind that he'd look forward to a visit from Bo Baladan but he's eager to hear a report on the flock and tend to the injured sheep.

Judith runs outside of the guild hall, hangs the corner, doubles over and loses her breakfast in the shadows. Evan slides behind a stall, but she catches a glimpse of his white shirt, blowing his cover.

Evan rallies to his sister's side to offer comfort.

"Must have caught a bug with the season change," speaks Judith from behind her hand.

"Hard to catch a cold locked in a guild hall."

"Sorry. I didn't mean to trouble you."

Judith runs back into the hall as if the sunlight scorches her skin.

Judith had yet to return to the market since judgment day and not one person came to visit the cursed widow. No letters arrived by messenger - not one note from Daniel's mother, who used to write poetry praising her beauty and sewing skills. The only sense of solace came from the black and yellow tapestry above the mantle for it reminded her of the last time that she laughed, watching Aden fall from the stool. It also made her think of Ben's bravery while she wondered about his adventures.

"Don't you get tired of staring at that rug?" asks Evan, gingerly positioning himself in the chair next to her.

"It used to annoy me when I'd hear the women ramble on after chancel about how much Jael resembled our mother. I'd never admit it, but I was jealous," admits Judith, redirecting Evan's attempt at small talk.

"You were jealous of Jael?"

"No. I was jealous because I was the odd one in the family."

"You!? No. Jael was the strange one. Remember her tic collection, how she'd spend all day in the stalls plucking them from the lambs?"

"You, Ben, Jael, our parents were all born with a sense of adventure, a sense of purpose. I was the only one to complain about our trips to visit the Keros family when we'd go to Tizra. I hated to leave the safety of the hall and the routine of my chores. Today, I'd give anything to get out.

I never belonged in this family. Tav never wanted me. The women used to criticize my dresses for being too neat, now they call me cursed... Maybe they're right."

Judith's emotions flush out her tears and they spill onto the floor. Evan's heart breaks for her, but he knows that nothing he says or does can heal her, for this would only be accomplished through time.

"Who's going to want me now?" weeps Judith.

Excited sheep stir in the stalls alerting their master of Bo's arrival. Judith hurries to her room, freeing Evan to tend to his flock.

Evan's excitement gets taken down a notch when he sees the scruffy shepherd with wild eyes cradling a lamb in his arms. His fluffy mother bounces about Bo's side. Only two sheep to tend to means that Bo comes bearing good news, instead of chores to occupy Evan's time.

Bo greets Evan with his typical stare of indifference. "You don't look too worse for the wear. I think those claw scars improve your ugly mug, Evan Tav."

"I was hoping to see one of your brothers, so they could tell me that wolves had crapped out your carcass. Since I'm denied such a good report, what's going on with the flock?"

"Age old struggles. A tinker tried to nab a ewe so we had to send him back without a finger. No wolf sightings. This little guy took a spill down a spring; I'm sure you'll have him back to good by winter. This is his mother. She can't take the mountain air, besides, I think she has a brother for this one in her belly. Resh sold you a good flock, a bunch of fertile lasses in the mix… So what's the word around Tav?"

"I've been threatened by the elders with the Law of Eviction," says Evan with a hint of pride in his admission.

"I assume because you keep such fine company," says Bo with a shine in his eyes.

"That, and Erez Elk visited my hall. Turns out that the girl I rescued is his daughter."

"It's a tall world after all," smiles Bo, taking steps toward the town square. "I'm going to head down to Shepherds Shack for some day drinking and probably stay over for some night drinking. Plus, I like that the inn doesn't have beds. Baladans never had much use for them."

"That's not a good idea, Bo. Me and my sister have a lot of eyes on us. You'd only upset the elders. Why don't you stay in the hovel with me? I'll uncork a barrel of mead for you. Heck, I'll even spot you another to take back to your brothers."

"That's a fair offer, but you're missing something in the negotiation… A lady. Unless you have some company in your hovel, I suggest you pay me my wage so I can be on my way."

All of his recent stress makes Evan overly cautious, but Bo upheld his end of the contract, so Evan relents and pays him.

A rapid WHAP! WHAP! WHAP! rattles Evan's hovel door. He rises from his bedding with fears that a wolf roams about. Evan flings open the door to find three elders with vicious glares in their eyes.

Upon seeing their crimson vision, he knows the next words out of their mouths are going to be 'Baladan' and 'Shepherds Shack.'

"Did you hear what a Baladan did at the Shepherds Shack tonight!?" roars an elder, drawing Judith from the guild hall.

Her eyes point to the grass at the sight of Ruth Gimel in the torch light.

"It was awful! The animal violated my son's wife!"

Plumpy Ruth stomps about like a duck in a puddle. "How could you invite this criminal to do such things our women? First, you send my darling Nabal to an early grave, now you force my precious daughter-in-law into isolation."

"Evan, we warned you about the Baladans," voices the spiteful elder with grey eyes and a bushy grey beard.

"Did you get his side of the story?" asks Evan.

"The criminal fled like a coward. Besides, we'd never trust a word from those filthy shepherds. All we know is that Merlen Gimel is devastated and his wife locks herself away in shame, as would any of our wives. All because you hire that filth! We have no choice but to bring charges against you. A gathering will be called to discuss the Law of Eviction."

Ruth Gimel uncoils like a tightly wound spring. "Yes, yes, eviction! I heard about this law at the market. The village would be a safer place without these two snakes. If we remove Evan and Judith from the guild hall then we remove this hex from Tav."

There's nothing that Evan can say in Bo's defense, so he lets silence make his case. He stands with Judith, the siblings refusing to hide in the hall. They wait in the cool night air until all of the torches disappear.

Evan knew that Ruth Gimel held a grudge, but he figured that it was laid to rest with his deceased uncle. Smoke emerges from the shadows and rubs his fluffy fur against Evan's leg. The mouser reminds him of an ancient shepherd saying: *Beware the claws of a scorned cat.*

Evan Tav had been mauled by two felines in one season.

Ezekiel's eyes follow a mouse across a crate. The outline of Tekoa grows larger behind the rodent as the schooner near the docks. The prophet whispers the mystical language and scurries the mouse across Seth's large nose. For the prophet's amusement, the critter dances atop Seth's face.

The grouchy bear awakens from his nap to swat the mouse from his face. "Stinkin' rodents never stop." Seth's frustration lessens when he finds the prophet leaning against his staff. "Did you see that mouse, Zek?"

The prophet shrugs innocently.

"You're lookin' better."

"My back is sore," admits Ezekiel.

"Well, you did hit a wall," says the warrior proud of the prophet for surviving such a blast. "That boulder could have been the end of me. How'd you do that magic?"

"I don't really know. It just happened. All I remember is getting angry when Zidon attacked us, then I thought about what you said to me in the mountains - patience over passion. I failed time and time again with ether magic in the seminary because of my temper. This time, I let patience take control."

"How are you able to do it, move the ether?"

"Ether is in us, it's in everything around us. Every element created by the Goddess has her ether, but it exists differently in what she has created. In rocks and metals, it's crude. In animals, wild. In humans, firm. In the ether fonts and vortexes, fluid. The ether that exists in us connects to the ether in all forms when we exist in spirit and not in flesh."

Seth marvels at Ezekiel's explanation, for the prophet's craft connects with the potter's craft. "Sounds a lot like pottery, Zek. Certain clays allow me to form it with ease, while other clays refuse to be shaped. Eventually, I melt with the soft earth and it becomes an extension of my hands." The observation sends his mind back to his wheel, and concern resurfaces about Aden making good on Emmerick's promise.

"Are you going to stay with us when we dock?" asks Ezekiel.

"My sister's invested in this fight. I'll protect her for as long as it takes."

Ezekiel's legs give out and he topples over his staff to the deck. He grabs his back in an attempt to quell the sharp needles pricking his nerves.

Seth cradles Ezekiel to his soft bedding and does his best to position his friend in a way that limits the pain. "Be still, Zek. Get some rest. I have a feeling we'll need you to face Zidon again."

After mentioning Zidon's name, the company and crew rush to the back of the schooner to see the Calcedonian fleet sailing over the horizon - hundreds of ships loaded with thousands of soldiers. Their hearts cease beating, their breath stagnates, and a bitter taste settles on their tongues. The anarchy of Elam nears Issur and the Remnant realizes that they'll be forced to endure another long night.

Chapter 15 ⁝ Survival

The admiral's head rolls across the deck. A trail of blood dots a path from the red plume on his helmet all the way to the steel boots of King Tartek.

The Calcedonian admiral had strayed too deep into the Cove of Carnek leaving too wide of gap in the strait, which allowed the Remnant's boat to dock safely in Tekoa.

The crew dare not eye Tartek on his return to the candlelit cabin on the command ship.

Tartek sits alone chewing on a hunk of rum cake. The sweet taste sends him back in time to his first birthday without his mother.

It felt like just another day when it should have felt special. Tartek was unable to cope with the awkwardness of being the only child at the party without a mother, so he hid under an isolated statue of a war hero. He covered his ears to drown out the playful sounds of children that filled the garden.

Lord Lars found Tartek in his wearisome state and knelt down beside his only son with a saucer of sweetbread inviting him to join the celebration - the frumpy boy begrudgingly accepting his father's treat.

"Tartek, I haven't checked the books but I'm certain that it's against the law to be sad on your birthday."

"Nothing feels the same without mother. Why did she have to die?"

"She fell ill. Sickness and death are part of nature, not just for humans but for all life. I've studied many types of plants and animals, all are ruled by a cycle of life and death."

"But why my mother? Why do all of my friends get to keep their mothers, but I have to lose my mother?"

"I don't have an answer but like I always tell you, I've never met a book that didn't have one. I'll find the right book in hopes of giving you a proper answer."

The birthday boy smiled, warmed from the sweetbread and his father's devotion.

"I love you so much, Tartek. I'll probe the mysteries of the universe to make you feel whole again."

Zidon enters the cabin jarring Tartek from his reverie, the magi sensing his melancholy. "I didn't realize that you had such a bond with the admiral."

The humorless Tartek wastes little time to throw a bad report in Zidon's face. "Your plot to kill Aden Tizra failed. Divine and Rothmore are dead, the Grand Chancel incinerated. Not to worry, I'll take Aden's head when we meet on the field of battle. I'm surprised that Melek didn't take your head."

"Where's yours, Tartek? You sit on the eve of destruction, a sad fool. Now is not the time for weakness."

"Must we cast off all that makes us human? Can't I taste a morsel of regret in memory of my father?"

"King Zimri Tizra wasted so much time on the past, despite my council to trust the future. Melek cares only about the future. The past if full of regret, the future full of anticipation."

"Magi, how can I avoid his mistakes?" asks Tartek with an earnest longing to know the answer.

"Strive for freedom by detaching yourself from your emotions - be bound to no one. When enough blood streams from your blade, you will rule an empire. Stop lamenting an indulgent father who did nothing to advance your ambition."

Zidon exits the cabin. He crosses the deck careful to avoid the mops that swab the admiral's blood from the planks.

Zidon finds Korah peering at Tekoa atop a tall crate.

"Is Tartek ready?" asks the nephesh of the magi.

"Like Zimri, he questions the decision to murder his father. And like Zimri, personal conquest remains his top priority."

Korah exhales a sigh of frustration.

"Still bitter about Zimri?" asks Zidon.

"All mortals disgust me, even you."

"It's not my problem that Neshama favors us and shares secrets with such a disappointing creation, unlike your noble race. Melek knows all about those mysteries. Why do you clamor for them?"

"I despise you, Zidon, because you speak to me as if we are equals. Your knowledge of ether makes you valuable to this mission, but don't assume that it makes you an equal. You are simply another piece of mortal trash."

"Why are you in this struggle, Korah?"

"If I tell you, will you leave me be and return to bloating the ego of another mad king?"

Zidon nods with anticipation to better understand the nephesh.

"You've read the prophecies so you're aware of what's to come. I refuse to be on the losing side."

"You're too craft and I'm too curious to let it die here. Truth be told, the prophets haven't the faintest idea who will win. If you're serious about ridding yourself of me, I demand better. Otherwise, I can show you the skill of my craft to prove that I stand atop of this dung heap that you call mankind."

"If we could but duel in the ether world… Since I'm down here, I must stay my blade and respect your craft.

Fine, I'll play along with your annoying curiosity. There's only one quality that permeates every being that Neshama has created - nephesh, mortals, animals - in this world and in the ether world. Every one of her creations has an innate will to survive."

Korah steps down from his crate to loom over Zidon.

"I abhor mortals and desire nothing more than to see them annihilated. Melek's disdain for them is what initially drew me to his cause. However, it's his knowledge, not his spite that binds me as his disciple because of my drive for survival. Even more than my survival - the survival of all nephesh. The Goddess herself won't be able to stop the coming reckoning."

"But I can. I'm the only one who can," says Zidon through his forked tongue, tossing his hood over his snakish eyes.

Korah snarls another sigh as Zidon returns to Tartek.

Aden stares at the sails of the Calcedonian fleet growing larger over the horizon when the company disembarks from their humble schooner.

Caleb dashes across the docks, grabs Aden by the neck and plants a kiss on his best friend's forehead.

Aden playfully pushes Caleb away from his personal space. "Glad to see you too, old friend."

"When I heard about Zidon's plot, I feared the worst," admits Caleb.

Aden looks beyond Caleb's relieved eyes to take inventory of the Remnant's dejected countenance. He quickly perceives their mission has gone awry.

After the final mariner exits the boat, reality confirms the warning that emanates within his intuition… Emmerick does not return home.

All of Aden's beloved kindred were dead - his grandfather, mother, and now, his uncle. The prince reaches into his shirt and squeezes his anguish into the stone medallion around his neck as tears form in his eyes.

Ben approaches Aden. He places the Signet Ring of Issur into the prince's palm and kneels. Everyone on the docks kneels likewise.

"Hail! The King of Issur!" proclaims Ben.

Before the heads of his subjects drop to the deck, Aden flails his arms in protest. "No! Stand! Do not honor me!"

Ben straitens and everyone on the dock follows his lead as Prince Aden stares at the ring in his hand.

The dock falls silent.

"The House of Tizra has failed Issur. I will only wear this ring if I redeem the Tizra name. Until then, I consider myself no better than any member of the Remnant.

We live in the Fourth Age. It's not an age of grace or justice. It's the Reign of Melek. He is king, until the Remnant proves otherwise."

The dire proclamation burdens the company as they disperse to prepare for the invasion, though Ben lingers over Aden's shoulder like another gnat in the swamp.

"You're relieved of your duty, Sentinel. You can go home to shepherd… Please send my regards to Judith."

"I fear that there will be no flocks left to shepherd, worse, no people left alive in Issur. If I recall correctly, a sentinel is bound not only to king but to country also."

The foreboding sails powering the Calcedonian fleet over the horizon offer evidence to support Ben's doomsday warning. Therefore, Aden heeds Ben's caution. "Concede Tekoa and Tamar. Evacuate the south; rally the precepts in the Grand Chancel. An army of ten thousand spears marches on Issur. Tekoa and Tamar don't have the fortifications to stop the Calcedonian army. We should make our stand in Tizra."

"We can evacuate the people; I'll send messengers… The precepts are no more. Zidon converted Amar Divine and Ur Rothmore; they turned to Melek worship and murdered the other three precepts. I went to the Grand Chancel for a confession. If it weren't for Shamgar Ram, I'd be dead."

"I thought that you said there are no more precepts."

"Shamgar killed Rothmore, putting an end to the inquisition. He then sought me at the Grand Chancel. The chancel caught fire and I narrowly escaped. Shamgar died after killing Divine in a duel, when the sanctum collapsed on him."

Ben takes a step back as the prospect of victory dims. The shepherd reveres Shamgar's sacrifice, but the volatile precept still shames his doubt from the grave.

Aden continues with his bleak report. "Tekoa got hit a few days ago, it would be nearly impossible to defend. I have a small force repairing the ballistas so that we might stall the Calcedonian landing. As for Tamar, forget that city… You're right, Ben. We must make our stand in Tizra. Pray that we slow the onslaught to protect the people."

✦ ✦ ✦

The first wave of Calcedonian ships crosses the outer markers bouncing in waters of the harbor. They sail under the cover of night over a string of barrels floating about in the choppy waves. Tartek's men slide down the thick ropes dangling from the ships, filling the rowboats in preparation of landfall.

Caleb and a handful of rangers surface in the waves near the barrels and uncork the oil within - a film of liquid instantly forms atop the harbor. The scout and his rangers submerse themselves unnoticed.

Caleb swims to shore and lights a torch, the glowing ball draws all eyes including Tartek's. The scout waves to the command ship before dropping the torch into the water.

The torch ignites a burst of flames across the harbor. The oil flares over the rowboats and the soldiers catch fire. Yelling in agony, Tartek's men leap from their rowboats. The flaming enemy provides the ballistas with an easy target and the Issurian bolts skewer the Calcedonian victims atop their rowboats.

Ben inspects his newly acquired hunting bow and arrows. He still longs for his lost bow from the royal armory, but the hunting bow reminds him of the one that he once held as a shepherd. He dips his arrow into a cauldron of flames and his detachment does likewise. They zing arrows into the Calcedonian troops; the tips that miss their targets hit the oily harbor, reinvigorating the blaze.

Caleb and his rangers join Ben to offer another flaming volley.

With the rowboats slowed, the fleet must lower troops directly into the swamp from nets. Arrows sink into the backs of the dangling targets. At first the task seems easy, but as the massive number of boats continues their approach, Ben's detachment tires, for their targets multiply rapidly scaling down from the sides of the ships.

Rowboats and swimmers reach the main dock for combat. As Tartek's men charge across the dock, Aden springs his second trap.

Seth and a handful of brawny soldiers grip a large rope that attaches to the main support of the boarding dock. The large rope fastens around the wooden cylinder chiseled out in the middle. Seth waits for the dock to fill with enemy soldiers before he yells, "Pull!"

The dock gives out and the iron-clad soldiers plunge into the murky water. Most do not return to the surface for their lungs and armor fill with water. Oars reject those fortunate enough to return for air; their eager Calcedonian comrades cruise over them as they prepare to make landfall.

Ben and Caleb continue to pelt the Calcedonians alongside the ballistas, their arrows stinging the swarm of soldiers.

Ashira fights among the ranks of Aden's regiment. They defend the shores from the Calcedonians, but the task grows hopeless as more and more boats emerge from the darkness.

A warning bell alerts all of the regiments in Tekoa to retreat across the land bridge on the northern part of the city.

Realizing that the city sits on the brink of destruction, a handful of stubborn Tekoans flee with the retreating troops.

The regiments rally behind a ballista on the land bridge. Sounds of shattering glass and crumbling mud-brick overpower the bellows of the bullfrogs while shops and homes burst into flames.

"They're dismantling the city with no concern for supplies," notes Aden, wearing a surprised face.

A few ranks meander through the narrow main street and onto the land bridge. A rapid bolt and a hail of arrows consume the enemy.

"Caleb, choose a dozen of the best archers among us. I'll need your help slowing the northern advance," advises Aden.

"Sure, maybe Tartek will surrender at the sight of a dozen men with sticks," snaps Caleb.

"Ben, I need you to gather a couple messengers and

return to Hallowed Hills. We need all of the shepherds that we can muster. The rest of you report to Captain Tamar and finish siege preparations in Tizra."

The ballista crew chucks another spear that claims more victims as Aden concludes his orders.

Seth slings Peacemaker over one shoulder and Ezekiel over his other shoulder, while Ben and Ashira rally to his side. The company flees the swamp alongside the troops.

The Calcedonian ranks swell at the city gate. They charge across the land bridge and fall into Aden's final trap.

The weight of the swelled Calcedonian ranks collapses the deliberately eroded dirt and the unit sinks into the swamp moot laced with poisonous snakes.

Aden shares a bittersweet smile with Caleb for his snares work to perfection. The prince feels certain that his Uncle Emmerick would have deemed the traps, *brilliant.*

Chapter 16 ✦ Evicted

It was the moment Ben dreaded the entire march north along The King's Highway, he even dreamt about it the night before, but the moment arrived and he had to face it.

Upon spotting the company, Captain Tobi Tamar dashes across the Tizra drawbridge. He grabs Ben by the throat for a greeting. "Refugees enter the city with lamentation that my king is dead! Sentinel, tell me this isn't true!"

Seth smacks the grip from Ben's jugular. His intense gaze demands that the captain stand down.

"He died by the hand of Melek. He was fearless in the

face of death as we must be. I'm sorry that I failed you, Sir…
We can't live in the past. The time is now," affirms Ben.

Listening to his own advice spoken from the sentinel that
he trained, Tobi calms his temper.

"A horde from Calcedon marches on Tizra. Tekoa is lost;
Aden and Caleb delay the fall of Tamar. We must stop their
army here or we lose Issur," informs Ben.

As a good soldier must, the captain detaches himself from
his grief over the loss of his king and the impending loss of
his hometown. "I have the city best prepared as possible. Visit
the armory and get some rest. I'll reassign this regiment."

Tobi orders a role call and the regiment jumps at his
commanding voice.

"I'll find Zek a bed. I fear that all of this traveling has
weakened him even more," frets Seth.

The prophet remains unresponsive as Seth carries him
away.

Everyone clears out except Ben, who lingers behind with
Ashira. The immediacy of the moment forces him to stay on
task instead of trying to romantically reconnect with her. "I
better find some horses and dispatch the messengers to Resh
and Tsadi, though I doubt we'll see shepherds from Ardon
Tsadi's clan. I'll return home to Tav."

Ashira keeps her request to herself, fearful to load another
burden on Ben's shoulders.

Ben's maturity overrides his jealousy to ignore her
unspoken request. "I'll let Evan know you made it back."

Ashira smiles before giving Ben an awkward hug goodbye.

Ben naps on a hay stack inside a dark stable while an
attendant shoes three horses for the trip to Hallowed Hills.
The blacksmith across the street lends a hand to the stable
attendant to quicken the task.

Hearing the pings of horseshoes and divine whispers, Ben's conscious and subconscious streams of thought flow in and out of time.

The divine voice strengthens, "Wake up."

Ben gradually lifts his eyelids to find Azor leaning over him.

An injection of adrenaline springs him from his rest. "Where have you been!? It's about time you return!"

The blunt greeting insults the cordial nephesh, causing his purple eyes to dim.

Ben's mind curses his emotions. "Sorry, things have gotten a lot worse since we last met."

"I hate to say the same about the ether world. The last two nephesh seen with Korah have vanished, and I fear a third may be in danger."

"Where'd they go?"

"I suspect Korah killed them."

"How can that be?" questions Ben, rustling his wavy hair. "I saw Korah in Elam marching an army towards Issur. Tekoa fell, Tamar's next, and soon they'll be at the gates of Tizra."

"Korah marches here?" The news forces Azor's fingers to rake the silver hair under his white hood.

Ben sniffles when an odor sours his senses. He identifies the source as the excrement under the guardian's boots. "You stink. Did you come from the sewers?"

"I did. The citizens might be given over to disorder if I were to travel the city in broad day light. I walked through the sewers under these stables to reach you... I have to go back down there. In time, I'll return to Tizra for Korah."

"You can't leave again, we need your help. What if you don't return in time?"

"My call is to bring Korah back to Neshama, and I will fulfill that call. I must warn my fellow guardians of Korah's betrayal."

Azor disappears, leaving Ben to ponder the fate of Issur.

Aden assesses Tamar from a shoddy wooden tower overlooking a smaller tower constructed of rotten planks. Grounded behind an uneven hip high stone barrier, dingy lumber completes the wall around Tamar. Rickety doors attach to the narrow gates, which cling to the walls by the rusted bolts.

The guards assist the refugees by loading their wares onto carts. Easing the burden of the elderly and lessening the fears of the little ones, the guards temporarily dismiss the peril that befell Tekoa.

The Plains of Tamar reveal no sign of life to Aden. No creeping things scurry within the tall grass that stiffens as if a winter's frost grips the blades. The ranger-prince perceives that even nature itself fears the coming purge.

Even if Aden had the numbers, the city would be difficult to defend. The wooden dwellings press against the shoddy walls, constricting guard deployment along the narrow ramparts.

Caleb Glade climbs the creaky steps of the tower to deliver the scouting report to Aden. "We set traps along the road, but the plains make it difficult to conceal them. We picked off a few of their spies about five lengths back."

"Five lengths! How's that possible!?" snaps Aden, rattling the tower with his shock.

"They're divided into two forces. A small one led by Tartek; I counted nearly two thousand. We clipped over a third of it in Tekoa. Tartek's force stops briefly for food and rest. The larger force doesn't camp, doesn't eat or drink."

"Why?" asks Aden.

Caleb resents the shrug, but it's all that he has to offer.

"Were Ben's numbers correct? Ten thousand soldiers?"

Caleb confirms with a regrettable nod.

"When do you expect an assault on Tamar?"

"At the break of dawn. It appears to me that they will use Tartek's army to eliminate Tekoa and Tamar, then, they will unleash that horde on Tizra."

"It's gonna be another long night," sighs Aden. "Make sure that the guards have plenty of torchlight to assist the citizens. Search for any supplies that you can find. I'll search Uncle Emmerick's place for any valuables."

Caleb exits the tower with haste leaving Aden to the sunset that dims on the rusted city gates.

It's not going to end well for Tamar, laments the prince.

Aden enters Emmerick's home through the unlocked front door. On the outside it looks like all of the other houses in Tamar, but on the inside it looks more like a museum than a residence. Maps, scrolls, artifacts, rare plants, and an elaborate chemistry set clutter the space.

Aden tinkers with the chemistry set and recalls the time that Emmerick spared his life in Tekoa. He shatters a beaker on the floor when Caleb startles the prince's thoughts about the poisoned wine. "Tartek's men form ranks less than a length out."

"Has the city been evacuated?"

"Yes. The rangers wait for us... Find anything worthwhile?"

"I'm sure it was to Emmerick. Nothing but clutter to me."

"Are those elk tongues!?" asks Caleb, gleefully staring at the large sealed jar - the heavy jar blocks a landslide of scrolls from cascading down onto the research desk.

"Those tongues must be decades old. They were my

grandfather's," informs Aden as if a vile taste burns his lips.

"Guess I won't know until I sample one of those delicious treats," says Caleb, reaching for the jar, only to get his hand slapped by Aden. "What's your problem? You used to eat them when we were boys. I loved that time when you, me, and Ishem went camping with 'Deerstalker.' Your grandfather made us eat every part of those elk... Well, almost every part."

Aden's face reddens with a humorous memory. Caleb lights up, recalling the same mishap.

"Do you remember when Ishem thought he was eating an elk tongue?" asks Aden.

"Your grandfather didn't have the heart to tell him," snorts Caleb.

"Remember how Ishem went on and on about how it was 'good eatin'?"

The two friends enjoy a long overdue laugh when Caleb lunges for the jar. Aden tries to stay his hand, but the hungry spy yanks the jar from the shelf.

Heaps of documents cascade down upon Aden.

A slow roller is the last to fall - it glides across the top shelf then bounces onto the table opening ever so gently as if it desires to be read.

Aden scans the plans, recognizing the layout of Tamar. A deeper glance details numerous notes scribbled by the hand of Emmerick.

"My attempt to discover the mysterious mating patterns of the rock badger was rudely interrupted the other day by the town council. There's a standing army camped outside of the city, yet they demanded that I do something about Tamar's defenses.

I embarked on a geological study concerning the foundation under the town, and that's when I made a fascinating discovery. Tamar sits atop a sink hole. If ever an army were to enter the city, Tamar would collapse. I concluded that funding the city defenses would be a foolish waste of money. Furthermore, the council should consider relocating Tamar three and one-third lengths to the south and start over.

Unfortunately, the city council disagreed with my conclusion, so I ordered a tower built instead. That seems to have distracted them, hopefully long enough to finish my research on rock badgers."

Aden smiles at a tiny sketch on the corner of the scroll detailing a warble of badgers.

"Brilliant," says Emmerick's nephew with a glimmer in his eye. "Assemble the rangers in the town square."

"Oh Goddess, no. Whatever you're thinking, Aden - it's a bad idea," says Caleb, returning the jar of elk tongue to the shelf, unsure of any scheme inspired by the random professor.

"Trust me. Or better yet, trust Emmerick."

Ben ties his exhausted brown horse to a trough of water and fills a feed bag with oats. The sheep in stall look upon their guest with suspicion for the steed chews loudly disturbing their sleep.

Ben peaks his head into Evan's hovel, but his brother is nowhere to be found.

Before entering the guild hall, Ben kneels to stroke Smoke.

The creaky doors open, startling Evan and Judith. They anxiously rise from their late night tea by the fire place, and Ben immediately senses the desperation suffocating the space.

Evan stares through Ben for a greeting, but Ben counters

the cold reception by addressing his brother's main concern, "Ashira is safe. She wanted you to know."

The good report soothes the main source of Evan's anxiety.

The sound of Ben's voice invigorates Judith. She runs to embrace him, her nails digging into his shoulders. Judith withdraws in embarrassment at the surprise in Ben's eyes. He had never seen her like this - strands of hair out of place, wrinkles in her dress.

"What's wrong?" asks Ben.

"If you cared, you'd be here. So don't act like you do," says Evan, stepping between his siblings. "Why'd you bother to come back?"

"King Emmerick perished on our journey to Calcedon, and I narrowly escaped with my life. I saw the army of ten thousand spears that marches from Calcedon and that now invades Issur. The southern isle will fall and Tizra will be next if I can't rally shepherds to help defend the city. I know you're not at full strength, but we could use your leadership and your sword."

Evan walks out on Ben, but before he clears the doors, his little brother offers a benediction.

"I want to thank you for everything that you've done for me. I understand that you hold Jael's death against me, and I respect your decision not to forgive me. I'm simply trying to find my way, be my own man. I have you to thank for that."

Evan listens to his brother's words. They slow his exit, but fail to halt him.

Judith serves Ben a cup of tea as he takes his place next to her chair. He gazes into her face as if she's a reflection of his doubt.

"My eyes have missed the view of these hills and mountains," says Ben.

"I have thoughts about disappearing into the mountains,

just like Miriam did once upon a time.

I think that I could find freedom in the mountains like she did. Maybe if I escaped this guild hall, I could leave behind the shadows of mother and father's death, Jael's death, Daniel's death. I could escape all of the judgment from the women, who call me the cursed widow."

Ben's soul quakes with worry over his sister, for she's not only poor in appearance, but also poor in spirit.

"Why do you stay, Judith?"

"The mountains deceive. The problem is not with Tav, and freedom is not in the mountains. The problem lies within me, and I will carry my burdens wherever I go."

"How will you ever free your soul?"

"I didn't choose to bear these yokes but I must choose to accept them."

Her faith warms his chest like the tea.

Judith reaches out for Ben's hand to share the worst of her news. "We're going to be evicted from the hall. Long story short, Bo Baladan got himself into trouble. He has only fueled the elders' suspicion of Evan, and Ruth Gimel's revenge stirs their wrath. The trial is at dawn."

Evan holds Judith's hand as they sit next to one another on small boulders - their faces as stoic as the rocks on which they sit. The spiteful elder proclaims a list of charges as he lays the foundation of his case concerning the violation of Merlen Gimel's wife. Merlen offers comfort to his mother as Ruth confirms each accusation with dramatic gestures.

Meanwhile, Ben enters the basement of the Gimel bakery in search of the maligned wife. He hopes to coax a testimony from the traumatized victim, for her statement may hold the power to stop the eviction.

Ben stumbles across the watchman.

Melvin Gimel sprawls across an empty mead barrel and snores loudly - the flab on his stomach sags off his body forming a blanket of fat. Ben winces at his epic gut. *That's a lot of dough in those rolls.*

The stench of yeast boils over in the cauldrons and overpowers the room, forcing the shepherd to cover his face with a hand towel as he navigates his way through the steam. Ben treads deeper into the basement and arrives at a barred door. On the other side, he hears the sound of a chair dancing about the wooden floor.

Ben kicks open the door to find Merlen's wife tied to a chair with a cloth bunched into her mouth. He unties the rope that secures the crumpled cloth from her jaw, and then frees her from the bindings.

"That rat and his witch of a mother!" yells the bride, before stomping upstairs into the bakery. She grabs a knife and marches to the gathering.

Ben pursues her for a statement, but the skinny lady handles the curvy Tav paths like a ferret.

Ben arrives two steps behind her when the frizzy-haired brunette interrupts the gathering, much to Merlen and Ruth's dismay.

The ragtag bride swipes the knife at her husband's neck nicking the scruff of his beard.

The elders disarm and detain her.

"You rat! Locking me in that room with no brew, no tobacco!" Merlen's wife rustles the arms of elders, who begin to realize that the woman may have been violated, but not in a way that Ruth Gimel accused.

"Mrs. Gimel, calm down. We need your testimony," says a soft-spoken elder.

"Don't call me by that name! Mrs. Gimel is my hustlin' witch of a mother-in-law!"

"Tell us the truth. Did Bo Baladan assault you?" demands the vindictive elder.

"Who's Bo Baladan?" asks the bride, relaxing her wiry arms.

"A wild lookin' shepherd with black features, even his eyes. He attacked you at the Shepherd's Shack," clarifies the vindictive elder.

"His name was Bo?"

"So you testify that this man attacked you?"

"No! We got to drinkin' and we… Do I have to spell it out for ya?"

A collective gasp exhales from the red-faced elders.

"I guess he got to drinkin' and forgot about his flock. When he woke up next to me, he flew out of the room like a bat on fire. I passed out again and woke up locked in a supply room."

"You willfully committed adultery?" asks the elder with a gentile voice.

"I had to find someone to meet my needs. Merlen is… let's say… doughy in the bedroom."

The embarrassed baker flees the gathering while the shepherds snicker at his dysfunction.

Ruth paces within her mind for a lie to counter the truth, but her lips stick unable to muster a sound. Ruth's contempt for Evan puts her at his mercy.

"Then, we've no grounds to evict the Tavs. The Gimels must be held accountable for their deceit. What does the guild master suggest in this matter?" asks the spiteful elder, reluctantly deferring to Evan.

Evan stands to promptly deliver a swift judgment, "This woman shall be released from her marriage contract."

"Thank the Goddess… I need a drink and a smoke," says the freed bride, making her way back to the Shepherd's Shack.

"Merlen and Ruth must never leave their property. Melvin may have access to the market, but that's it."

"You're not gonna to kick us out of Tav?" asks Ruth, her

eyelids blinking with disbelief over Evan's mercy.

"Get out of my face before I rethink myself."

The guild master's stern response repels Ruth and disperses the crowd.

Evan winks at Judith before sharing their father's favorite saying. "Never a dull moment in Tav, eh Judith."

Judith offers a faint smile, grateful for the exoneration granted by the scorned wife's testimony. Figuring that Ben played a role in producing the witness, she thanks him with an extended hug.

Evan offers his hand in gratitude. Ben grips it firmly along with his brother's attention. "You can accuse me of whatever you want, but don't ever accuse me of not caring about my family." Ben unfastens his grip and returns to his mission of enlisting recruits.

Tartek opens the gates of Tamar to the screeches of rusted metal, grinding his teeth at the painful noise. When surveying the abandoned walls and streets, his intuition reminds him about Tekoa and the traps that claimed a third of his force.

"Make certain that the city is clear of defenders before we burn it to the ground. My gut doesn't feel right about this," orders Tartek to an officer as they walk timidly through the barren streets.

Caleb and a handful of rangers spring from behind a corner to loose arrows. Caleb's dart pierces the officer through the neck, dropping him dead at Tartek's boots.

Aden's ranger regiment assaults Tartek's unit from the other flank. Another shaft lodges into a soldier's lung and he falls alongside the officer.

Another volley rains down from both flanks to claim more casualties.

"Patience," says Tartek, steadying his anxious infantry.

After a final volley, the Issurian archers retreat with Aden and Caleb into the narrow Tamar alleyways.

"Cowards!" yells Tartek, motioning some troops to fan out down the side streets.

The king continues his march down the main street with the bulk of his force behind him.

Aden, Caleb, and their rangers rally at the north gate. Their arrows pummel the cautious Calcedonian troops.

"Patience," demands Tartek once more, peeling his eyes for traps.

Aden sinks an arrow into Tartek's left forearm.

"Charge!" yells the king.

His army thunders through Tamar toward the north gate.

Aden, Caleb, and the rangers flee the city.

One piper among the Calcedonian ranks bellows the Rygar and Rex battle-anthem to proclaim victory over Tamar. The dose of patriotism brings about celebratory dancing. The victory jig ceases momentarily when the ground shifts subtly. The soldiers look at one another, then, look at the ground.

Unfazed by the shifting ground, the swelled Calcedonian ranks return to their victory jig.

Abruptly, the earth shifts, falling out from underneath the Calcedonians.

Tartek's intuition puts his legs in motion and he dashes for the north gate. As the street erodes underneath his feet, he leaps onto the ledge of the sink hole.

Aden and Caleb watch in amazement when thousands of Calcedoian warriors plummet into the depths of Issur.

"Curses! I forgot the elk tongues," grieves Caleb, drawing his bow and setting his sights on Tartek.

Tartek pulls himself from the hole with a dust cloud billowing behind him.

Caleb zings the shot into the king's shoulder pad. The rancid Calcedonian roars insults at the Issurians as he rips the arrows from his forearm and shoulder.

Aden and the rangers respond with another volley of darts that soar through the dust cloud.

Tartek hits the ground as the arrows whiz over his armor. The exposed king crawls for cover behind a slither of the rock wall.

Aden considers an assault on his compromised rival, but that notion ends quickly when Korah's ranks emerge on the horizon and the sheer terror of such an army paralyzing the prince.

The unexpected package arrived before the rooster crowed, the messenger galloping in and out of Tav as fast as her steed would carry her.

Sitting on the corner of her neatly tucked bed, Judith unties a strand of twine wrapped around a small box covered in brown paper. As soon as the twine unwinds, the paper falls to the floor. She unfolds a note attached to the top of the box, which reads, *One family heirloom for another.* Her brow wrinkles deeper and her mouth gapes wider when she peaks into the box to find the Signet Ring of Issur. The golden sun-face atop the ring peeps at her, before she quickly closes the lid.

Her smile fades after wondering why Aden refuses to wear the ring of kings. She tucks the box securely under her pillow before joining Evan for breakfast.

Judith sits at the table and tries to stomach the three bites of oatmeal in her bowl, but she finds the oatmeal a lot harder to stomach than Evan's callous attitude.

"I'm going to join the next rotation, see if I can make it a week. Maybe if the elders see me in the hills a bit more, they'll back off."

Judith's eyes pierce him from within her eagle-faced stare.

"You're mad because I didn't go with Ben," guesses Evan.

"I'm mad because you didn't even say goodbye."

"That's between me and him. It's none of your concern…

Now, do you want anything from the market before I leave?"

"You're not going to ignore me, Evan. Ben is my concern; he's the only family that we have left."

"I told you, I'm going north into the hills."

"No. Go south," pleads Judith with desperate breath.

"I'm not going on a fool's errand to Tizra."

"I'm not talking about Tizra."

Evan's wits catch up to Judith's geography concerning another city south of Tav.

"No. No way. Out of the question."

Evan gets up and moves for the door, but Judith blocks his exit. "Go to the Forest of Elah. Make Erez honor his debt to you for saving his daughter's life."

"We were nearly evicted from the guild hall. If I get caught going into that forest, I'm through as guild master."

"Quit making excuses for your anger. I'm angry too. They were my parents, Jael was my little sister, Daniel was my husband… My little brother faces grave danger!"

With his mask lifted and true feelings exposed, Evan flees toward the exit.

Judith blocks him once more.

She lightly places her hands on Evan's chest. "If you turn your back on Ben, you turn your back on me." Judith removes her hands and steps aside.

Evan gathers his gear on the top step of the guild hall. "I'm headin' north. I don't see things your way, this time. Sorry, Judith."

"I don't need your apology, but Ashira might. You not only turn your back on your own blood, you turn your back on Ashira."

The shepherd's wolf-skin boots remain firmly planted on the top step of the guild hall while Judith's words convict her brother's loyalty.

"Never a dull moment in Tav, eh Evan."

Chapter 17 ✦ Confrontation

Ezekiel could not rid himself of the voices no matter how much he focused - the shouts, conversations, whispers. The shouts didn't bother him as much because they didn't sound like her voice. The Goddess was in the whispers and the whispers vexed him the most.

Imriel's face troubled his memory. Ezekiel couldn't rid his mind's eye of the beastly prophet and the image of his purple flesh wound from the ether bolt haunted him.

Though his aching back begged him for a good night's sleep, his mind and spirit refused to afford him such a luxury. Ezekiel knew her conviction because he felt it before. After failing to master ether in the seminary, he decided to quit.

Neshama squeezed his soul to remind him of the hands that he'd entrusted his life.

Ezekiel wanted out again. He felt guilty for pumping Ben with false hope, he felt insignificant for thinking he could live up to Othniel, and he felt doomed by Zidon.

Ezekiel gathers his belongings strewn about his chamber while storm-bolts shock the night sky to illumine his room.

He scans the halls as he makes for a way out of the palace.

"You are the last prophet," whispers a woman's voice.

Ezekiel moves down a corridor away from the voice.

"You are not a fraud, you are pure of heart," the whisper continues.

Ezekiel finds an exit, which fills with the large frame of Seth Keros. The prophet's loyal friend returns to check on him.

Ezekiel scurries up a flight of stairs in the opposite direction.

"I will mark you like I did Imriel and empower you to solve divine riddles," the woman's voice whispers once more.

The whispers bring Ezekiel to his knees on the stairs, and he prostrates himself before Neshama. He pulls himself up the steps and opens a hatch to the tower above. Rain pelts his face as he uses his staff to return upward. Lightning rides the clouds and the wind rustles his robe.

Ezekiel looks to the sky as rain mixes with his tears. "You are my Goddess and I am your prophet."

The black cloud overhead fades to a deep purple, then a violent bolt of magenta strikes Ezekiel above the right eye, searing his flesh all the way to his shoulder blade - the ether chattering his teeth and rattling his bones.

A burst of heat energizes his ether.

The force of the bolt smacks Ezekiel down the hatch and across the staircase. He clutches his back when it reminds him of his mortality.

Ezekiel's shout bursts an echo throughout the corridor summoning Seth to his side. The wide-eyed warrior shields his stare at the sight of the pierced flesh and the purple pulse that pumps in the prophet's cheek. "Cover that up. You'll scare off everyone. Seriously Zek, they'll flee the city with one look at you."

Seth pulls Ezekiel from the floor and returns him to his chamber. Realizing that his humor does nothing to normalize the moment, he refuses to press the prophet for the answer concerning the purple pulse.

"I'll find you a robe with a hood before I have to report for deployment. The Calcedonian army assembles in Fog Swamp. Zidon is with them."

Zidon puffs smoke from his black pipe. After a final flare, he reloads the pipe with a dash of crispy tobacco leaves. The relaxed magi stands next to the uptight Korah with his ether sword resting across the back of Tartek's neck.

The morning fog caresses Korah as if it were ether. The nephesh gets a whiff of Zidon's smog, and with one glare from his yellow eyes, he forces the magi to retreat a step.

"King Tartek 'The Destroyer.' You have been aptly named," mocks Korah. "More like King Tartek 'The Half Wit' for your father's brains, you did not inherit."

The insult brings a rare grin to Zidon's face. "Tekoa and Tamar lie in ruins; your army hasn't been scratched. Tartek did what was required of him."

"You, like Melek, put too much faith in mortals," snaps Korah.

"Melek crafted these soldiers through his mastery of the ether arts. The Remnant has no chance to defeat them."

"Don't manipulate me, Zidon, because you can't. I know full well the joy you'd feel to see Tizra razed to the ground

- the Remnant along with these ten thousand Calcedonians buried beneath."

"Maybe it's you, Korah, I should fear. Perhaps I've been serving the wrong nephesh."

"Do you think that I'd ever tolerate one of your ilk as my servant? The very thought sickens me."

"If you truly hated Tartek then you'd let him live," says Zidon, lifting Korah's sword from the disgraced king's neck.

Zidon gets Tartek to stand and backhands him across the mouth with such force that blood and teeth scatter into the bog.

"Do you hear this? The nephesh mocks you because your faith in Melek is weak… You mock me. Before this campaign started you wanted to know how to avoid the failure of your father, yet you cling to his memory like that little boy who used to cry himself to sleep over his dead mother."

Zidon cracks another string of knuckles across Tartek's skull to remove those memories.

"You must detach yourself from all emotion, be bound by nothing, no one. That's the only way you'll ever earn Melek's favor. If you want to honor Melek, present him with the head of Aden Tizra and end Josiah's line. You'll not only earn the respect of Melek, even I will bow down to your greatness."

Zidon places Tartek's enormous claymore across his hands as a signal to dismiss.

Korah peers down at Zidon with a hint of pity in the bend of his neck. "I despise mortals, but let it be known that no mortal has ever hated himself more than you hate yourself."

The black ether of the nephesh fades into the thick fog lifting off of the swamp as he assumes his place as general in the front rank.

"I don't understand. How does a siege army fail to bring siege equipment to a siege?" asks Aden, giving Caleb his serious face. "You figured ten thousand troops and not a catapult among them."

"No catapults, trebuchets, or any contraption capable of flinging a boulder."

"No rafts to cross the river, either?" presses Aden.

"No rafts, boats, canoes, dinghies," answers the scout, his immature mind failing to repress his smile.

"Enough with the dinghies," admonishes Aden.

Caleb's smile twists with concern as he recounts the events from previous night. "That's what my favorite wench from the Robber's Den told me after a few pints."

"Can we get serious?" pleads Aden.

"That's the next thing she said, but Caleb Glade ain't putting a ring on any finger."

The company's disposition matches the prince's and Caleb heeds the hint to shut his mouth.

"Maybe they're going to cross at Bera's Bridge," says Ben.

"If we could be so lucky. An army that size on such a narrow strip of land would be a tactical disaster," says Aden before another optimistic thought pops into his mind. "Maybe the siege engines are delayed; perhaps a storm hit the fleet."

Seth and Ashira sense the anxiety passing between one another.

Tobi studies the layout of Tizra scanning for any overlooked tactical advantages.

Aden lets out a sigh that breaks the suspense of the uncertain defense plans. "I think Tobi's plan puts our men in the best position to succeed."

Ashira clears her throat to remind the prince and the other men in the room about who else serves in the ranks.

"Sorry, puts our men *and* women in a position of strength."

"Men *and* women in a position of strength," sarcastically chides Caleb.

"For the love of the Goddess, will you shut your mouth!?" shouts Tobi, hammering his fist on the map.

Aden waits for Tobi's echo to die down before issuing orders.

"We have to thin their ranks, and the only way we can do that is too keep the catapults firing from the main towers. Tobi and Seth, I'm going to need you to get the most of out those crews."

Tobi nods with a sense of duty, Seth with disappointment, for he prefers to smash skulls on a face to face basis, not from a distance.

"Ben and Ashira, I'll need you to lead the shepherd army in the south plaza in case they breech the city. If these five hundred shepherds can fight with the fervor of their brethren who perished in the revolt, we'll have a chance to keep the archers clean on the towers. I'll put the halberdiers on the wall to bookend the archers as a double measure of security. Caleb will patrol the walls with me."

"Nicely done, Sir Aden. I do think this plan to be our best chance," affirms the raspy-voiced Tobi.

"Is Ezekiel going to be able to neutralize Zidon when the time comes?" asks Ben of Seth.

The question raises a lot of eyebrows at the allusion to ether magic.

"He's in pretty bad shape," admits Seth, still wrestling with the ether-lightning phenomenon from the night before.

"His back?" assumes Ben.

"Yep, back still hurts."

"Seth Keros, out with it," says Ashira in the same tone as their mother.

The truth sits on the tip of his tongue, but he finds a way to swallow it. "He's got a bad case of diarrhea. Are you happy now? Embarrass the poor guy."

After Seth's revelation, the company awkwardly disbands from the dining hall to take up their positions. Most pretend like they never heard the diagnosis, except Caleb. The jokester smacks a hunk of cheddar in Seth's hand.

"I hate you!" yells Ezekiel with his left cheek blushing to match the purple glow of his right cheek.

"It's the first thing that came to mind. I was afraid to tell them about what happened to your face."

"So you told them I have the runs!?"

After the prophet removes his palm from his face, Seth presses the hunk of cheese in his hand. "Compliments of Caleb Glade, guess he thinks that you like cheese."

The wittier prophet realizes once again that the inner-workings of human digestion are lost on Seth.

"By the way, where did you get these robes?" asks Ezekiel, holding up a purple-hooded silk robe with gold trim.

"Zidon's old chamber. I thought the color matched your face."

"It's a moon festival garment, like the one that we were almost killed at."

"You complain too much. The city's about to get sacked and I'm runnin' around lookin' for robes. Not too mention, I haven't been able to eat a full meal or ask Aden if he's gonna make good on Emmerick's promise. Now, I must lead a catapult crew."

"And I complain too much."

"For whatever it's worth, Zek. How are you feeling?"

It's a simple question, a kind one, but it's the wrong question to ask a prophet freshly marked by Neshama. What was Ezekiel feeling lay at the root of Seth's curiosity.

The prophet sits with the heightened senses of his rebirth

stirring within. "The atmosphere shifts, and I'm not talking about fall giving way to winter. Something stirs in the clouds above the city and it's not a storm. I can feel the ether in my lungs when I breathe the air outside of the window. Likewise, the smell of rain settles in my nose. I don't know what's coming to this city, but the Goddess help us all when it arrives."

Ashira inspects her steel knives as she fastens their sleeves to the front of her armor. She takes a few swings to get a feel for her swords before she sheathes them behind her back.

Ben quietly tightens his sentinel armor before he straps his hunting bow on his back and Kurion to his side. The tension rising in the ranks behind him stifles his optimism.

Ashira gazes fondly upon the standard's banner. The angry ram's head embroidered into the yellow cloth reminds her of the banner that Shamgar Ram placed in her hand during the revolt. The memory bolsters her faith as she recalls his encouragement about the power of one.

Ben joins her to admire the colors and crest of Hallowed Hills.

"How's Judith?" asks Ashira.

"Lonely. I regret that my visit was so short, but as she always does, she made my goodbye guilt free. Judith would never admit it. I bet she hasn't even considered it, but she has more heart than me or Evan."

"How is your brother?" asks Ashira, adjusting her bootstraps to avoid eye contact with Ben.

Ben wants to feel slighted by the question. He searches his soul for his companion, jealousy, but he fails to find her within his heart. He finally reaches a point where he realizes that grace is at work within in him, and in such a profound way that Othniel would be proud. Even though he still desires to be with Ashira, he doesn't feel the desire to judge her.

Ben leaves his adolescent ways behind. He now feels it more important for Neshama to have her way in molding him and less important for the Goddess to change the circumstances around him.

"His ribs heal slowly. The elders have been after him too, about the same criticism that they accused our father… He misses you. He didn't say that, but he didn't have to."

Well aware of Evan's stoic nature, Ashira smiles. "How'd he act around you?"

"It's going to take time before he forgives me."

"You seem sure that he will."

"If I've learned anything these past two seasons, it's that Neshama can bind my wounds as if I were an injured lamb in the arms of a shepherd. I must trust that her grace will prevail, even in the darkest situations."

Ashira shines her whites within her soft smile, offering an innocence that forces Ben to deal with his guilt.

"I'm really sorry about the way that I treated you lately. It was with contempt, not grace. I was jealous of Evan."

"Ben, for the first time in my life, I'm trying to live in the moment. I'm not too good at it. You don't have to apologize for my indecisiveness."

"I must. Rejecting Melek's freedom empowered me in way that I never thought possible. If I can't find freedom in this call then I never will. I must seek forgiveness and I must forgive before I can accept who I am and what I must do."

"How will you know what to do when the time comes?"

"I hope that I'll face it with grace. At least I'll be free to choose when I face my decision."

The stomps of ten thousand troops quake Tizra, interrupting their conversation.

Aden rushes to the edge of the wall to see the horde break

into siege formation outside of the city. As the fog lifts, his spirits dampen. The iron-clad warriors glisten under the sun like a million diamonds spread across The East Sea, their spearheads twinkling atop their long poles.

The hopeful sun blazes down upon Melek's wretched chosen troops. Yet, the image brings a smile to Aden's honest eyes. In the moment he thinks on Emmerick's mantra, *Oh, the irony is grand.*

Chapter 18 ✦ The House of Elk

The crimson pebbles scattered across the banks of Lake Resh had yet to be washed clean. They stained the shoreline in the same manner that the memories stained the souls of Evan and Judith. Evan passed quickly by the scene of the attack, but he didn't anticipate how the memories would continue to hunt him in the forest. Had Evan known, he would have taken the longer way to Elah.

Evan was disgusted with Ben, heartsick over Ashira, and convicted by Judith. He missed his flock and the last task on his list was to ask a favor of a forester. He felt physically weak and willfully pathetic. His fractured ribs absorbed the shock of his strides, and he couldn't figure why he conceded to Judith's demand to travel south.

A gust of wind rattles the forest causing leaves of red, yellow, and orange to burst over Evan when he approaches the north gate of Elah. The gigantic timbers that row the walls intimidate him, sternly warning the other guilds to stay out, but the smell of hot apple cider blends with the autumn foliage to offer an inviting aroma.

To his surprise, no guards stand post at the narrow north gate. Based on the growth atop the path, Evan assumes that the entrance doesn't welcome the steps of many visitors.

Evan wanders into the town square. Though a guild master of shepherds, he concedes that his hall doesn't compare to the majesty of the Elah architecture for the shops and homes are woodworking-masterpieces.

In the center of the city, tower four gigantic carvings of a Boar, Elk, Owl, and Wolf - one for each of the prominent houses of the Foresters Guild.

Enraptured in the comeliness of the city and the grandeur of the statues, Evan becomes oblivious to the raised eyebrows of the inhabitants. The stares intensify to the point Evan feels them, but the proud shepherd would never give a forester the satisfaction of showing any signs of self-consciousness.

"A pint, please," says Evan, offering a coin to a cider vendor. The furry-faced lumberjack ignores the shepherd, as do the other customers who rudely cut in front of him.

Evan takes his business to another vendor.

"Pint, please."

"All out," rebukes another furry-faced woodsman.

Evan realizes that his coin is not welcome in Elah, and by the gazes of residents, neither is he.

Evan looks about the cityscape for Erez's Lodge. He identifies a great banquet hall with a vaulted roof shingled in green squares. A red-brick fireplace the size of a tower puffs an aroma of apple pies.

As Evan makes for the lodge, the men and women that he passes on the street bounce him back and forth. They crash into his shoulders, blocking his path. He keeps his head up, but refuses to make eye contact. His cocky disposition antagonizes the citizens of Elah.

After a few dozen bumps and bruises, he arrives at the steps of the lodge with any newfound admiration for forester culture jostled out of him.

"Where do you think you're goin'!?" roars Sorek Boar, Erez's guardsman. He shakes his bearish-face in disbelief when Evan turns to make himself known. "You're a fool for comin' here."

"I was invited, remember. My reward for saving Erez's daughter."

"The invitation was your reward, you greedy pig."

Evan turns his back on Sorek and begins his ascent up the long flight of stairs. He acknowledges the truth in the guardsman's words, but he had come too far to heed the warning.

The giant looms over the shepherd to monitor his every step up the stairs, taking note of the brittle ribs that demand the shepherd's caress in order to complete the trek.

"Since you're so stubborn, I'm probably wasting my breath. I suggest that you let Erez do all of the talking. Stuff your chops, leave Elah, and never return," advises Sorek, ushering Evan into the grand hall.

The exploits of prominent guild masters canvass the walls each assigned to their ancestral houses of Boar, Elk, Owl, and Wolf. Scenes of great hunts honor the creatures etched into the wood. Majestic elk heads encompass the entire hall and antler-chandeliers dangle from the vaulted ceiling.

The servants stop at the sight of an outsider, but a quick glare from Sorek presses them back to their duty.

Three of Erez's daughters emerge at the far end of the hall. The damsels share their father's green eyes and their reddish hair flows in shades from bright to dark. Though a set of twins perch on the same branch of the Elk family tree, one might suspect that the sisters are triplets. Their ages span the range of adolescence suggesting otherwise.

Unlike her refined older sisters, Iana playfully enters the hall by trotting about like a pony. She lays eyes on Evan and dashes through the lodge.

Iana knocks over a servant, who spills hot apple cider across the floor. She leaps into Evan's arms and latches onto him as if he's her favorite climbing tree, her curly red locks dangling behind her back and her fiery orange freckles glowing atop her fair skin.

"Iana Elk! What did I tell you about running in the hall!?" yells Erez, entering the lodge.

"I told you he'd come, Papa! You missed me, didn't you?" asks Iana, burying her head into Evan's chest.

"Evan Tav, you're as bold as your exploits boast," admits Erez behind a rare smile. "Pumpkin, get down and take your place at the table."

Iana jumps down. Taking Evan's hand, she pulls him to the seat next to hers, which displaces the oldest sister from her usual spot.

Evan awkwardly sits down between Iana and Erez.

Within moments, three highbreds sit at the table. The noblemen represent the three prominent houses of the guild.

It's a full hall with Erez, his daughters, Sorek, Evan, and the three highbreds feasting at the oaken rectangle.

The chair to Erez's right remains vacant. Evan realizes that his wife has yet to join them and he worries that he may have erred in his etiquette. Therefore, he waits for Erez to take the first bite of venison.

Despite his desire to know the whereabouts of the absent wife or his interest to know the names of everyone at the table, Evan heeds the advice of Sorek to keep his chops shut. The lack of hospitality makes Evan assume that it's part of forester culture, like chewing loudly with an open mouth.

Iana happily crunches her sprouts while she gazes into the brown eyes of her hero.

Erez catches Evan observing the vacant seat. "My family has been stewards of this guild hall for five generations. My wife died giving birth to Iana. She produced no male heir, so I will be last in my line to oversee the guild."

Evan chews his venison hoping to find the words for an appropriate condolence, but he keeps his silence along with everyone else at the table.

The daughters, guests, and servants exchange few words and the silence irritates the typically quiet shepherd. Peering up from his plate with cautious eyes, Evan notices that Iana isn't the only Elk daughter admiring him. The oldest daughter with flowing auburn-colored locks smiles at him through the flecks of her emerald eyes.

Evan's food settles in his throat and not even the hot cider can scold it down. When the servants begin to slice the warm apple pie, Evan realizes that the feast will soon end. "The meal was quite filling and your hall is unlike anything that I've ever seen. But I didn't come here simply to enjoy your table. I've come to ask a favor."

Erez's daughters exchange worrisome looks with one another, before they lower their mouths to nibble on their knuckles.

The offended nobles drop their utensils.

Sorek rubs his raised forehead with his thumb.

The servants plate the last pieces of pie. Their quaking hands serve the saucers before quickly removing themselves from the hall.

Erez's white skin catches fire and burns as bright as the embers in the hearth. "I don't entertain favors from lesser guilds and that includes shepherds. You spared Iana's life and for that, I'm grateful. That's why I offered you the finest meal in the finest hall in Issur. I think that it's time for you to go."

Sorek connects his furled brow with Evan's eyes and nods his head to remind the shepherd of his warning.

"Your reward lacks equity," says Evan.

The remark ignites Erez from his chair. He slams his fist onto the table causing the dessert plates shatter on the floor.

His daughters flee from the table, the eldest whisking Iana from her seat. They race to their rooms on the other end of the lodge. Iana screams along the way in protest of her exit.

"We are not equals, shepherd! Must I take my fists and smash that understanding into your thick skull!?"

"This is not a favor for me, it's for Issur. A Calcedonian army is at the gates of Tizra and if that city falls then my hills and your forest will be destroyed."

"I dare anyone to invade this forest... You and your guild of warmongers, you're just like your father. I'll hear no more of this, get out now, or I'll throw you out."

Evan's gut convicts the shepherd to make for the door and never return to the Forest of Elah. Evan's honor refuses to budge. Though this time, his sense of honor roots itself in respect - not in selfishness. His respect for Judith grounds his honor. She'd endured so much disappointment, yet she deserved none of it.

Evan understands that he can't return to Tav without first exhausting every fiber of his marrow in Elah. He recalls a tale that his father once told of how the houses of Boar, Elk, Owl, and Wolf determined the first master of their guild - a gruesome bludgeoning by oaken planks in a fatal contest.

"I challenge your honor, Erez Elk. Guild master to guild master."

Erez thinks on the offer.

The fire in his pale skin dies down when he comes to a conclusion. "Very well. Prove your worth and I will afford you the privilege to plead your case as to why I should lead my guild into battle. If you can't, you die."

Sorek and the three highbreds tilt the dinner table, placing it against the far wall. They stand to watch the contest from the near wall.

A summoned bard sits next to the hearth and raps his palms against a drum to fill the hall with the beats of war.

Evan stands near the entrance with a wooden plank resting on his shoulder. Erez stands opposed with a larger wooden beam fused to his fist.

Sorek steps forward. "The House of Elk Rules of Contention allows each man a shaft of lumber, chosen according to his liking. The rules do not permit armor. No blows below the waste. Only cowards seek quarter, so mercy may be granted but never asked."

Sorek retreats to his spot, and then blasts his horn to begin the challenge.

The two combatants circle slowly waiting for the other to take the first shot. Evan hopes to utilize his speed to negate Erez's strength.

The impatient forester strikes at the shepherd, who turns aside the beam. The follow up shot comes at Evan much fiercer and dislodges the shepherd's board into the mouth of a highbred.

Evan kneels to reclaim his weapon, but the bloody-lipped lumberjack kicks it away with a laugh.

The shepherd dodges a few swings on his way to reclaim his plank.

Erez strikes downward with a crushing blow that Evan blocks, but he grips his beam too tightly and the vibrations from the strike incinerate the nerves in his hands all the way to his elbows before shooting out of his arm bones.

The mighty forester gets a clean shot when he splinters a piece of his wood across the shepherd's shoulder. Though, he misses his next shot and loses his balance, allowing Evan to make use of his speed.

Evan cracks a flurry of blows across the forester's back, then, ducks a spinning return shot. Evan unleashes another flurry into Erez's stomach.

The bruised woodsman rushes the surprised shepherd and plants the broadside of the plank into Evan's mouth.

At the sound of the nasty slap, Sorek shares a laugh with the bloody-lipped highbred from the House of Boar.

Erez slams his boot into Evan's chest, wrecking him into the floorboards. Evan's brains rattle as he tries to determine the legality of the kick. A plank across the gut tells his brain to quit contemplating challenge etiquette.

Evan uses a tactic of the flock and crawls under the legs of the forester, which draws a belly of laughter from the onlookers who mock Evan with bahs.

As Evan gets to his feet a crushing blow thumps his ribcage. The force is so great that it dislodges a blood-filled cough.

Erez finds the same spot and again bashes his inferior foe. Evan falls to the floor paralyzed by the pain.

The highbreds continue to mock the wounded guild master, but Sorek Boar's amusement dies down for he knows what is about to befall the stubborn shepherd. He has witnessed the mightiest of oaks buckle under the power of Erez's ax; the sapling-shepherd doesn't stand a chance.

"Mercy may be granted but not asked," says Erez to Sorek.

"It is as you say, Master."

"What say the men of Boar, Owl, and Wolf?" asks Erez of the highbreds.

Evan's nerves reconnect with his muscles. He musters the strength to roll over and sprawls open to show the foresters his broken and bloodied body as a plea for mercy.

The highbred from the House of Boar dabs his crimson lips.

"I think I speak for the other nobles when I say you've bent over backwards for this fool. You offer him your table and he vomits your meal back in your face… Lay the lumber!"

Erez raises his plank high and sends it crashing down toward Evan's face.

The desperate shepherd grips his hands on the far ends of his board and pushes it forward to block the death strike. The towering blow splinters both men's beams, which burst into a thousand pieces that spray across the hall - slivers of wood rip the flesh of the shepherd's neck and shoulders.

Sorek and the highbreds gasp in amazement at Evan's feat of strength to block a chop from the unrivaled Erez.

Horrified by the cracks of the wood, Iana flees the pursuit of her oldest sister when she returns to the hall.

"Papa! Stop! Why do you hurt him!?"

Iana's plea ends the contest.

She takes her dress and wipes the blood from Evan's face. A closer look at her fallen hero overwhelms her fragile emotions and her tears flood his wounds.

The brokenness of Iana melts Erez's heart, for he could never weather the sadness of his daughters.

"Speak, Shepherd," offers Erez.

The concession of equality stuns Evan, but his unheralded feat of strength gets Sorek and the highbreds to nod in agreement.

The concession momentarily stays Ian's tears.

"Go on, plead your case," encourages Erez.

Evan gets to one knee before he can return to an upright position. His wheezes keep his lungs from gathering enough air to form words.

Iana clenches his hand to squeeze a word from his lips. Her embrace grips his heart instead, providing him the answer to why he journeyed to Elah.

Like his father, he cherishes the women in his life. He

loves Judith and Jael, and hopes to love Ashira as deeply as Oren loved his wife, Rachel.

"I risked my life for your daughter because she was helpless. I had to protect her from the wolves. There are some among my people that are in the habit of war, my father and brother are among them. Trust me. I've little patience for these religious wars. They've cost me my parents and a sister. My betrothed escaped death once, but she's in the clutches of death, yet again. I need you to protect her from the wolves. A life for a life is all I ask."

Erez studies Iana's freckles while he contemplates the request.

"What do the other houses say to this?" requests Erez, continuing to look deeply into Iana's green eyes.

The three nobles talk under their breath.

Sorek withdraws out of respect for their rank. He scoops a pint of cider, and with a grin of admiration, serves it to Evan.

The noble from the line of Owl peers up from his bushy brows and narrow eyes to address the hall, "This debt to settle with Evan Tav is yours, Erez Elk. Pay it as you see fit, for it was not our daughter who was spared. If what the shepherd said is true and the Calcedonians are at the gates of Tizra, it would be in our best interest to stop the enemy before they spread to the north. We shall offer half of our fighting men and we choose Sorek Boar to serve as general."

Sorek turns to the highbreds with grateful eyes, honored by the opportunity to lead over eight hundred foresters into battle.

"With all due respect to Sorek, I will serve as general and settle this debt with Evan. Though, I welcome your ax, good friend," says Erez.

"I'm going too," adds the battered shepherd.

"You're a stubborn one indeed," crows Sorek.

"Sorry, Evan. It would be a worthless agreement if I spare

the life of your betrothed, only to watch you perish. You'll be lodged here. My daughters will tend to your wounds until my return."

Iana frolics around her champion at her father's announcement. Failing to conceal her infatuation with Evan, the oldest daughter blushes the same shade as Iana's hair.

Erez's hand swallows Evan's as he finalizes the pact. "A life for a life."

Chapter 19 ✦ The Fallen

Bright rays shine across the clear blue sky boosting the morale of the Remnant with a touch of hope. The guards atop the Tizra walls find it difficult to be on edge, for the siege equipment has yet to appear among the Calcedonian ranks.

"This is a waste of time. When do the catapults and rafts arrive from the fleet?" asks Tartek.

"We don't need catapults and rafts. Zidon is the only siege equipment that we need," answers Korah.

As soon as the final word lifts from Korah's lips, the atmosphere begins to shift. A frigid stream of air shoves aside the comfortable fall breeze and dampens the stone of the city.

The white rays fade along with the blue sky when grey clouds invade the horizon. Once the grey clouds conquer the sky, they blacken like a storm. The wind picks up and violently thrashes the banners among both armies.

Bolts of red lightning pulse through the clouds. The current of crimson circles like a tornado and the ominous stratosphere transitions into a hypnotic flow.

The ecstasy of the moment enraptures Zidon, his eyes rolling back in his head, his soul tingling as the vibes of pleasure pulsate within. The magi expands his arms and lifts his head back while the wind ruffles his grey robe.

Ezekiel rushes upward from a deep sleep, his eyes widen and the hair on the back of his neck heightens. He wraps himself in his robe, tucks Othniel's book underneath the purple fabric, and clutches the notched-staff.

Ezekiel moves to the tower to witness what he already confirms in his spirit - an ether vortex the size of Tizra swirling above the city.

The swirling vortex uncomfortably enthralls Ben, before his calling stirs his soul.

The question. Every Issurian desires to know *the* question. Yet only one person within the city walls knows the answer. Ben kept his promise to his father by never ceasing in his inquiries, but he's learning that there's a price to pay for asking questions - the burden of knowledge. Ben knows the answer and it shreds his insides. He refuses to voice it. Instead, he makes his supplication into the wind with a wish to unlock his divine mystery.

"Neshama. Are you there, are you listening?"

His prayer takes him back to the desperation that he felt when chained alongside Othniel in The Pit. He recalls the master prophet stringing a strand of Korah's ether through the metal shackles to free them.

The memory provides a glimpse of the future, but Ben has no way to alert Aden, positioned so high on the walls of Tizra.

Zidon emerges from the ranks with outstretched arms. He widens his hands and begins to channel ether as he approaches the drawbridge.

It takes Aden's wits a moment to shake off the ominous conditions hovering over Tizra. "Shoot him!"

Like the prince, the archers must pull their heads from the clouds before the command registers. They draw arrows, but their adrenaline-loaded volley soars over the magi's head.

"Protect him, you fools!" scolds Korah, pushing the Calcedonian soldiers towards the vulnerable target. They form a circle around him and serve as pincushions when they absorb the next round of arrowheads.

"Form ranks at the gates!" yells Ben, waving the uncertain shepherds forward to plug the entrance.

Zidon weaves the ether down the gate well. The ether entangles the pulleys and levers as it wraps around the chains like a vine. 'The Absolute' yanks the ether strands, which drop the levers and rattle the chains to dislodge the drawbridge from the gate. The massive wooden planks slam down across the Tizra River with a thunderous BOOM!

"Charge!" blasts Tartek in sync with the horns of battle.

The Calcedonian King runs ahead of the army with his steel claymore out front, eager to shred armor.

Once the horde makes range, Tobi and Seth order the catapult crews to launch boulders into the ranks of Melek's chosen. The bouncing boulders crush the soldiers as the rocks roll across the ranks.

Aden's and Caleb's archers land perfect targets that only stun the enemy. What seem like kill shots are shaken off like bee stings by the Calcedonians. The pain threshold of the Calcedonians baffles Aden and Caleb.

Aden adjusts his strategy, "Head shots! Aim for their eyes!"

Caleb leads by example by placing a direct hit through a helmet and into the pupil of his victim.

The enemy ranks wreck into the snug shepherds locked shoulder to shoulder in the gate. Their tight formation holds off the surge and keeps the Calcedonians on the drawbridge vulnerable to the archers. Most of the arrows continue to sting the swelled ranks, while a few fortunate shots prove fatal.

Unruly boulders fly from the towers and bound through the ranks of red banners, scattering spearmen in all directions.

Tartek maims three shepherds with the first swing of his claymore. Ashira slides into the front rank to halt his deadly charge, the speed of her blades slow his slaughter. An exact counterstrike from Ashira removes Tartek's left ear. The enraged king knocks her backwards and readies his claymore for payback.

Ben moves in for support.

Both heroes hold off his offensive, giving a morale boost to the shepherds around them and allowing them to maintain the initiative in the gate.

"Mortals," says Korah with disgust for Tartek, parting the ranks on his way to the drawbridge.

Korah reaches the fighting rank and both sides pause in awe of the presence of the nephesh. He unsheathes his ether sword and points it at Ben.

"What did I ever do to you?" questions the sentinel as the battle lines reengage.

The shepherds fail to match Korah's skill as he clears a path towards Ben.

Ashira's swings glance against Tartek's armor and she struggles to land a fatal blow. Her speed annoys the impatient king as he swings for her head, only to miss three times.

Ben feels his boots slip northward away from the gate as Korah wills his troops to advance. The Calcedonians push the entire shepherd regiment into the south plaza.

"Clear the walls," orders Korah, as Tartek leads half of the army up the gate towers.

Tartek finds fierce resistance, for Tobi's plan proves formidable. The halberdiers hold their ground, allowing the archers to continue their barrage of arrows.

Zidon takes cover within the gate at the drawbridge. He channels more ether and fires it into the palace walls; debris tumbles down upon the ranks of the shepherd regiment.

Ezekiel scurries along the city walls to offer protection to the shepherds below.

Seth's catapult crew absorbs a quick pottery lesson before creating a distraction for beleaguered shepherds. The crew heats clay jars with torches and launches the jars down upon Korah's ranks; shards of clay spray the enemy to slow their advance.

With a swift blast of ether, Zidon cracks a corner of brick and mortar.

Ashira shields her face when a hunk of debris nearly blinds her.

Seth sees the peril of his sister below and the potter hurls his clay vessels with deadly accuracy, draining the vitality from his victims.

As the enemy spearmen overwhelm the Issurian halberdiers in the gate towers, Tobi and his crewmen feverishly stir iron cauldrons filled with scalding tar.

"There's no Azor to save you this time," mocks Korah, clashing his ether sword against Kurion.

The blade of the nephesh whirls like a windmill in a storm, yet Ben manages to repel the onslaught. His discipline to master swordplay becomes evident when he rips through the black robes of Korah, Kurion dazzling a vibrant color of red.

Ben slices the back of Korah's leg, dropping the nephesh to one knee.

Zidon launches a gigantic onyx ether-ball that crushes the corner of the palace and dislodges chunks of brick intended to crush Ben, Ashira, and the shepherd regiment.

Time slows for Ben, and his muscles tense with the anticipation of death.

Suddenly, a white net of ether shoots over the heads of the shepherd regiment to deflect the boulders. The rocks bounce through the Calcedonian ranks, narrowly missing Zidon on the drawbridge.

The magi steps forth from the gate and lowers his hood, revealing to Ezekiel the malice in his eyes. The prophet lowers his hood, revealing the purple scar seared into his flesh. The divine mark agitates Zidon, so he channels thicker amounts of ether. Ezekiel follows suit, preparing to counter.

Aden, Caleb, and their dozen of faithful rangers retreat along the east wall beyond the catapult tower manned by Tobi and his crew.

The bowmen feverishly draw from their quivers in an attempt to spare their engaged comrades from the clutches of death. The enemy on the adjacent wall proves overwhelming when the Calcedonian spears skewer the lightly armored archers.

After the last bowman falls at Tartek's feet, Tobi orders the catapult crew to load the cauldrons of blistering tar into leather bands stretched across the tower. They pull back the bands and let fly.

The black tar scolds the flesh from Tartek's face.

The maligned king rears up in misery as he rips tar and tissue from his skull.

Tartek fans out his arms in two directions - one finger points towards Seth's catapult and his claymore points at Tobi's.

Tartek, along with half of his possessed swarm, storm the tower. The other half of his swarm absorbs more shards of clay when they assault Seth and his catapult crew.

Seth grips Peacemaker and readies his men for hand to hand combat.

The distraction of Ezekiel's ether-net allows Korah to return to his feet and blast a shot at Ben. The powerful swing removes Kurion from his hands and plants the shepherd into the cobblestone plaza.

The nephesh swiftly drops his blade on Ben's throat when Ashira thrusts her blades under the ether sword to stop the attack.

Korah rears back to cut through her defenses. The brute force of his strike bends her blades.

Ben detaches his bow from behind his back and returns her favor. He blocks Korah's blade, but the strike shreds the wooden bow. The blade slows, failing to pierce her armor, but the might from the swing throws her into the palace walls.

Korah spikes the crown of Ben's head with his elbow, spinning the dizzy warrior to the ground alongside Ashira.

Zidon manipulates barbed edges around his ether-orbs to shred Ezekiel's ether-nets. He unleashes his jagged onyx orbs at the dwindling shepherd regiment.

Ezekiel outwits him by casting an opal shield.

The ether collides and radiant colors burst over the soldiers. The prophet labors to halt the magi's orb, for his position of weakness makes it all the more difficult. Zidon's direct attack on the shepherds in the street below proves problematic for Ezekiel's diagonal angle on the wall above.

Ezekiel's arms weaken and the opal ether fades. The prophet's ether proves potent enough to spare the regiment but not potent enough to quell the orb. The black ether soars into the palace wall, unsettling the infrastructure.

A large crack shoots down from the highest tower, all the way to the cobblestone plaza.

Seth slugs another crazed warrior from the catapult tower, sending him to his death on the street below. His muscles ache from the strength it musters to land a devastating blow on the superhuman enemy. His legs grow weary beneath him as the mass of soldiers swamp him and his crew.

His biceps bulge as they muscle him out of the sea of hands and back onto the tower platform. His comrades are not as fortunate.

Seth abandons his catapult and dashes for Ezekiel on the west wall. A black ether-stand removes the bricks from under his feet and Seth surfs the landslide to the street below.

Zidon zips another blast at Ezekiel.

The prophet pulls it into his palm and sends it back to the magi. His shrewd uncle yanks an unassuming Calcedonian into the line of fire - the shot knocks the warrior backwards off of the drawbridge.

Steam billows from the remaining tar embedded in Tartek's skull when he engages Tobi. The captain's crew stands their ground, enabling Tobi to receive the challenge.

Aden, Caleb, and their rangers offer support as they cut down a handful of soldiers with perfect targets.

Claymore connects with halberd and the blast echoes throughout Tizra.

Tartek rattles Tobi's confidence when a swift cut from the claymore removes a portion of the captain's red beard. The king buries another dent into the captain's war-torn cuirass with his shoulder pad. The king knocks the captain down a set of stairs and onto the rampart.

With the legendary Tobi Tamar removed from their ranks, the catapult crew falls to the possessed Calcedonians.

Their sacrifice emboldens the captain's resolve as he reengages the king. Tartek's claymore blocks a shot from Tobi's halberd, but the blowback of the claymore cracks against Tartek's mouth. The king swallows his teeth and rolls his tongue around his lips to wash them down with his blood.

Tobi buries his halberd into Tartek's right shoulder with such power that it sinks into his bone.

Tobi tugs the oak shaft but his weapon sticks in the marrow. Tartek lunges his claymore through the newest dent in Tobi's cuirass, the blade sinking into his clavicle.

Unable to free their weapons the two veterans latch onto one another with powerful grips. They struggle atop the wall trying to overpower one other. The snorts of their breath sting the other's eyes and the blood from their wounds stream down their arms into a pool of crimson beneath them.

Tartek bashes his forehead into Tobi's bald head with such force that the captain collapses into the bloody pool underneath. The king's red eyes glow hotter with each bash of his forehead. Tartek continues to crush Tobi's skull until blood gushes down the psychopath's face.

Tartek gets to one knee and feels no pain when he rips the halberd from his shoulder. He grips the halberd like a spear and plants it into Tobi's chest as if to claim territory.

Aden, Caleb, and their archers exhaust their quivers at the same time Tobi exhausts his breath.

It becomes obvious to Aden as he stands upon the rampart that the dark tide swells, ready to wash over his men, and not even the elite among them will withstand the enemy wave.

All of the pieces fall into place for Melek, and Aden has the perfect vantage point to see the master's plan - no precept to lead a crusade, no prophet to match the magi, no hero to best a nephesh, and no Issurian king to challenge the Calcedonian king.

In the midst of the hopelessness, Caleb secures a rope and drops it to the street below. Caleb nods to Aden to scale down, but the corpse of Captain Tamar delays his decision.

Tartek forces the choice when he clears the loyal rangers with two swings of his red-stained claymore.

Aden decides to place his kingship into the hands of fate. If the Signet Ring of Issur were to ever slip onto his finger, it'd be placed there by the hands of fate.

Aden draws Royal Blue to Caleb's surprise.

The pommel of the sword causes the scout to lose his balance and tumble off the rampart. The tips of Caleb's fingers find the rope to reel him into the wall, but he pays a price when he smacks against the wall twice on the way down to the street below.

As a little prince who grew up Issurian royalty, Aden knows all too well about the feats of champions in challenges - storybooks laced with gory details of survival. He wonders if he'd be worthy of such a tale.

The essence of Korah's ether tingles with a heightened sense of satisfaction. To the lofty nephesh all mortals are scum, but slaying Ben Tav offers a rewarding mix of accomplishment and revenge.

Decapitate, impale, mutilate. Quick, methodical, longsuffering. The method of the execution lingers in his thoughts as his ether sword hangs over his incapacitated victim.

"Mortals. So frail, so finite."

Korah raises his blade with a twinkle in his yellow eyes.

The sheen in Ben's brown eyes dims.

Suddenly, Azor soars from a tower above. The breeze from the flight rustles Ben's hair as the white nephesh latches onto the black robes of Korah. Azor drives his rival into the cobblestone causing bricks and debris to spray the warriors around them. The celestial beings grind to a halt a quarter of a length away from the battleline in the southern plaza.

Korah escapes Azor's grip and engages him with a violent swing that's narrowly turned aside.

"Damn your cheap shots!" shouts Korah, his black robes flowing in the breeze that swirls about his blade.

Azor goes on the defensive in disbelief of how quickly he lost the initiative. He labors to slow the barrage of attacks as his feet retreat down an alley away from the shepherd regiment and the Calcedonian horde.

Ben's heart returns to function and pumps blood through

his excited soul. He reclaims Kurion and lifts Ashira from the street. Ben arms her with a sword from a fallen brother.

The shepherds slowly fragment down the street when Ben and Ashira join the flight. Retreat wars with Ben's will to fight, and he can no longer bear the tension. "Hold the line!"

The verbose command grips the core of the shepherds and they rally instantly as if they were sheep heeding the voice of their master.

The regiment locks shoulder. Ben and Ashira file to the center and the ranks swell behind them in the cramped street.

The Calcedonian spearmen pause for a command from their distracted nephesh general. Zidon fears losing the impetus and orders the troops down the narrow street. The surly warriors grudgingly respond to the wizard's command. They knock into each other as they make a final push to destroy the defiant shepherds.

Caleb Glade regains consciousness and his initial view reveals sparks flinging from atop the wall. He pops his backbone into place and rolls over onto his hands and knees. He grabs the dangling rope to ready his climb but his biceps offer no support and his hamstrings numb. Caleb burns his hand on the rope as he returns to his weakened state on the street below.

A cry of horror rings out from above when Royal Blue slides across Tartek's face.

A thick drop of blood plummets down, splattering on Caleb's forehead. He reconnects with his humor to make light of the situation. "It's only blood, could have been a head or an arm."

"I'm going to put that sapphire on my crown after I run you through with that blue steel!" mocks Tartek.

Aden remains silent, focused on every attack from the claymore. The prince maintains his defense as Tartek hacks and slashes. Aden finds it more and more difficult to hold his sword as the madman gains more and more strength with each blow. The prince nicks and cuts the armor and flesh of the Calcedonian King, but fails to weaken the monster.

Aden adjusts his approach to take the fight to Tartek. He lands a vicious shot that connects precisely where Tobi severed his shoulder from his body; his attack hits so accurately that it nearly detaches Tartek's arm.

Tartek freezes from the shock of the wound, allowing Aden to rip another exact cut across the wound. Aden's blade removes Tartek's arm and the appendage falls from above, landing on Caleb. Tartek's claymore rattles across the cobblestone below, before disappearing into a gutter.

Caleb squirms from under the chopped arm as chills shoot up his spine. "I should have brought a parasol into battle."

Aden moves in for the kill when Tartek yanks him close with his left arm. The king grips the scruff of the prince's neck and slams his forehead into Aden's face. Both men drop when Tartek plummets down on top of Aden.

Royal Blue flies from the wall like a spear, pinning itself to the street below in between Caleb's leg. The charmer's eyes grow large as he grabs his crotch in relief.

Tartek grinds his gauntlet across the side of Aden's head, raking the steel like a garden hoe, trying to dig up the brains of his enemy. Aden's dark-blond waves rip from his scalp as the metal tears his flesh.

Tartek presses his seared flesh and exposed skull into his Aden's cheek while he grinds and digs with the gauntlet. The possessed king punches the prince betweens the eyes, which stuns him and deadens his muscles.

A delay in the struggle allows Tartek to slide back his gauntlet to reveal his dagger. He places the onyx handle in his fist with the tip aimed at Aden's heart.

Tartek's arm rears back and slams the steel downward into Aden's chest.

The thrust penetrates Aden's black armor, but violently recoils when the dagger shatters the stone medallion that dangles from the prince's neck.

Judith's gift of the shepherd relic splits in half when a fault line cracks the engraved lightning bolt.

The medallion not only spares Aden's life, it sends a jolt of redemption through the bones of the blessed prince.

With wit his only weapon, he plots his next move.

While the distracted Tartek shakes out the painful vibrations that dull the nerves in his arm, Aden grabs the rope secured to the wall. He wraps the cable around the pale-skinned neck of the Calcedonian king. Then, he leaps off the wall putting all of his weight into the rope.

The rope cracks, Tartek's neck snaps, and his corpse crashes down to the stone below.

Aden jumps from the line and lands next to his abused scout. Aden offers his hand to Caleb and pulls him up.

The two friends take a moment to unwind some tension. Caleb looks over the mangled corpse of the fallen King Tartek before offering an odd look to Aden. "You really need to sort out your daddy issues."

Chapter 20 ✦✦✦ The Ether King

The heap of the deceased piles high as the shepherds dwindle the Calcedonians in the street between Josiah's Palace and The Pit. Though, the enemy ranks run deep and require vicious strikes to fell them.

The Lord of Swords blackens with each corrupted soul it harvests in Ben's skilled hands. Ashira's joints ache from the fevered day of combat, yet she shines in combat among the warriors in the shadows of the palace.

Zidon shakes the boulder dust from his robes. In a fit of rage, he channels a quick mass of the divine substance and fires it into the soldiers that scrap in the street. The ether rips through the ranks of spearmen, narrowly misses Ben, and cuts down a handful of shepherds. The surprise attack unsettles both regiments and the fighting ranks disengage.

Ezekiel moves down a flight of stairs and onto the street below to face Zidon's ether head on.

Zidon's next blast scatters a row of Calcedonians, but before if reaches the Issurians, Ezekiel deflects the blast with an ether shield. Another row of spearmen fall when the strand reverses course before it weakens and dissipates.

Frustrated by the energy from Zidon's ether attacks and Ezekiel's defenses, the animosity of the Calcedonian horde activates - nudges to avoid the strands become pushes, and pushes strengthen to shoves. Within moments, the sound of gauntlets clashing with helmets ping off the palace wall.

Ezekiel steadies himself with his staff and pulls ether into his ever-widening shield.

Zidon harnesses the ether like lightning and shoots black bolts into the white disc. The protective wall weakens with every bolt. The magi's strikes pack more energy, chattering the prophet's teeth. Ben rushes to Ezekiel's aid and absorbs a flurry of bolts with Kurion. The ether sword allows the prophet to strengthen his defenses and forces the magi to rethink his strategy.

Aden and Caleb watch the siege unfold from the northeast tower. Helplessness, mixed with guilt, sickens Aden's stomach. "We should take to the streets and join the shepherds."

"We've no clue the number of friend or foe between palace and pit," says Caleb, fearful to act without proper intelligence.

"So that's it, then? We stand here and watch the Calcedonians destroy Tizra?"

"I'm not that bright, but last I checked. A king…"

Aden interrupts before the letter g leaps from Caleb's lips. "A prince."

"Sorry… A *prince* needs an army to fight a war. There are thousands of spearmen, who would love nothing more than to impale you for dismembering their king because your father didn't hug when you were a little boy."

Caleb relishes Aden's glare.

"Troops, if you only had troops, Sire."

"I have a trooper," notes Aden, unwilling to relinquish his glare. "Maybe I'll lead him into battle."

"Or you could send him into exile, preferably to some place tropical, renowned for their rich beer and beautiful women."

The conversation comes to an abrupt end when the sounds of clanging iron rings throughout the city.

Aden and Caleb look across the southern towers to see the animosity of the horde spread to the walls. Without Tartek or Korah to issue commands, and with Zidon's attention occupied in the ether duel, the Calcedonians begin to quarrel.

"Mutiny," says Aden behind a wide grin.

One bold warrior claims generalship of the army. A rival emerges from the ranks and clasps the general's shoulder pads; he hurls the warrior to the streets below promptly ending his term.

The new leader climbs to the pinnacle of the tower. He trumps the dead general by declaring himself the new king. He boasts of his conquests, demanding that all of his comrades bow to him.

A boulder flings from the catapult on the southeastern tower. Soaring over the ramparts, the rock launches the self-proclaimed king into the horizon and sinks him in the Tizra River.

Booming laughter billows from the ranks of the Calcedonians. Even Aden and Caleb chuckle at the braggart's demise.

The sunken soldier's misfortune plants a universal thought in the dull minds of the horde. Both towers turn their catapults inward on Tizra. Each crew heaps a chunk of stone onto their machines and let fly. The first boulder slams into the palace, but the second misses high.

Caleb yanks Aden by the arm and the two men dive out of harms way as the catapult behind them splinters into a thousand pieces.

A senseless competition thwarts the prince's wish for mutiny. The catapult crews boast at one another while they sling boulder upon boulder into the palace walls. As hunks of ore cripple the infrastructure, the Calcedonians chant from the towers, "Bring it down!"

Bleachers splinter as Azor attempts to incapacitate Korah with a heavy swing. His nemesis counters with a mighty hack that hews more wood outlining the arena floor. Korah makes a bold move and takes hold of Azor's left arm; he tosses him down the stairs and onto the earthen floor of The Pit.

Korah sheathes his sword, yet stays aggressive. He throws Azor into the Zimri's cement box seat. The white nephesh smacks into the slab and the structure crumbles down upon his back.

Korah readies his blade for the kill.

Azor heaves a chunk of cement that crashes into Korah's hooded-face. The stunned nephesh stumbles backwards and Azor dashes at him. Azor clings to Korah and drives him through post after post planted in The Pit - red ether sprays when each mast disconnects from the ground.

Azor blasts Korah through the wall of the training room.

The explosion causes Og, the pit boss, to swallow his tobacco before fleeing the scene.

"Come back home," pleads Azor.

Korah lays claim to a shield on a weapons rack. Zipping the disc, he catches Azor in the throat. Korah ramps up his attack by throwing a mace that shatters against Azor's shoulder and hurling a stone pillar into his torso. Korah yanks spears from the wall and barrages his nemesis - golden ether-flares brighten the dim space as the white nephesh fades.

Azor claws his way across the floor and plops down into the sewer through the unsealed grate. Korah's nose jerks back at the grotesque smell of Azor's escape route. His ears sharpen to the sounds of chaos in the city.

Korah's obsession to best Azor overrides his duty as a general, so he splashes down into the filth beneath.

The animosity of the Calcedonian horde scuffling in the street lessens at the distraction of the massive onyx ether-orb forming in the rear of the regiment. Zidon puts the orb into motion and the ranks of spearmen drop to the cobblestone as the ether soars over their heads.

Ezekiel casts white magic with command - his eyes widen, his purple ether-pulse deepens within his scarred-eye, and his pearl shield thickens.

Ezekiel drops his staff and extends both hands to advance his defenses. The ether collides and sparks spray, illuminating the dark street. Ben and Ashira pause with the shepherds to marvel at the dazzling colors above.

Seth moves covertly through the alleyways of Tizra in hopes of surprising Zidon. Though Seth doesn't care for such tactics, he trembles at the notion of taking another ether-blast.

Seth reaches the final corner between him and Zidon. He calculates the distance and his slowness to figure the risk involved. A sense of sadness prompts Seth to look down the street. The sadness stirs within him at the sight of the anguish on Ezekiel's face.

Ezekiel feels his spine bending and his knees buckling, even worse, his mind drifting. The throes of the duel no longer engage him and he questions his worthiness on the battlefield. For the first time, he recognizes his responsibility for the care of souls - for Ben, Ashira, and the shepherds huddling behind his shield. An abundance of doubt lingers in the air like the thick amounts of ether flooding the atmosphere. Ezekiel feels it emanate from the Remnant. Doubt nags him like a dog that won't stop barking.

Ezekiel tries to seek Neshama's grace to balance his unbelief, but the noise of battle makes it impossible to quiet his mind. In his youthful naivety, Ezekiel thought himself worthy of Othniel's duty but now that he bears it, he can't handle it. The eager prophet finally found the necessary patience to manipulate the divine magic, but he lacks the perseverance to defeat Zidon.

The ebb and flow of faith and doubt washes out the balance when a crashing wave of disbelief drowns Ezekiel's self-confidence. Zidon feels the weakened state of his nephew through their ether connection. A sense of relief soothes the magi as Lilith's offspring collapses to the ground and his ether shield fades.

Seth places Peacemaker behind his back to make for a quicker jaunt at Zidon. He scoops two handfuls of dirt from the rubble while rushing the magi.

Zidon catches the charging bull through the corner of an eye, which he slams shut anticipating the pitfighter's dirty antics. The filth collects in his beard and fails to settle in his eyelids, so Zidon mocks Seth with a grunting laugh.

Zidon's irises reappear and get buried in the follow-up fist full of crud causing him to lose control of the enormous orb. The meteor of ether wrecks into the palace with a thunderous BOOM!

The weakened structure cannot absorb another blast and the construction collapses. The Caledonians rumble out of the street as the palace debris falls down around them. Many unfortunate foreigners find themselves permanently embedded in the Tizra cobblestone.

Ben slings Ezekiel over his shoulder like an injured lamb. Ashira grabs his staff. They join the three hundred shepherds lucky enough to escape the falling infrastructure.

Seth has no time to detach Peacemaker to remove Zidon's head when a hefty slab of stone explodes between them. Another heap of rocks rains down on them forcing Seth to shelter in place.

Zidon fires a quick ether-shot into the corner of a shop to carve out a refuge. He dives into the haven as large amounts of debris bury him within.

Seth's strength empowers him to survive the debris as he emerges from the heap of rubble. He scans the wreckage for Zidon, but after no sign of the magi, he moves through the Tizra rubble-maze towards the North Plaza.

Aden watches as the final bricks of his ancestral home topple down upon one another. Streams of dust puff into the cityscape. A range of feelings stir within him as the palace powder disperses into air - a sense of sorrow at the happy memories of his mother and grandfather buried beneath, a sense of relief at the iniquity of his father buried beneath.

Caleb puts his arm around the shoulders of the conflicted prince. "Well, look at it this way. With all of your daddy issues, you were bound to remodel at some point."

The explosion above the surface quakes the sewer walls as bits of dirt speckle Korah's black robes while he stalks Azor in the tunnel system.

A quick slice zings around an angle and sparks flare from

an ether sword. The black nephesh ducks the return swing and readies his defenses for a third.

Instead of the sound of a whirling blade, Korah hears the splashes of fleeing footsteps and sees the ever-fading robes of Azor retreating deeper into the void.

The smell thickens with rancor as does Korah's malice.

A hill of rubble divides Tizra.

The ominous grey vortex above swirls intense flashes of red bolts as if eternity opens above the city to stop time. The noise of war dies when the palace rubble settles - no more sounds of catapults, no more sounds of mutiny. Only the rushing sloshes of the Tizra River and the rumbling of the ether clouds echo throughout the city.

The final fifty citizens complete their transition to refugees, loading their possessions on carts and fleeing north.

Ruben, the palace chef, and his staff remain out of loyalty to Aden. The famished shepherds gratefully partake of the hot tea and griddle-cakes while Aden gratefully eyes his leftovers of an army.

Ashira's countenance crumbles when Seth passes on the fare, using both arms to prop up the lifeless frame of Ezekiel. He adjusts the purple hood of the robe to cover the ether-scar.

Benjamin sits on a stool away from the regiment, admiring Ashira's beauty but careful not to get caught in a stare. For whatever reason, her tossed hair and sweaty complexion makes her more attractive to him. But not even her brown eyes can keep his gaze, for the ether vortex demands his attention.

The hypnotic flow numbs him into a trance.

Benjamin Tav never expected his calling to bring him to such a common moment in his journey. Maybe it was because his parents were revered heroes in Hallowed Hills and their legend was larger than life itself. Maybe it was because his calling was delivered by a nephesh and he got caught up in the majesty of such a being.

After his duels with Korah and the encounter with the leviathan, it seemed like this very moment in the journey of his calling would have felt extraordinary, instead, the day felt rather ordinary.

He remembers that Captain Tamar once said, "Heroes aren't born, they're made, crafted in the depths of a barracks." The shepherds, the hopeless prince, the unsure cook, the broken potter, and the doubting prophet appear no different - everyone seems so ordinary.

Ben wonders about the day that Josiah triumphed over the magi Zithri, and when his parents confronted King Zimri - were these epic days actually ordinary?

A vision strikes him in the midst of his trance with force, and Othniel's words convict his heart, "Grace nor justice, but sacrifice." The death of 'Wayfarer' flashes in his mind - the prophet drawing the black ether to his frame, the substance launching him into the wall, shattering his bones, and his life draining from him as he enters the ether world. Ben reasons that Othniel was ordinary, just like those present in the rubble of Tizra, but he gave life to the Covenant, to the Remnant. For in that moment of sacrifice, his human life became divine.

As his mind calms in the trance, the faces of the Remnant became brighter to him, their reasons to fight become clearer. The shepherds fight to protect all that is dear to them in Hallowed Hills. Aden fights to redeem the Tizra name, Ashira for the moment, Seth for peace, and Ezekiel for the prophetic narrative. They are common humans infused with a divine purpose. He fights for freedom, but he was not yet free, for Melek still reigns.

However, for the first time, Ben understands freedom. Evildoers must face justice, but only the Goddess can break the cycle of evil through grace. Justice and grace will only become a divine force when humans make the choice to sacrifice, and pass through this gateway that leads to freedom.

Am I willing to do it?

The question liberates Ben from the grip of the trance.

Caleb Glade bounces through the tranquil afternoon to liven everyone's curiosity of his scouting report. The regiment gets to their feet to receive the news - only Seth remains on the ground with the incapacitated prophet in his arms.

"The only way to the other side of the city is across the walls or over the rubble-hill, but I'm not sure if we want to stir the hornets over there."

"How many hornets?" asks Aden.

Caleb hesitates to answer, afraid of how much damage his report will inflict upon the Remnant's morale.

"Three thousand," sighs Caleb, pointing his eyes to the ground.

The three hundred shepherds hang their heads in disappointment at the large number of remaining Calcedonians.

"Any sight of Zidon?" asks Ben

"No. Hopefully, he was crushed by the rubble."

"They were on the verge of mutiny; maybe we can use that against them. The refugees fleeing north will be slaughtered if we do nothing," says Aden, hoping to gauge the morale of the shepherd regiment.

"But three hundred against three thousand," says Caleb, hoping to quell any delusions of victory.

Caleb's argument weakens when the clanging of gauntlets against cuirasses crescendos throughout the Calcedonian ranks – the buzzing sounds of mutiny stir in the nest of the horde.

Ezekiel's eyes flash open, startling Seth - the purple ether-pulse within his eye pumping faster and faster. All faces lock onto the prophet - his body convulsing within Seth's arm, his lungs pounding, jaw buckling.

Ezekiel tries desperately to discount the omen, but his teeth chatter and he exhales the warning, "He's here…"

The mystery baffles the shepherds.

Aden and Caleb exchange inquisitive looks, while Ashira and Seth pass perplexed glances.

Ben looks once more to the vortex, knowing full well the magnitude of the warning.

"Melek."

The ether vortex above blackens, the red ether-flashes become more vibrant and violent, and the wind viciously thrashes the yellow banner with the embroidered ram head. The vortex howls as if a pack of timberwolves spin within.

Melek descends from the void like the manifestation of dread, his obsidian robes fluttering in the turbulent sky as he touches down atop the rubble heap.

Melek surveys the destruction for Tartek and Korah while the possessed Calcedonians form ranks in the south plaza as if Melek commands their minds. The troops on the towers and walls exit their domain to complete the back ranks of the troops in the south plaza. In unison, they lift their eyes to their divine master.

"The Remnant rejects me. I offer deliverance from a vain deity, yet they clamor for the Goddess. Where is Neshama? Where are her nephesh? You must extinguish her light!" orders Melek with such vigor that the ether vortex booms with thunder.

His chosen warriors begin their march up the rubble hill.

Ezekiel's eyes roll into his skull as his last drop of energy drains from his body.

Seth taps his cheek, "Zek, wake up! We need you!"

Ben peers deep into Ashira's dark brown eyes as the wind sends ripples through her raven-colored hair. She puts her hand on the hilt of her sword to ready the weapon to charge alongside him. Ben lightly shakes his blank face in hopes that she'll reconsider her decision. Ashira's fears heighten, sensing the desperation in his soul.

"Melek is wrong. The Goddess is here. She's within me and I will answer her call," proclaims Ben to Ashira's fears.

Benjamin Tav is the son of Oren Tav and now, he is ready to take his place as the son of Neshama. If sacrifice is required, then he will serve as the offering.

Ashira's current reconnects with Ben's heart. The unexpected energy hits him like a flock of nightjars calling out to one another in the darkness of Abilla's Orchard.

Ashira cautiously lowers her defenses to unfetter her feelings for him. For the first time since her parent's death, she casts off the yoke of indecision and becomes lost in the moment.

Ben moves toward her. He wraps his right arm around her waist and pulls her to his chest. His left hand slides down her silken hair and across her flush face - eyes lock, noses touch, lips seal. Warm sensations tingle beneath their skin as they sink deeper into one another's being.

Love kindles in their hearts until the chill winds from the ether vortex and the frigid presence of Melek ices their fleeting moment of romance.

"Goddess keep you," whispers Ashira.

The blessing returns Ben's mentality to the task at hand.

The sentinel draws Kurion and charges up the hill. Loyalty hastens the boots of his shepherd brethren as they follow their champion. Seth gently lays Zek in Ashira's arm. He detaches Peacemaker from his back, and charges with Ben. Aden readies Royal Blue, but Caleb yanks his arm.

"I figured a way that we can put a hurtin' on them," informs Caleb. The scout's eyes show no signs of a bluff, leaving the prince with no concerns about following him.

"We need your help," demands Caleb of Ruben and his cooks. The regiment of chefs faithfully follows.

Aden, Caleb, and the cooks rush to the rope and scale the wall.

Melek effortlessly channels ether in a way that Othniel and Zidon would be envious, weaving it through his fingers like silk, as smooth as a spider spins a web.

Melek rockets into the ranks of the shepherds, picking them off one at a time, as if he flicks over toy soldiers.

The hasty charge grinds to a halt when Melek pulls back his robes and grows four black ether tentacles from his torso. The obsidian lashes scan for victims with their arrowheads.

Three tentacles stick into fateful shepherds, allowing Melek to begin his soul consumption. The fourth misses his target when Ben ducks the strike.

The fourth lash, instead, finds a suitor in Seth. It penetrates his heavy armor on its way into his chest bringing the warrior to his knees. Peacemaker bounds down the rubble pile and lands at the feet of Ashira and Ezekiel. Seth's roar of agony disturbs the morale of the shepherds as he fights the consumption with every tendon.

Ben moves to aid him, but Melek fires a fury of blasts at the fleet of foot hero. Rubble sprays in all directions as he leaps and dodges the blasts.

A handful of his shepherd brethren reach the nephesh and land a few blows, forcing Melek to draw his ether sword. A mighty blow removes three heads that bounce down the boulders.

The valor of the shepherds allows Ben to hack and slash the ether lash that devours Seth's soul. The Lord of Swords tears through the divine substance severing the arrowhead. The tentacle flails about as it puffs a haze of ether-smoke.

The lash seals slowly before regenerating a new head.

Seth collapses across a stone slab - his soul spared from consumption, but his muscles consumed by exhaustion.

The Calcedonian possessed reach the summit of the hill

to fight alongside their master. The shepherds ward off the surge, though their nerve cracks as Melek's sword claims more casualties. Their countenance shrinks when the legendary Seth Keros slides down the debris a diminished presence.

Ben steadies their fears with vicious strikes against Melek's chosen. His precise attack-points remind his men how to best their battle-hardened foes.

Suddenly, a boulder rips through the ranks of the Calcedonians, flinging warriors through the air. A handful of casualties smack into Melek like a wall. Others soar over the heads of the shepherds and down the other side of the rubble-hill.

Aden, Caleb, and the chefs reload the catapult and fire another shot that explodes against Melek's shoulder, causing red sparkles to burst atop his black robes.

Melek sheathes his ether sword. Taking both hands to gather an enormous ether orb, he lifts it above his head and hurls it across the cityscape.

Aden and Caleb have the wits to scurry out of the way, but the untested chefs are not so fortunate. The enormous orb collapses the tower consuming the catapults and the cooks. Only Chef Ruben clings to a brick. He pulls himself up onto the rampart and makes an executive decision to join the refugees.

A biting slice from Kurion hamstrings Melek, and the giant drops to a knee. A follow up shot removes another tentacle. Red ether oozes from his leg and black smoke puffs from the lash.

Melek unsheathes his defenses to repel a third whirl from Kurion. The nephesh puts both hands into his retaliation swing and plants Ben into a hunk of stone.

Korah lurches deeper into the sewer tunnels.

An exact shot from Azor's downswing racks Korah's ether sword above the hilt. The blade shifts in Korah's fingers, but he maintains control of the weapon.

Azor pays for his failure to disarm Korah when the dark nephesh strikes back and lands a devastating blow into the frame of the guardian. Bright gold ether flares, Azor's divine substance contrasting against his dimmed exterior aura.

Azor falls to his knees, his head smacking down upon Korah's boots. He labors to breathe as traces of his bright gold ether seep from his wound beneath his robe. Azor raises his purple eyes to his executioner. "Guess I'm your next."

"My next what?" questions Korah, staying his sword.

"Your next victim. I know about the nephesh that have disappeared from the ether world, the ones to last have an encounter with you."

Korah's yellow eyes brighten with intrigue as Azor reveals his findings.

"Three dead nephesh… We were created to protect life and you take it, Korah. Not only from humankind, but now your own kin."

Korah's yellow eyes fade into his black hood at Azor's false assumption. "For a masterful nephesh, your knowledge is yet again misplaced… I didn't kill them, I converted them."

Azor's purple irises dim with disappointment.

"And there are more than three… There are thousands."

The revelation cuts Azor's ether deeper than Korah's blade, and his head bows low once again. "You must give an account before Neshama."

"Join me, Azor. We fought side by side once before. Besides, you haven't the faintest clue of what Melek is capable of accomplishing."

"All must give an account before Neshama, so shall it be with you and with Melek."

"No account will need to be given once the Goddess

ceases to exist. The time is coming when the nephesh will serve a new master. That is why I answer to none but Melek."

Korah raises his sword in judgment above the neck of his condemned. Azor quickly motions to his side and rips a canvass from sewer floor. Underneath the canvass swirls a white ether vortex.

Azor's last pulse of energy pushes him upward and he clings onto Korah's frame. The executioner loses his attack point when the guardian's head presses into his robes. Azor latches onto Korah and falls backwards into the ether vortex.

Korah slips on the slick stones. He drops his ether sword and uses both hands to cling to a metal grate in the ceiling, his black boots violently thrashing the chest of the white guardian. With each heel to the heart, Azor loses his clasp and his hope of returning Korah to Neshama.

Azor desperately clings to the corner of Korah black robe. The vile nephesh reclaims his sword to render judgment. Azor releases his grip and vanishes into the ether vortex.

Ben raises his head from the cool stone to survey the slaughter of his brethren. Few remain to challenge the onslaught of their possessed foes. The uncomfortable rock forces Ben to remember his training session under the fallen Captain Tobi Tamar. *Heroes aren't born, they're made.*

The words hit a nerve and challenge everything that Ben understands about sacrifice. He's no hero. The lifeless men strewn about the rubble count for heroes and know far more of sacrifice than he does. Being born a son of Oren Tav did not make him a hero. Raising his exhausted mind, body, and soul from the rock heap, answering Neshama's call, and issuing a challenge to the ether king might afford him such a title.

His imagination fuels his courage to stand. Logic tells him that challenging Melek will be his end, faith tells him otherwise.

Unexpectedly, war horns blare throughout the north plaza of Tizra and a rush of wind blasts across the rubble-hill invigorating Ben and the Remnant. Erez Elk and his army of foresters stampede up the hillside like a herd of wild beasts.

Melek swings his head to the unforeseen threat. He readies his tentacles and channels ether.

Ben runs across the hill directly in front of Melek, his blur causing a distraction as the shepherd leaps onto the adjacent temple. "This son of Neshama lives! She remembers the Covenant, and I will end your reign!" shouts Ben at Melek.

The challenge insults Melek's motive to free humans from the Goddess. The obsidian nephesh glides across to the temple that bears his name.

Melek channels his ether down through the roof of the temple and raises the marble Melek altar through the ceiling. The black and grey marble alter crashes down at Ben's feet as the lid slides off. "I will preserve your remains within this tomb, a reminder of misplaced love for an inferior creation," condemns Melek.

With Melek out of the way, the foresters gain a clear path to the Calcedonian horde. Their banners of brown embroidered with evergreens and oaks tatter a marching beat while their emerald cloaks take flight. The emerald woodsmen collide with the crimson horde, cloaks contrasting, banners clashing. Erez Elk strikes down a harvest of warriors as blood blots his fur raiment. Sorek Boar protects his flanks with mighty blows, shattering the beams of spears and splitting helmets in half.

One chip at a time, one chop at a time, the Calcedonians lay down to the vicious hacks of foresters.

Suddenly, another blast erupts in the far ranks of the foreign foes. Calcedonians scatter from the rubble hill and splatter against the city walls. A nervous energy pulses throughout the horde as Caleb smiles at the direct hit.

"Come on, we've got to reload." Aden's command sours Caleb moment at the thought of laboring another boulder onto the machine.

Ben rushes Melek.

Kurion absorbs ether orbs as the shepherd weaves in and out the ether lashes that whirl around him. A precise swipe removes the spearhead of another tentacle.

Melek loses a hand to cast ether as he grips his sword to repel Ben's charge. The nephesh crushes a counterattack that burns Ben's hand and scorches the veins in his forearm all the way up to his inflamed shoulder.

Ben holds fast and Kurion flashes a bright crimson when it tears through Melek's ether, an oozing chasm appearing on his wrist. The red ether envelops his black hand.

Melek pulls his wounded appendage into his chest and unleashes a furious swing at Neshama's favored. Kurion absorbs the blow that blasts him backwards into the marble casket; the shock of the impact penetrates his armor, numbing the nerves in his back and legs.

Melek sheathes his sword and straitens the altar with his right hand, his left still pressed to his chest as the red ether fades to black. Melek yanks Ben into the coffin, lining up an ether lash to consume his soul. "This will be most satisfying."

The sentinel returns to his senses and sees the lash peering down on him as if it has a will of its own. The spearhead strikes like a viper.

Ben turns to his side to avoid the tentacle and it recoils off of the marble.

Melek rears back in agony when a boulder removes a chunk of his shoulder. Red ether spews from his shoulder like a volcano, streaming down his left arm and across his chest. The ether drips down upon Ben, dashing out from under the nephesh.

The ether king turns to Aden and Caleb's catapult with hatred in his grimace. He channels an ether strand so swift and so deadly that the blast explodes the catapult, burying Aden and Caleb underneath the debris.

Melek's frustration flares at the site of his slaughtered chosen strewn about the hill of rubble. He tries to stomp the life out of Ben as he did Zimri, his thunderous clomps weakening the infrastructure of the temple - tiles sprinkle down from the ceiling, and cracks meander down through the columns and walls. Dust sprays from the roof with each imprint as Ben dodges and rolls away from each stone-crushing stomp.

The quick sentinel circles back around to the marble altar, survival causing his confidence to soar as a smile returns to his face. "Your pride is my ally."

Ben's words fail to crack Melek's stoic face as he retracts the ether lashes underneath his black robes. Both hands grip his ether sword as every fiber of his focus sharpens his swordplay. Melek's golden gaze glows within his thick hood - it beams through the ether fog floating about in the atmosphere as a warning beacon to the brash mortal.

Ben courses his chart to the crag, but rock-face swiftly rejects him with a force so great that it shatters his nerve.

CLANK! The clash of ether blades summons everyone's attention to the challenge.

Erez removes his axe from the skull of the final Calcedonian fallen. Sorek admires his lord's handiwork before his attention joins all of the foresters peering across to the fractured temple.

In unison, Aden and Caleb heave a plank off of their chests and over their heads. They rise from the catapult wreckage.

Aden and Caleb scan the debris maze of Tizra for a path leading to Ben, but no such path leads to the stranded sentinel.

Seth regains consciousness and rolls onto all fours. His strained muscles remind him of his near consumption and fall down the rubble hill. He uses Peacemaker like a cane to push himself upright.

The violent crimson bolts brighten with vigor, jarring Ezekiel's awareness from his dream to the living nightmare.

Ashira stands with the prophet to offer support, returning the staff to his grip.

Ashira, Seth, and Ezekiel stare at Melek lording over Ben.

Zidon digs out a jagged window from his cell of stone-shards. He attempts to manipulate the haze of ether within in his tiny chamber to clear an exit, but the lack of the substance avails nothing to the magi. His attention shifts to the temple and Melek's dominance over Ben.

Korah emerges from the sewer, the hopes of refreshing his senses sour, for the stench of death suffocates the city. His army of chosen lay slain across the rubble of Tizra, brown banners and emerald cloaks fluttering triumphantly over their victims. Korah connects with his master's essence to offer a hint of serenity in the midst of such slaughter.

Melek grips his blade with both hands on the hilt and raises it high above his head. He sends it crashing down upon Ben.

Ben rolls away from certain death, but the devastating shot rips a rift through the temple splitting the pantheon in two.

Kurion's well-placed retaliation strike reopens Melek's maimed shoulder causing yet another eruption of red ether. Ben's next attack aims to penetrate Melek's heart, but the nephesh repels his advance with a spiteful strike that awakens the doubt in the shepherd's soul.

The fog of uncertainty clouds Ben's imagination of possible victory. The notion of winning the challenge becomes impossible to envision. His faith offers no comfort and his friends, no support. He looks to the tower above with visions of Azor racing to his rescue, but no celestial guardian appears to aid him.

Ben looks to the raging ether-storm overhead with hopes of a blinding white light piercing the darkness and cutting the dreary clouds. "Neshama. Are you there, are you listening?"

"Neshama is there, but she does not care… Of all mortals, I feel the most sorry for you. I will now free your tortured soul," boasts Melek.

Ben drains the last of his energy in another fatal stab at Melek's heart. The nephesh deflects Kurion with his blade and plants his boot into Ben's chest, blasting him into the altar.

Melek towers over the compromised hero, raises his blade high above his hood, and drives his ether sword though Ben's armor – flesh – bone – soul. The color purple flares from the shepherd's soul illuminating the blade of the nephesh. Ben clinches Kurion to his chest as his last breath exhausts from his lungs.

Ashira's shriek of horror fills the vacuum of sorrow that Ben's death creates within the spirits of the Remnant. Her soul empties as his soul lifts from his body. Ben's current of energy ceases, leaving her heart to waver once again.

Ezekiel's faith shatters like waves on a coast and he struggles to reclaim his identity as Neshama's prophet. Ben's sacrifice shakes Seth to his core. The sentinel spared his life, but now, no way exists to repay this debt.

King Emmerick Tizra, Captain Tobi Tamar, Sentinel Ben Tav - Issur's heroes dwindle like the hope within Aden. Caleb senses a shift in the atmosphere as the frigid winds howl like wolves devouring the fallen shepherd.

Zidon smirks at the destruction of Othniel's favored son of Tav. Korah watches unfazed, for his master keeps his promise to free Ben.

Melek channels ether strands that gradually lift Ben's body from the coffin. He wraps the corpse, the ether strands serving as burial cloth. They gently lay on top of one another until the divine substance completely encases his trophy.

Melek returns the marble lid to the altar when the temple shifts sharply and the roof gives way - the columns collapse, the pantheon shifts, and the implosion consumes the altar-coffin.

Melek leaps from the temple and floats atop Tizra in the ether winds. The ether king surveys the city to calculate his odds of victory. His initiative vanishes now that the foresters hold the high ground. Melek's command roars down to Korah, "Summon the Corrupt!"

His adherent bows his head in obedience. Korah removes his black ether disc from behind his back, and jettisons into the ether vortex causing a flurry of crimson flashes through the grey vapors.

Melek slowly ascends into the furious currents. The whirlwind gathers speed, violently whipping around their maker.

The turbulent winds impel the foresters to seek shelter on the rubble-hill as pieces of debris toss about Tizra. The wind pushes against the stone slab that imprisons Zidon. The magi shrewdly assists the liberating force by throwing his body against the rock. The slab tips over and shatters on the ground allowing Zidon to escape Tizra.

The wind dies when Melek disappears into the vortex and the ether dissipates around him. The grey ether-clouds give way to a plum horizon that welcomes an autumn sunset while a soft breeze carries colorful leaves of the same tones through the silent city streets.

Erez marches the foresters directly towards Ashira.

The aggressive action summons Seth to her side uncertain of their motives. Sorek stands at eye level with Seth and marvels at an outsider of such stature, though Ezekiel feels like a sapling in the midst of the lumberjacks. Ashira suspects Evan's intervention as Erez approaches.

"We return to Elah to tell your betrothed - honor for

honor, a life for a life." Erez raises his axe into the air. Sorek and the foresters follow his lead as he parades his men out of the north plaza.

Aden sprints and leaps across the rubble in hopes of halting Erez to show his gratitude towards the House of Elk, but the Tizra wreckage proves too treacherous and he fails to reach the foresters in time. Caleb labors to catch his breath; the air burns his lungs, reminding him of the drastic seasonal shift. Aden questions with a furrowed brow.

"The air. It's crisp, like winter." Caleb scoops a handful of leaves to breathe their scent. "The land is cursed. Autumn ends too soon, and winter's caress is now upon us... We should flee Issur."

"I won't abandon my people," affirms Aden.

"I'm just sayin' what everyone's thinkin' - that *thing* is bent on destroying Issur and the Goddess does nothing. Now the heart of this movement is dead and there's no bringin' him back," acknowledges Caleb.

The Remnant concedes to Caleb's honest assessment with downcast faces, except one.

"Such a way may exist," cryptically speaks Ezekiel.

Before the stunned tongues can stammer how to the enigmatic prophet, Ezekiel walks toward the mound of pantheon-rubble and stares at the corner of the Melek altar peaking out of the debris.

Ezekiel closes his eyes to connect with the blackness locked inside Ben Tav's tomb. He bows his head to offer a eulogy over the son of Neshama. "Darkness can only exist in the absence of light."

www.ingramcontent.com/pod-product-compliance
Lightning Source LLC
Chambersburg PA
CBHW021138110726
47900CB00002B/401